DEADLY PEDIGREE

DEADLY PEDIGREE

Book One

by

Jimmy Fox

Top Publications, Ltd. Co.
Dallas, Texas

Fiction

To my parents, Sylvan and Rosalyn,
for the freedom to dream,
the passion to learn,
the courage to write,
and love beyond words.

Top Publications Paperback

Deadly Pedigree

This edition published by Top Publications
12221 Merit Dr., Suite 750
Dallas, Texas 75251

Jimmy Fox

ISBN#: 1-929976-08-9
Library of Congress No. 2001 132363

Prologue

Murder has a family tree. Its ancestors and descendants are causes and consequences. Every act of murder gives birth to an eternal bond, spanning countless unwitting generations, scorning the limits of mortal time. This bond, this spawn of murder, instantly and forever alters all that has passed, all yet to be, insatiably reaching across the ages to lock events and individuals together in unbreakable, deadly kinship.

The frail man slowly pulling himself up the stairs needed no words to comprehend this truth. He heard, always, in every tongue devised by man, the weeping of the dead, without number, to confirm it. Language was irrelevant, impotent to express what he knew with every cell of his being, what it meant to be a member of this fatal family.

The stairway was steep, and nearly as hot and muggy as the New Orleans summer afternoon outside. The old man touched his chest and stomach alternately, as if not sure where the pain was worse. Sweat covered his blanched face. He clung to the handrail for support. His breath came short and shallow.

More than once the old man froze after ascending a few steps and covered his face with trembling hands.

Darkness. Cannot breathe! Is it the grave, so often escaped? Those voices, long ago. The same today, but different. Were they not utterly destroyed? Do they yet live? Yes. They rise up from the blood they spill. Black rivers, oceans of blood, pressing down upon me now.

"Let up dude. You're gonna kill him."

"So? One less kike in the world. Big fuckin' deal."

"Give him some air, dude. Old man, can you hear? You gonna stop what you been doin'? Hey, old man! Listen: keep your mouth shut, mind your own business, or

we'll be back."

"Yeah, asshole, and next time we won't use a fuckin' pillow."

Cannot . . . breathe!

Each time the terror assailed him, he shook off his fear and proceeded upward, drawing strength from a secret source.

Now, his chin set defiantly, his gaze fierce, he pushed up the left sleeve of his outdated but carefully preserved sport coat. His shirt cuff rode easily up his bone-thin forearm to reveal blue-green tattooed numbers.

"You think you have won again?" he said bitterly to the echoing staircase, as if to an old invisible adversary. "No, no! I will have the final victory. You will remember, you will all suffer. This time, this time it will be *you*." He fastidiously rearranged his damp shirt, tie, and coat.

From an inside pocket he removed a slim, dimpled silver flask. He coughed and took a furtive swig. Then he smoothed the two clumps of white hair on either side of his fragile skull and resumed the struggle toward his destination.

Chapter 1

New Orleans dances to its own addictive music, Nick Herald mused, as he angled the latest issue of the New Orleans phone book to catch the light from the windows along the east wall of his office. The Yellow Pages ad he'd placed was supposed to perk up his business. It wasn't working.

There was an article somewhere under the debris on his desk, where his feet were propped, that said genealogy was fast becoming America's favorite hobby, rivaling stamp collecting.

Not here, buddy! New Orleans—another world, another reality.

Clients were not exactly getting busy signals from his office phone, or lining up at his door, here in the Central Business District of the enigmatic city he had considered his home for the last fifteen years.

The ad had been a foolish waste of money, he now realized—more proof of his lack of commercial smarts. Despite the hyena pack of resentment that ate at his soul, he wished he were back in a familiar classroom at Freret University, preaching to uninterested undergrads the gospel of English literature. The paycheck had been regular.

"Can't even see the damn thing," he grumbled, squinting at the ad. Louisiana mosquitoes were bigger than the phone number and address. What a rip-off.

**NEW ORLEANS GENEALOGICAL
SERVICES WORLDWIDE, INC.**
J. N. Herald, Certified Genealogist, Ph.D.

He looked up. One of these days, he would get around to

changing those blown light bulbs. He refused to admit he was succumbing to failing eyesight, yet another symptom of encroaching middle age.

Sure, it was the bad light. He shifted the dozens of folders on his messy desk and found his drugstore reading glasses.

The ad, in better focus now, seemed to strike the proper dignified tone he'd wanted, even if it was too small. Lawyerly, doctorish. So what if it strained the nature of his set-up here? He ran a one-man operation, yes; but he could call on genealogical stringers all over the country, all over the world. At least those lucky few he'd paid on time and in full; the others wouldn't give him the local time of day. And so what if he wasn't really incorporated? On the battlefield of business, as in the ivory tower of a college English department, Machiavellianism ruled supreme. In his former career, he'd learned that lesson too late.

Was his minor deception ethical? he asked himself, as he stood up and walked over to the windowsill for the dregs of the coffee. Hey, it was an imperfect world. Nobody had elected him to fix it? *Next question, please.*

The tooting of a big ocean-going ship on the river, the faint roar of a streetcar and other traffic clamor, and ephemeral brass-band notes from deep within the French Quarter merged with the asthmatic drone of the window air-conditioner. If it rained later, as the white anvil clouds rising above the humid city seemed to promise, he could jog down St. Charles Avenue without risking a heat stroke. That would be better than sitting in his office, breathing stale memories, wasting electricity.

Nick still dressed with the indifference to taste of a college English professor; but because he seemed younger than his thirty-eight years, he looked more like a dissolute graduate student at the end of his monthly stipend. Today, as usual, he wore baggy khakis, a wrinkled once-white Oxford shirt, and a pair of Clark's sand-suede desert boots that had seen better days. When he needed a touch

of formality, he donned a coat and tie hanging in a closet
of the outer office. Too much thinking, too much drinking,
and twenty years of jogging had left him a bit too lean for
his 5'10" frame. His hair was dark brown with only a few
irascible gray ones; he wore it a bit longer than was wise
for a professional genealogist, who, as a rule, dealt with
people of a more conservative bent, especially here in the
South. But haircuts were expensive.

That morning, in the office bathroom, he'd scraped
his morose face with a dull razor; already he had an early
five-o'clock shadow to go with the dried blood of nicks.
His thick eyebrows extended in a nearly continuous bar
above his brown eyes, which now surveyed the dusty still
life that was his office.

Stacks and stacks of books, manuscripts,
documents, and letters leaned precariously against the
office walls and crowded every inch of shelf space. His
apartment was full, too. He collected indiscriminately,
compulsively. It had all started after his ejection from the
faculty of Freret University.

Why did he impoverish himself gathering this
material, traveling wherever in the area there was a likely
repository of irreplaceable genealogical material about to
be consigned to the dump? He saw his collection as a
kind of witness protection program. These yellowed and
crumbling products of human interaction were those
witnesses. Someday, they would reveal a lost connection,
rescue a reputation, or resolve a mystery. His own career
might have been salvaged by just such testimony.

As a genealogist, though, he'd learned never to
trust a written record without question; false records, like
mindless machines, repeat the lies of their creators.
Doubt everything was his credo, as it had been for
Descartes. He kept a small bust of the seventeenth-
century French philosopher in a place of honor, high atop
a section of shelves; it was a souvenir of a happier time,
the summer he directed a study group in France and
England. The bust had become something of a household

god for him, a constant reminder that we can know only part of any story.

Nick's humble office occupied two rooms on the fourth floor of a 1920s building, on an easily missed oblique street of downtown New Orleans, across Canal from the French Quarter. He had chosen the neighborhood precisely because it was off the beaten track. His address allowed him the solitude that, more and more, he had come to treasure, while still keeping him somewhat accessible to intrepid clients. If he lacked the acquisitive drive to be a genealogical tycoon, at least he could enjoy his marginality.

The neighborhood was a perennial casualty of the boom-and-bust cycles of the Louisiana economy. Empty lots, with tile floors of the buildings that had once occupied them, spoke of surgical arson. Nick had a relatively good view of the river through one such gap. New Deal-Art Deco government buildings and neo-Doric banks hulked over the modest, short block—symbols of power and success Nick envied and at the same time despised.

Lately, this section of downtown had become a mecca of affordable addresses for small businesses. The buildings now wore "For Sale or Lease" signs for only weeks instead of years before they were snapped up. It was a seller's market. Somebody was making a mint where yesterday tourists were advised not to walk.

Between "Gemstones" and "General Merchandise," his ad was nearly lost in the clutter. Nick now admitted to himself that he had bought the ad in the hope of striking up a friendship with the young saleswoman. A date would have been cheaper, he thought now, looking at the bill that had arrived at his post-office box that morning.

He sighed and opened a drawer in his desk. It wasn't the first time he'd done something stupid in the name of love—or lust. And it wouldn't be the last bill he swore he never received, when the dunning began. He crammed the bill into the drawer, among the many others, and slammed it shut.

Then he turned to his typewriter and got back to work.

His research was finished on this project. A thousand dollars waited for him—if he could justify the inflated bill. That feat was going to be trickier than the project had proved to be. It was big money, for him. Yet he hated to see the job come to an end, since it was the only one he had at the moment, phone-book ad notwithstanding.

He had been commissioned to do an extensive family tree for a woman who believed, based on family lore, that she was descended from the royalty of Sweden. Nick had found that this certainly was not the case. The truth was that her forefathers had been blacksmiths and shepherds since the dawn of history in Ireland.

There was no disgrace in the lack of royal ancestors; most of the world's population was in the same boat, not to mention the fact that once, every royal family was non-royal. But Nick knew it wasn't what she wanted to hear. He could do more if she wished, follow other limbs, twigs, and roots by mail and fax and phone, but it would be even more expensive, and of course, this extended research wouldn't change his findings. The facts of genealogy, he'd learned from his studies, can't be forced, though force might make genealogy.

But genealogy could be *delayed*, through a bit of fudging by a creative, needy researcher. All he had to do was carefully withhold certain information, and then maybe he could milk this project—

A noise interrupted his ruminations.

Was that his office door? Maybe his old typewriter had a new complaint. He certainly wasn't expecting anyone. It was two-fifteen. He could use some lunch, he suddenly realized, as he continued to listen.

There was definitely someone in the office now, Nick was sure. Maybe the janitorial crew, back for something forgotten that morning. Hell, it used to be all they did was empty the trash can, and that rarely. A new vitality had energized the neighborhood, which probably explained this annoying, unusual zealousness of the cleaning guys.

The wooden floor in the small anteroom gave a few initial creaks, and then there was silence.

"Is someone there? Can I help you?" Nick said, at once irritated, curious, and a bit apprehensive.

"Where . . . where are you?" replied a quavering voice.

Before Nick could reach the doorway that separated the two rooms, an elderly, unsteady man stumbled around the corner, taking mincing steps in the shackles of age and pain.

"Oh my! Such a nice office you have here," the old man wheezed. "So many books . . . everywhere! That's good. You are a smart fellow. And it is so cool in here! Thank God! Just give me a minute, just a minute, to get my breath." He leaned against a section of the tall bookcases opposite the windows and wiped his forehead with an extraordinarily fine handkerchief. Nick saw the initials in ornate letters: M C.

He wondered briefly if the old guy was a member of his reading classes at the public library, or an escapee from one of the nursing homes where he sometimes gave genealogy lectures. He certainly wasn't a janitor. From the old school, one of those who still dressed up, in their own sad way, to go downtown. A dandy once, probably, judging from the handkerchief; but he'd lost the knack.

No, Nick couldn't place the old fellow. It was obvious to him, however, that his visitor was in serious respiratory distress. He must be feeble of mind, too, if he thought the office was blissfully cool, with that one pitiful air-conditioner.

"This is where they do the research, the research on the family?" the man asked finally.

"Yes, that's correct. I'm Jonathan Nicholas Herald, and my business is genealogical research. People call me

Nick, though I've been called worse—mostly by my ex-wife's mother."

The old man apparently didn't catch the humor in Nick's efforts to put him at ease. Maybe he couldn't spare the breath to laugh.

"I do all the work myself," Nick explained, trying to polish his image a bit. "It's more efficient that way, I find . . . would you like to sit down?" He cleared papers and books from a chair in front of his desk. "How about some coffee? It's no trouble, really."

The old man might very well be in the early stages of a heart attack. *Great! Just what I need: MAN FOUND DEAD IN GENEALOGIST'S OFFICE . . . another scandal to bust me out of another career.*

"Thank you, no, no coffee. Just the chair. It is so hot on the stairs. You know, it is bad for my cough." Having sunk with exhaustion into the offered chair, the old man coughed and made use of the silver flask from his coat for a few medicinal sips.

Nick was amused, but didn't want to insult the old fellow by showing it. He remembered a great-uncle who had the same trick: a chronic, probably fake, cough to sneak in nips of whiskey.

"Maximilian Corban. Max. That's me," he began. "I am an old, sick man, alone in the world. I want that you should find someone who has my blood on—who has my blood in their veins. I am getting close to the end, and I want to go to my rest knowing there is someone who might say Kaddish for me."

Not the way most people refer to their relations these days, Nick thought, this emphasis on blood. But the old man's native language was obviously not English. Relieved his visitor seemed to be recovering, Nick sat down at his desk. He didn't have to ask what the Kaddish was; he had inexpertly stumbled through Judaism's sacred prayer for the dead over a few departed family members and friends. Nick's father was Jewish; and once, in those sunny days of youthful optimism before he had reached his present exalted level of skepticism, he had considered himself a believer in the undemanding Reform variety. But that time was as distant to him as a two-hundred-year-old census. Now, he no longer believed in very much that didn't pay the rent.

"Well, Max, my services and fees are all laid out here on this sheet, along with the accrediting organizations I belong to, and a little bit about my academic qualifications. I'd be happy to work for you, if you find my terms acceptable."

And I'd make a perfect heir, if you're looking for someone to leave your estate to, Nick thought but did not say.

"This seems very high," Corban complained. "What is this, brain surgery?"

"Genealogical research isn't brain surgery, but it is a specialized field. I assure you, my work is worth it. You'll notice that I'm a published genealogical author."

This guy's no dummy. He disarms you with pity, then pounces. Careful, don't scare him off; you need this old fellow. Nick glanced at the drawer of bills as a reminder to remain civil. He concentrated on the businessman's mantra: *The customer is always right. The customer is always right* . . .

Corban shook his head, fidgeted, seemed on the verge of leaving–if he even remembered where he was, which Nick doubted. He coughed, put up a shaking hand to beg a moment's pause, and then brought the flask to his mouth. Apparently refreshed, he leaned forward with startling intenseness on his face.

Where had that come from? Nick felt irresistibly drawn forward, too, for he suddenly sensed that this old fellow had led an interesting life.

Nick was curious by nature, and he'd been in this business long enough to understand that oral history often revealed facts which written history missed. He unobtrusively foraged for a pencil and pad to take notes.

"Very well, young man," Corban said. "We work

something out, yes? But first, I will tell you how they bled my family tree dry. Hah! and they call *us* blood-suckers, even today."

"I'm sorry, Max, but I don't follow—"

"Listen; you will. My father and mother owned a nice little hotel on the Bodensee—you may know it as Lake Constance—on the German side. The wrong side."

"You mean, because your family was Jewish?" Nick asked.

"Yes. Oh, but we were Germans, too! Jewish Germans, weren't we? So we thought. I was a youngster at the time, working at the hotel, of course. And going to school, dreaming about the rich lives of the guests who came to fish and swim and sail on the lake. Chasing the good-looking girls of our village. Expecting to go to university." Corban gave a wistful sigh.

"Do not think we were blind to the signs of what was coming. Everybody knew. They approved of what was going on, most of them. At first, it was gradual, but a secret? No, no." He waved his hands as if refusing a second helping of something.

"We were so sure that they considered us Germans first, not simply Jews who happened to be unlucky enough to be living in the Reich. We loved German culture, thought we shared it with the Gentiles. We worshiped the culture, just like we loved the Fatherland. To tell the truth, we were Jewish only in memory; my father and mother had nothing to do with the old ways. Oh yes, we were very modern. God help us!

"A little cut here, a little cut there. That's how it was. First came the pamphlets and posters with the Jews as vermin. Then we heard of the state propaganda films and the rumors against Jews, no longer just whispered, either. They had become bolder with their successes. We listened to the madman Hitler on the radio. We were shocked but still we did not see what was to come. How could anyone believe such craziness?

"Soon, our loyal guests started to treat us like we

were dirty, less than human. Then came the boycott, the Anschluss, the swastikas painted everywhere on our property. My father kept saying if it got too bad, we'd cross over into Switzerland. If it got too bad . . . it was bad enough already! When, when? He told us he knew some people who would get us through. I remember Kristallnacht like it was yesterday; I can hear the glass shattering, I can feel it crunching under my shoes. It got worse. There was blood in the streets, in the synagogues. When, when are we to leave, Papa? Already it was too late."

Corban raised his sleeve to reveal the blurred number. "You know about concentration camps?"

"I, uh . . . yes, I know something about them," Nick said, feeling suddenly like a student who hadn't done his homework.

Corban shook his head. "You cannot know what it was like, what any of the camps were like, unless you were there. I never saw my parents or my two brothers or my three sisters again. All my aunts and uncles and cousins disappeared. Up in smoke." He made a swirling gesture in the air. "You know, at the end, it happened so fast. We had no time to question, we didn't know *what* to ask. Overnight we had become cattle led to slaughter.

"The rest is like a dream to me, a nightmare that will not leave me. Why was I allowed to live? I do not know. Sometimes I wonder if I am not dead." He looked around the room, as if he didn't recognize matter and form anymore.

"I worked in factories at first, because I was strong then, like you are when you are young, you know, a hard worker, determined to stay alive. I became ill, but I managed to hide it for a time. They moved us as the fronts shifted. East, east I went, into the rising sun. It was cold, colder than I thought possible. Even the summers were without warmth and life. Don't ask how long I was in this camp or that; I do not know. Time stopped for me. Somehow, God kept me alive, though there was less of me than you see now, thin and sick man that I am. I buried and burned the corpses and sorted the gold teeth and the hair for the Nazis as long as I could stand."

Corban had a feverish look in his pale eyes, though the rest of him seemed exhausted. Nick moved his hand nearer the phone, ready to call for an ambulance. But the old man continued his story, his fervor hardly abated.

"And then it was my turn. The war was going bad, very bad for the Nazis. They could not kill us fast enough, but they did not want the Allies to see what they were doing to us. Trains were scarce, so they marched us on the snowy roads. You see, they hoped we would drop dead and save them a bullet. I think we were going to Chelmno death camp. That was the rumor, anyway. One day, when there was nothing left of me except bones, a rag or two, and a weak pulse, I looked up—it was a sunny, cold, sparkling spring day, I remember—and there, there were horrified Russian soldiers in place of the Nazi guards."

He blew his nose with startling, loud vigor.

"Acch, the things I could tell you."

The trance broken, Nick took a deep breath and shifted in the chair, making it squeak loudly in the sudden quiet of the room.

Nick was strongly moved by Corban's narrative. A hundred questions formed in his mind, the foremost being, *If all of his relatives are dead, what the hell am I supposed to find?*

"Look, Max," Nick said, "I know this is painful for you. You don't have to tell me more. Let's just move on to the specifics of the project you want me to—"

"It helps, sometimes, to talk. No one wants to hear about it anymore."

"I understand. Well, if that's what you want. What happened after the war? What did you do? How did you get yourself back together?"

"After a few years in the displaced-persons camps, learning how to live like a human being again, for a while

I cried, and a while after that I screamed in rage at the
Nazis, all Germans, mankind, my parents for being so
stupid—even at God. I got married to another survivor; she
was French. God rest her soul, she is gone now. We came
here, to New Orleans. You see, I liked the music and the
river and the warmth; she liked the food and the street
names." He smiled sadly. "That is what we told
ourselves. But really we both hoped that a few thousand
miles would help us forget. It did not." He paused for a
minute, looked down, his eyes filling with tears.

"She could have no children. The Nazi
devils—'doctors'—they called themselves—they did . . .
experiments on her. For many years she worked at a nice
place on Royal, selling lace things and gifts for the
tourists. This handkerchief, she gave me, for our forty-
fifth wedding anniversary . . . I was a traveling dental-
supplies salesman." Corban wiped his eyes and looked
up, a trace of an ironic snicker shining through the tears.
"It was the one trade I learned in the camps. I had to do
something," he said, shrugging.

"I'm sorry, Max. That's the saddest story I've ever
heard. You're right, I can't know what it was like.
But—and I hope you won't take this the wrong way—as a
genealogist, I'm fascinated. There are few more difficult
tasks in modern genealogy than tracing families torn apart
or destroyed by the Holocaust. I've never actually worked
on such a case, but truthfully, I've always wanted to. And
more than that, since my father is Jewish, I understand
your anguish on a more personal level."

"*Mazel-tov*. Welcome to the club. Wait until you
see the dues. *Oy*, they're murder!"

"Well, I'm not a religious person. Currently, I
mean."

"When you shed your first real tear, you'll come
crawling back, young man, back to God, whatever you call
Him. Like me. Mark my words."

Nick felt sorry for the guy. How had he survived
with those memories and remained sane? Was he sane?

Well, clearly, he was eccentric, to put it charitably. Despite his compassion for him, Nick felt compromised, tricked into revealing such personal things to a stranger. He also believed he'd shed a sufficiency of genuine tears himself, thank you very much.

Nick was a private person by nature; his humiliation at Freret University had made him even more so. Though he rooted around, sometimes literally, in the basements and attics of other people's lives, he didn't want anyone doing the same in his.

"Max, if we could talk genealogy for a few minutes. From what you've told me, I think the best place to start is with your parents, and with whatever European records may have survived. It's possible some line of your family escaped. There are several excellent archives in Europe and Israel which—"

Corban suddenly lost his temper.

"No! I have had enough of eating the dust of my past in Europe! I know what you will find there: a dead vine, uprooted and burned and scattered to the four winds. You must find the new shoot, the graft that may have been saved from the fire. No, forget Europe, I tell you! I have seen the death of more genealogy than you can know. The Nazis—may they rot in Hell!—made us carry a card—"

"The *ahnenpass*," Nick said. "I've heard of it."

"Yes, that's it. It had the names of ancestors, so that even they became informers on you. 'Look, he's a Jew!' the Nazis made them shout. They wanted it all written down, so there would be no trouble in a German mind when it came to denying us freedom, travel, property, love, livelihood, life. It's the law, you see, and the law must be followed. Cut, cut, cut, until our lifeblood flowed from us. Oh, it was all very properly done, stamped and signed and filed. They were rounding us up, drawing in our history to the ovens.

"My every waking and sleeping moment is a vision of what they did to those I loved. What they are still doing to me. You will find nothing in Europe, young man, or in Israel. Take my word. But there was a story among my family that a cousin of my grandmother's came to Louisiana from Alsace and made good."

"When was this?" Nick asked, glad finally to have something to write down.

"In the 1840s or '50s. I remember only his last name: Balazar. It is all that is left, except me. This man's name is the last prayer in an empty boxcar."

Damn! Nick thought. There went his chance for some outrageously overpriced overseas research.

"Okay, Max, I'm on the case—that is, if you want me. But I can't promise any definite timetable. For one thing, I'm extremely busy with current projects"—a slight exaggeration bordering on a lie; Nick had already missed one utility bill. "For another, this is likely to be a bit complicated—and, I might add, worth more than I'm going to charge you. In your case, there are special problems. Usually I begin a pedigree search with fairly specific information on identity or locale. One line is involved, and you work backward from the client himself. Another thing—most of my clients don't especially want to meet their newfound relations. They're just curious, or looking for something in their family history that makes them feel important in their otherwise ordinary lives. Say, descent from an early distinguished colonist or from a soldier of the Revolutionary War. Your search may involve several lines, hundreds of people. But I think I can keep within a budget of"—he took a quick look at Corban to gauge the effectiveness of the sales pitch, and doubled his original idea for the fee—"fifteen hundred dollars. A turnkey job."

"You really should make it $750, young man."

"Let's say a thousand, then, plus expenses." Might as well throw that in, too. "I don't mean to be rude, but I'm offering a professional service, not a piece of furniture at auction. It's not too late for either of us to change his mind."

His words had come out more harshly than he'd

intended. It was the old imperiousness he once used so effectively on students who mistook his kindness and willingness to help as weakness or a sign that he'd do their work for them. He'd always hated himself for a few minutes after crushing a student's fragile blossom of self-confidence.

With a sour expression on his face, the old man capitulated: "Yes, yes, all right!"

"You can pay me when I finish. I'll keep you informed of any expenses, which I expect to be minor, anyway. If you would write down for me the spelling of the ancestor's name, as well as your phone number." Nick handed him the pencil and the pad, turned to a fresh page.

"Who? What ancestor?"

Great, the old guy's got Alzheimer's, on top of everything else.

"The ancestor you mentioned, the one who might have immigrated to Louisiana. Remember?" The one who sounds suspiciously like the well-known fictional Cajun, Belizaire, Nick almost said, wondering if Corban's ancestor was a fiction, too.

"Oh, *that* ancestor! Why didn't you say so."

Corban hesitated, then wrote the information.

Still terrorized, watching over his shoulder, after all these years, Nick was thinking. A strange little man. He'd be a bit addled, too, after such horrors.

He decided he'd better accompany Corban on his trip down the stairs, and to the streetcar stop, which was his stated destination. But Corban waved him off.

"Young man," said Corban, "I survived the Nazis. New Orleans I can handle."

"Well, okay, if you're sure—oh, one more thing. Where did you hear about me?"

"A retired dentist who used to be my best customer told me you were good at whatever it is you do." Corban mentioned the name. Nick remembered the job. "Also he said you were reasonable. Ha! What does he know? These dentists and their fast cars." He left, shaking his head.

So the Yellow Pages ad still had not produced.

Standing at the open door of his office, Nick listened for a few minutes to make sure his new client made it down the stairs safely. He heard Corban's not quite convincing hack echoing up the stairwell, and regretted not having asked for half of the money in advance.

Chapter 2

This was crazy, really crazy. She knew it was. What a chance she had taken! It was all highly illegal.

But the money! *There* was the power that had fortified Elzbieta throughout the seemingly interminable train and plane rides.

She worked at the District State Archives in Poznan, Poland. Her long journey had taken her to Zurich, to New York, and finally here, to New Orleans International Airport.

Hunger pangs pulled at her stomach. She forced herself to stay away from all the tantalizing aromas wafting from the restaurants that seemed to fill every niche. There would be time for such things, later.

She encountered no delays in Customs, but she did witness a drug bust in the line next to hers. Some very nervous young men were apparently trying to smuggle heroin into the country in condoms they'd swallowed.

Elzbieta knew this would be the most momentous event of her life; she tried to memorize every detail.

What a day! What a wide, astounding world it was! What a lot of money this strange errand of hers would bring. A hundred thousand American dollars! It was almost unbelievable that she had found the courage to make the additional demand. The future belonged to the bold in the new Poland; and, in truth, she had done worse things during the nightmare years. Now, she would be able to take her son for the operation in Germany; she could buy new clothes; some jewelry; she could maybe even get a car. Some new glasses. Yes,

she would buy them here, before she went home.   A
small indulgence, but she deserved it.

The richness of the rest of the world had shocked
Elzbieta anew twenty-four hours ago; but now she was
just plain numb from exhaustion and sensory overload.
Though she was only an assistant librarian at the
Archives, she had already seen something of the world.
She'd attended a small religious college in Virginia on
an American Baptist scholarship just after the Wall
went down and communism imploded.   She had not
actually been interested in being a Baptist, but a
Western education was worth the four-year charade of
faith for the benefit of those earnest Americans.
Especially an education that gave her a knowledge of
English.   A very peculiar, difficult language, but a
definite asset that got attention. Elzbieta went after
what she wanted.

Angry with herself for having allowed her
language skill to slip since her college days, she
struggled with the direction signs.   Announcements
from speakers distracted her; she couldn't help trying to
figure out what the superfluous words meant.

Concentrate, concentrate! she berated herself
silently.   She was looking for the taxi area, where
someone would be waiting for her with a sign with her
name on it.

Everybody except her seemed to know where to
go. Would her contact wait? This was like a spy novel,
more fun to read than to enact.

She struggled through crowds of people, lugging
her one small taped-together suitcase.   It contained
most of her meager worldly belongings–a few precious
bootleg cosmetics, grooming items, two changes of
underwear, one blouse, one pair of old, mended, but
genuine Levis, which she coveted from her college years
and could still fit into, almost without pain. In Zurich,
using a good deal of her advance money—$200—she'd
loaded up on over-the-counter medicines she'd never

heard of; she could sell them when she returned home. Not that she would need such piddling sums then. Just a habit of survival.

In her other hand was a briefcase, with the merchandise she was delivering. One hundred thousand dollars' worth, though you'd never know it to look at it! On the jet, she had sat protectively on it at first, and had reacted perhaps a little too violently when a Swiss Air stewardess politely offered to stow it under the seat in front of her.

TAXIS, and an arrow. Then other signs with the same thing. She didn't have to consult her dictionary for that. At least she was going the right way. She quickened her steps, in spite of her exhaustion. Soon she would be rich.

These Americans and their craze for genealogy. She couldn't understand it. Didn't they know? They were the envy of the world. The future was theirs. Why try to be something else? Most of the world is trying to forget its past, but not these Americans. They are like children who must have something, even though it will probably make them sick.

Since the opening of Eastern Europe, the requests and the seeking tourists had poured in, an avalanche, a flood. At the Archives, where the pace was, well, relaxed, they had years of American genealogical work piled up. And it wasn't just those haunted Jews whose relatives had been exterminated. It was all kinds of people.

Elzbieta considered herself an intellectual of heightened sensibilities, an exponent of unpopular ideas. Unlike many of her contemporaries, she felt modern Poland was not feeling guilty enough about their Jews. For her, in spite of the fact that she wasn't even alive at the time, the Kielce pogrom of 1946 was a raw wound on her country's honor. She gritted her teeth whenever she heard the old ones—some in her own family—mumble that Hitler had done the country a favor; now some in her son's generation weren't mumbling. Let them hate. She was just one woman, who had grown tired of ministering to sick consciences. Anyway, the dead Jews were beyond harm, and there were hardly any live ones left in Poland today.

Somewhere in this complex of moral indignation and weariness lay her reasons for stealing the documents, she reflected as she made her way through the crowd. To make amends, somehow, in her private way; to give back some of the past to those who had lost so much of it—even if by proxy.

Only she, the Deputy Director, and the Librarian spoke English with any fluency. By chance, Elzbieta had taken the phone call that winter afternoon. It was a woman on the other side of the Atlantic, an American. A rich American from New Orleans, who wanted very specific genealogical information on her Jewish ancestors in seventeenth- and eighteenth-century Poland. "Information" wasn't exactly the correct word. She wanted the real thing, the actual documents. She wanted them *stolen*, and sent to her. Anything dealing with the surname Balazar.

Elzbieta didn't tell anyone. The enterprising budding capitalist that she was, she took it on herself to make the deal—$10,000 the woman offered—a sum which quickened Elzbieta's pulse.

She found everything requested and more. She even had to do some traveling, paying out her own money, which she had decided not to mention. Soon, she sprang her counteroffer. It was her big chance to change her life, perhaps even to leave dreary Poland. The price had gone up, but Elzbieta would assure the safe arrival of the documents by carrying them personally. Otherwise, who knew what would happen to them? She had worked it all out: her vacation month was coming up. Several phone calls followed. Finally, her veiled threat worked. Surprising the dickens out of Elzbieta, the woman agreed.

Funny thing . . . she would never give her name;
just a phone number. Perhaps these weren't even her
people, these Balazars. Maybe she was only a
secretary, didn't want to get involved further than
giving telephoned instructions. Elzbieta didn't care.
She just wanted that money.

So many signs, so many unfamiliar names.

There! There was her ride: two men standing
next to a big car. One man held a piece of cardboard,
but she couldn't quite catch the name on it. The man
scanned the passing pedestrians, showing his sign
quickly only to certain young women, as if it were a
dirty photograph.

Her relief turned to wariness. Both men seemed
impatient, angry for some reason. Was she the cause of
their annoyance? She recalled the nervous young men
in the Customs line; each second of delay could have
cost them their lives. She hoped these men would not
be mean to her. Maybe she was later than she thought.
What time was it at home? Had she set her watch back
too far, failing to account for Daylight Saving Time?

These men . . . she held back. Both of them were
big, muscular, rather handsome, in fact. Good teeth.
One was blond, the other was darker, vaguely Siberian
looking. Then she remembered there was a lot of
aboriginal stock in the population, here in the South.
What did they call them—Indians? How can all these
people live together in peace? she wondered.
Europeans can't seem to do it. Since New York, black
people, especially, had fascinated her. She had seen a
few in Virginia, on campus, of course, but now she
noticed them in all their variety of colors and facial
constructions. What a wonderful country!

But these men scared her. Their eyes were cruel,
hunter's eyes. She remembered that look in the eyes of
the worst of Jaruzelski's security forces, that late fall of
1980 when martial law was declared. Recently, she had
seen the look in the eyes of the Russian and Ukranian

gangsters. Such eyes looked on horrible things and did not blink.

"My name is Elzbieta," she said. "You are here for me?"

'Yeah, babe, we're here for you," the fair-haired one said, a troubling leer on his face.

He tried to take her briefcase, but she clutched it to her.

"Suit yourself. Get in." She heard him say something to his darker friend, and she thought it ended with "dumb polack bitch."

Surely she had misunderstood.

The car amazed her. The president of Poland himself probably didn't have one this big or nice. All this comfort, this elegance. She was embarrassed. She knew she did not smell all that great; it was so warm here, and she had been sweating. She checked her breath. She began to worry about her jaw-length light-brown hair—a disgrace; she had tucked it behind her ears because it refused to do anything else. A bath, a long, luxurious bath in a clean American hotel room! That's what she most wanted right now. She should be living like a queen, she was so rich!

The dark-featured man drove very fast. He ran red lights. Neither of the two men spoke. They stared straight ahead.

Elzbieta had a guidebook with a foldout map. She prided herself on her map-reading skills. The car was going in the wrong direction. She was certain her reservations were at a hotel downtown.

"We should go that way?" she said, pointing over her shoulder.

No answer. The blond one turned up the radio. Spunky modern jazz. Elzbieta would have enjoyed it in other circumstances.

"You are mistaking," she said. Fear made her chin quiver. "I am staying in hotel downtown. That way. Here are my papers." She held up her hotel confirmation for the blond man to see. He didn't turn around.

As she looked back in the direction of downtown New Orleans, through the heavily tinted rear window, she understood that there was indeed a mistake, a terrible one, and *she* had made it.

Elzbieta frantically yanked the door handles. Both doors were locked. She began to cry quietly.

Chapter 3

"Nick," Una Kern said, after one of those long, observant, nearly telepathic lulls in the conversation that characterize the meetings of longtime friends. They were sitting around a shellacked salvaged cable reel that served as a table at the Folio, a favorite hangout of diverse groups from the adjacent Freret University campus.

At the Folio there was a boozy truce between highbrow and lowbrow, professors and students, art and science, social dissidents and establishmentarian frat members, aesthetes and athletes.

Nick's earlier plan to jog had lost out to an invitation from Professors Una Kern and Dion Rambus to meet here.

"Dion and I have a proposition for you," Una said and waited. She adjusted her glasses, leaning forward on the table in earnestness, her blue eyes daring him to take the challenge.

Nick raised an eyebrow in suspicion. He put down his beer mug with a thud. "Hey, I was just sitting here, tending my own psychic garden, enjoying the music, and the whole time you two have been laying a trap for me . . . oh yeah, I definitely smell a conspiracy. What is it this time? An office job in the geology department? Somebody at the library on maternity leave? Assisting a Ph.D. candidate in his research? Hey, friends, please: you don't have to throw me scraps anymore. In fact, I *like* my work. I haven't been able to say that in a long,

long time, have I?"

They nodded in unison.

"Look, I know it must be unnerving for pampered, tenured, grant-rich scholars like you to acknowledge that; it does violence to your self-image; but I am actual proof that there is life outside the shaded groves of academe."

Always focused on the higher motivations, like one of her long-suffering Victorian literary heroines, Una ignored his self-defensive outburst: "We've noticed that you're overworked. The rat-race doesn't agree with you. You're too thin . . . those circles under your eyes."

"Just allergies, that's all," Nick replied.

"For a minute there, when I came in, I thought Una was sitting with Keith Richards," Dion Rambus said. "He's coming to town for a performance, so the posters stuck all over campus proclaim."

"Ouch! That hurt," said Nick, wincing in feigned discomfort.

"'Oh, how full of briers is this working-day world!'" Dion continued. "Listen to Una, Nick. You need our help. I remember the days when you would outpace me, in spite of my longer legs, on our brisk walks across campus. And outtalk me! Now, you're stooped and brooding like a medieval monk in a scriptorium. What a horrible yoke it must be to have to work *twelve* months a year." Dion shook his head and tisked.

"*I* remember a time when I thought you were somewhat handsome, in a tragic-hero way," Una said.

"'Somewhat'!?" Nick said.

"You miss appointments, you don't even answer the phone most of the time."

"It's positively infuriating that you refuse to hook up that answering machine we bought you for Christmas," Dion complained.

"I mean, really, Nick," Una said, "you're living in the past, yours and mankind's. It's 1993, not 1893 or

1793. It's a new world out there, full of possibility, and you're stagnating, cutting yourself off! You need an infusion of fresh ideas."

"Hamlet asked Horatio to absent himself from felicity," said Dion, "but only for a while. Haven't you done enough penance?"

Una continued the verbal assault: "You probably aren't even aware we have a dynamic new president—"

"Grover Cleveland?" Nick asked teasingly.

"That's rich," Dion said. "But you've proved our point precisely."

"Okay, okay, what's going on?" Nick said. He had tried to hook up the answering machine but had given up in frustration. They didn't need to know that.

"Dion and I have come up with a solution to your dilemma."

"Which you've conveniently manufactured."

"Her name is Hawty Latimer." Una let the name sink in a few seconds and sipped her daiquiri—her first drink to the men's fifth. "She's a junior, with a double major, English and computer science."

"I don't like her already," Nick said. "Computers?" He contorted his face into a grimace.

"A Blakean nightmare vision, eh, Nick?" Dion asked through a mouthful of pretzels. "Our invention has made us its slaves."

"Be nice, now, Nick. Don't be so quick to judge. She had a two-year scholarship, and now she's exhausted her family's abilities to help her. What talent! Quite an overachiever."

"Una's right, Nick. Seriously, I've read her stuff. Her papers are so well reasoned and innovative she could replace any one of about half our staff. For instance, that incompetent philistine—"

"Dion, shhhhh! Someone could overhear," Una cautioned.

Dion bit his lower lip in suppressed rage. "Yes, yes, I'll muzzle myself. Anyway, Hawty's poetry is damn good, too. She's an exceptional lass . . . and, uh, spirited."

"Spirited? What's that supposed to mean?" Nick demanded.

"Her true intellectual loves are literature and history," Una said, avoiding his question. "And I'm certain she has a vocation for teaching. This past semester she taught an introductory English course. The kids loved her. The review group gave her high marks, too. She had some, oh, slight medical problem, and missed out for a summer course. Nick, I'm afraid that this time, if she goes home—a tiny village in north Louisiana—she won't be able to return. We'll lose a fine future teacher. What you're doing will mesh very well with her developing abilities and interests; and she could really, really use whatever small salary you could pay. By the time fall gets here, I should have some funding lined up for her." Una held up crossed fingers.

"Pay! You got to be kidding," Nick protested with a laugh. "Most months I can't handle my rent. Or as President Cleveland would say, it's the economy, stupid—mine."

Smirking in disappointment, Una looked at Dion, as if to confirm their suspicion that Nick had turned into a hardhearted capitalist swine. They contemplated their drinks while Nick fidgeted and the loud, eclectic, alternative-alternative music of the Folio swirled around them.

"Just think about it, okay?" Una said before lapsing into a pout.

❑

How could he refuse? Nick asked himself between sips of his beer, as Dion launched into his standard diatribe against their perennial arch-foe, Frederick "the Usurper" Tawpie, currently the assistant department head of the Freret University English department.

He owed these friends so much. And for a time twelve years before, he and Una had been much closer than friends—lovers, in fact.

She had just joined the department then, a rosy-faced, diminutively sexy, enthusiastic young professor, who frolicked like a nymph through the wordy marshes of Thackeray, Dickens, George Eliot, Hardy, Meredith, and Trollope. There had been three or four years of passion and cozy togetherness, many late nights of nakedness and laughter and wine and both Brownings aloud by candlelight. A lifetime of love seemed the logical outcome—at least in her mind. And Nick? Well, he merely let things go on their course, feeling naively blessed and smiled upon by the universe, feeling the very focus of creation in his unvanquished egoism.

But the happier he told himself he was, the more dissatisfied he became. He changed, became moody, solitary; life lost its savor. He turned into a cad, though his students continued to crowd into his classes. Everybody who cared said it was too much Shelley and Byron, the subjects of his graduate seminar that fateful semester. Just an affectation, a Romantic pose he would grow out of. Now, looking back, Nick supposed it was nothing more unusual than a normal professional burnout, which would have been temporary had malice not worsened his circumstances, had Tawpie and computers not given his wheel of fortune a gratuitous damaging turn.

He had enemies he never suspected, who resented his youth, his popularity with the students, his relationship with Una—who knows what. Does jealousy really need a good reason? One thing he did know: jealousy takes more insidious form in the minds of highly educated people.

There was a charge of plagiarism. He wasn't sure to this day who first made it; it permeated the department, as if someone had broken wind. He had always suspected that Tawpie had something to do with not letting the matter drop, as some of the school's heavyweights, on and off the faculty, wanted to do.

An article Nick had published in a literary journal seemed to echo too closely an obscure article by a long-dead critic. Nick was no paragon, but he did have a deep respect for words in the service of art and knowledge; that's what had drawn him to the study of literature as a profession in the first place. He had never read the earlier article and maintained that fact through it all.

They sicced the new department work station on him. The computer found an unacceptable number of similarities of phrasing. Today, Nick would tell them how dangerous it could be to trust coincidences, especially in the field of genealogy.

His depressed mood undermined his defense. It was his word against a growing prejudice, until he grew disgusted with the whole thing. He *wanted* them to can him, to give him his freedom at the cost of his former identity and livelihood.

The judgment was rendered. Thumbs down.

Una and Dion defended him to the last. They lobbied successfully for the dropping of charges without comment in exchange for Nick's quiet departure. Quiet, that is, if not for the unkind, self-serving mouth of then-Assistant Professor Frederick Tawpie. Because he was chairing the departmental affairs committee at the time, and willing to speak for attribution, reporters sought him out. In his statements to the school paper and the *Times-Picayune,* he was mostly concerned with parading his own righteousness, though he was supposed to be protecting the honor of the school. It was chiefly because of his high profile in Nick's case that, later, some gullible but powerful alumni pushed for his promotion to the position most department staffers thought Una had earned.

And it was Una who sailed him into the calm cove of genealogy after the storm of disgrace. He had never given the subject a minute's thought, wasn't even sure what it was. It just so happened that a cousin of hers had contacted her about their family origins, and Una rashly volunteered Nick as an experienced genealogical researcher—which, of course, he wasn't. The new challenge was just what he needed. Two published family histories were the result in the following year and a half; these initial works of scholarship kindled his interest in the subject, and cinched his certification.

But after that promising initial splash, Nick now found himself floundering. He had lately begun to wonder if he could stick with anything—or anyone—long enough to find fulfillment.

❑

"Hawty Latimer, huh?" Nick said, rubbing his chin as if deciding, trying not to appear to surrender too easily. "Fine. You win. Send her over. But I can only give her minimum wage."

Victorious at last, Una raised her glass for a toast; Dion and Nick did likewise.

"She may turn out to be very helpful, if she's as sharp as you say. I've got this big project for a little old guy who wants me to track down an ancestor he knows hardly anything about. I might have to do some traveling on this one. I've rushed through my most urgent current projects and lied to the clients who—"

"Zounds! You, lie?" exclaimed Dion, with counterfeit surprise on his expressive face.

"You heard right. Hey, by common consent I'm already a scoundrel, so what do I have to lose? My conscience and I have come to an amicable arrangement: we look the other way when necessary. So, there's a lot someone with a little intelligence could do for me while I'm tied up with my new client."

"If only Messieurs Shakespeare, Jonson, Milton, and Tawpie—he doesn't deserve to be in that august company—would allow me some leisure for such fascinating pursuits! Maybe *I'm* the one who needs Hawty."

"Dion means that we spend quite a lot of time

reading incessant inane memos from the Usurper," Una said.

"What an intellectual titan!" Dion declared. "He concerns himself with things like the price of Twinkies in our snack machine. Sends out polls craving our opinions on parking arrangements. A bad teacher makes a worse bureaucrat. Ah, Nick, in a way I'm glad you aren't soldiering on with us under the new regime, forced to endure the mindless pettiness to which we have descended!"

Dion twirled his flamboyant mustache as he spoke. His bony limbs were splayed across his chair. Beneath his frizzy black-and-gray hair, his thin bearded face had the jaded look of a Renaissance rake in a London strumpet shop. A face from a sixteenth-century miniature. The substantial gap in his front teeth served to enhance the eccentricity of his appearance and gave his speech an engaging sibilance. He was immensely popular with most of his students for his ice-breaking histrionics and brilliant presentation in his difficult classes; others, less interested in the substance of the course, liked the ease with which he could be reduced to caricature in their notebooks.

"Well, we do have our little weapons to fight back, don't we, Dion?"

As Una described the latest guerrilla tactics of their band of departmental subversives, Nick listened with divided attention. Their concern for his state of mind touched him, as usual, and he wanted to put them at ease, convince them he wasn't going to swan dive off the Huey Long Bridge. Yet, he didn't want to let on how much he had begun to love genealogy; he still could not shake a certain feeling of inferiority—even among his best friends; a deeply ingrained idea that genealogy was pap for the masses, junk food for the mind, on a par with astrology.

Yes, he wanted to tell them that genealogy was a synthesis of history, sociology, anthropology, psychology, economics, even literature. That, long before language, there were the rudiments of an appreciation of genealogy in the behavior of proto-humans. It was the mother of biography, the father of heraldry, the thinking ape's response to the genetic imperative to love one's own kind. Religions and dynasties have risen and fallen on the real or faked facts of genealogy. Billions have perished over slight differences in armorial bearings. Nick wanted to say that genealogy should be considered the original social science, the flesh and bone of myths and sagas, perhaps the first application of that uniquely human faculty, memory.

He'd lounged back in his chair, in his typical posture of contemplation: hands locked behind his head, eyes staring at an idea floating somewhere in the music and smoke and dimness.

Una watched him a moment and then said, "Nick, you're . . . all right, then? Really?"

The d-word, depression, was unspoken among them, but on their minds. A mutual friend who'd moved on to another university had recently committed suicide.

"Yeah. Really," Nick assured her.

"This genealogy stuff," Dion said, "he's into it, Una, bastard discipline that it is. That's a sign of emotional health."

"It has its moments," Nick said. "You *have* been secretly reading up on the subject. Bastardy is certainly a frequent topic in genealogy."

"I wish I had the time, as I said. But, my friend, one of these days I'll ask you to address my classes. The synergies could be absolutely mind-blowing. For instance, imagine definitively identifying Will Shakespeare's grandfather, or finding a direct descendant of the Bard after 1670. You would join the ranks of the very greatest Shakespearean scholars. I'll personally write the foreword to your book."

Nick knew he meant it. He was drawn to people

like Dion and Una precisely because of their intellectual curiosity, which allowed them to ridicule dogma and cheer originality.

"By the way, here are two tickets to our production of *As You Like It*, week after next. I play Jaques and a couple of other knavish extras. You would have made an excellent Jaques, misanthrope that you are. Anyway, I expect you be there. Bring someone you wish to impress to our Forest of Arden." He looked at Una with meaning. "It's going to be an excellent effort. Waiter . . . say, I know you. You were in my Tuesday-and-Thursday class last semester. Bring me another Guinness. Make sure it's a cold one, too, none of this room-temperature crap. This is New Orleans not Stratford-on-Avon! And stop by my office the next chance you get. I still have a paper of yours. Frat brat," Dion confided as the young man left. "Wants to 'go into the media,' whatever *that* means. Everything he knows comes from Cliff Notes and CNN, so I suppose he'll make a good television bubble-head. I'm still trying to hammer the soft metal of his soul into a shape more useful to society. Turn him from the Dark Side," he intoned in his best James Earl Jones. "But, alas, some of these children are such difficult cases."

Una's one drink had done its work. "Let's all celebrate the expansion of Nick's business," she said brightly. "I volunteer him as chef for the evening. *If* he can clear out enough room for us among his priceless collection of genealogical junk. We'll stop off at a grocery store on the way. Agreed?"

"Oh, I have . . . to rehearse my lines. Yes," Dion stammered, "very difficult part, you know. Afraid you'll have to count me out."

"That was just slightly obvious," Una said. She smiled anyway and glanced at Nick, an old question in her eyes.

Nick noticed the stronger glasses Una wore; the new depths of wisdom and disappointment her lively and intelligent blue eyes showed; the vocational paleness and mid-life aridness that had replaced the ruddiness and ripe plumpness of her younger days; the wild gray strands that rebelled against every part and wave, where once there had been luxuriant dark honey hair. He wished he had been with her during all the changes he now saw in her, during all of his own changes, too.

He felt the hot closeness of the futile desire to alter the past. But the consciousness of irrevocable mistakes was not new to him. He was not the first to have made bad decisions; there had been countless precedents, and he saw them every day. He'd learned to live with such feelings in part through the solace of his new studies, by imagining the sighs of regret in the frozen spaces among the records he researched.

Genealogist becomes artist, transforming family history into a kind of poetry, when he can give voice to the hope and sadness fossilized in mute statistics of migrations, disappearances, feuds, bankruptcies, births, deaths—the mere punctuation of existences otherwise forgotten; when he can convey some sense of the glory and misery that once filled each unchronicled moment between two heartbeats, those "impossible gaps" as short as a thought, as long as decades, that no one can ever fully know second hand, though the best genealogists never give up trying.

"Nick, we almost forgot to tell you," Una said. "Have you heard that Frederick is doing television commercials, now?"

"Figures." Nick relished more proof of the Usurper's despicable power-hunger. "He's utterly sold out, hasn't he? Tell me all. I want the gory details."

"'I invest with Artemis Funds. Words are my business, but Artemis knows the language of capital growth. Blah-blah-blah-blah,'" Dion said, doing a remarkably accurate imitation of Tawpie at his most pompous. "I wanted to puke the first time I saw it."

"What's Artemis?" asked Nick.

"Oh, you *are* out of the loop, aren't you?" Una said, patting his hand. "He can't help it, poor boy. Artemis Holdings, Nick. Ring a bell, now? You can scarcely go down a New Orleans street, open the local newspaper, or turn on the television without seeing some reference to Artemis. Real estate, stocks and bonds, shipping . . . and he's wheedled this huge grant from Artemis for a new edition of Pound, poetry *and* prose. Heaven help us!"

Dion suddenly became a fast-talking television pitchman: "'Order now and receive at no extra cost the complete Italian Rantos, those infamous World War II radio addresses, in which the poet proved himself a traitor and a quack. Yes, the loopy, anti-Semitic bombast that even Mussolini turned off . . . delivered to your home! Call 1-555-T-A-W-P-I-E for your own no-risk copy.'"

They all had a good laugh.

Una said, "Frederick has made a name for himself as one of old Ezra's foremost modern apologists."

"Beshrew me if that isn't Malvolio himself fouling our happy refuge with his vainglory," Dion said bitterly, having spotted Tawpie. "No more cakes and ale here, my boon companions, I'm afraid. Excuse me. I'm going to play some music. I'd probably say something actionable were I to stay. The fiery Tybalt always was one of my favorite roles." He unfolded himself to his considerable lean height and strode off into the smoky shadows of the bar toward the jukebox, parting the crowd as he brandished an imaginary rapier.

Tawpie, in an ugly lime green blazer, stood just inside the doorway, letting his rabbity eyes adjust to the darker interior of the Folio. It was after seven, and outside the air had taken on a lazy lavender summer glow. He took off his sunglasses, put them in a case and the case in his coat, and then donned another pair of untinted glasses. His hair was an unusual orange color, thick as a mass of snakes. Lighting a cigarette, lolling his head back to exhale voluptuously, he seemed an overgrown, freckled, pudgy kid.

"There's a boy like him in most neighborhoods," Una said, staring with distaste at Tawpie. "He's the one who throws rocks at small animals and younger kids, denies it, and gets away with it, thanks to his hoodwinked mother's intervention."

Tawpie stumbled down the steps that tripped up everyone who wasn't a regular, and searched in vain for a certain face.

His eyes found Nick and Una instead. He made a barely perceptible movement, as if to turn away. But then he swaggered up to their table, a false smile on his face.

"Una, Nick.   How are you?" Tawpie said. "Surprised to see me? Well, this isn't exactly my choice of drinking establishments, you know. I'm supposed to meet someone here, for . . . thesis coaching . . . but she doesn't seem to . . . " Tawpie scanned the crowd, no doubt hoping his friend would rescue him.

"Probably told you the wrong bar on purpose. I sure would," Nick mumbled. Una kicked him under the table. "Probably they moved on to another bar," Nick said louder, in atonement.

Nick, enjoying the awkwardness of the moment, didn't invite his former colleague and probable betrayer to join them.

"Well, Nick," Tawpie said challengingly, seeming to have given up on any invitation to sit down, "I haven't seen you in a long time. What are you doing these days?"

"I don't suppose you really care," Nick said, matching Tawpie's feistiness, "but I'll tell you anyway. Got nothing to hide. I've started a genealogical research firm. Quite successful, several employees."

Una cleared her throat and swirled the melted remains of her drink with her straw.

"I'm so happy for you! It's wonderful when someone can pick up the pieces of a broken life like that. Genealogy. Hmmmm. Somehow, the image in my mind is of a group of blue-haired ladies drinking weak tea and discussing the exploits of their common ancestor, a shopkeeper who once sold General Washington some denture adhesive." Tawpie laughed heartily, lolling his head back on his round shoulders. "Oh, I'm sure it's more significant than that. I certainly *hope* so. You know, I always thought you might seek another teaching position, somewhere out of town, out of the South, of course, where no one would know of the whole sordid mess. But I can see that you might feel uncomfortable in the fold of real scholarship again, with such a disgrace hanging over your head."

"Bad news travels fast along the academic grapevine, Frederick, especially with a little help from back-stabbers."

"I hope you're not implying that I have been anything but professionally neutral in the . . . affair of your departure. You don't seem to need any help destroying your own career."

Nick stood up. He was slightly taller than Tawpie, but the shorter, stockier man was far from backing off; he was as aggressive as a hungry pig, red faced and scowling. Nick had wanted to punch the jerk for a long time, and now seemed just about right.

"There's one thing I really hate, Frederick: a phony who hides behind innuendo and sarcasm."

Una stood up hurriedly and pulled Nick to her. "Take our table, Frederick," she said. "We were just leaving. Don't stay out too late tonight. We need you sharp for our departmental meeting tomorrow at 7:30."

The situation thus defused, Tawpie returned to his disgusting urbanity. "Thank you, no, Una. But I'll have the coffee waiting for *you* tomorrow morning, my dear, in the conference room. We have quite a full agenda."

A waitress struggled by under a loaded tray. Tawpie grabbed her shirt sleeve, almost upsetting the tray; he ordered a Virgin Mary and slipped the waitress a couple of dollars to find a back-corner table.

"Goodbye, Nick. No hard feelings?" Tawpie then turned his back on them and walked away.

Una tugged Nick toward the door. "My job, Nick!" she whispered desperately. "Swallow your anger, for me and Dion. *Please.*"

Nick glanced back over his shoulder. "Hard feelings?" he snarled, too low for Tawpie to hear in the tumult of the bar. "Oh, yeah, Frederick, there certainly are. Lots of them."

At that moment, a loud whistle pierced the lull between songs, and the bar grew momentarily hushed. It was Dion, who had a remarkable facility for whistling through the gap in his teeth, signaling across the room that his selection was coming up.

The bell-like revival-organ chords of Dylan's "Positively 4th Street" filled the cavernous barroom, the words bristling with scorn for yesterday's enemies turned fair-weather friends.

Nick hoped that Tawpie, though famously devoted to Wagner, would pay enough attention to catch the insult in the Dylan song.

They waved to Dion as they left the Folio and stepped onto the quiet sidewalk in the humid evening.

"Virgin Mary. Perfect," Nick said. "He thrives on the blood of innocents."

"That certainly describes his marriage, as everyone knows," answered Una.

"I guess I shouldn't let him get to me like that. Hey, people lose their jobs all the time, and the powerful have stomped on the little guy from time immemorial."

"You're only human. That's why I still love you."

❏

She was late for the meeting the next morning,

and hung-over. Ignoring the terrible throbbing in her head and the indignant stare of the Usurper, she smiled with a private joy and inhaled the invigorating aroma of her coffee.

Chapter 4

Balazar. An uncommon name, Nick found over the next week. He checked a few favorite reference sources first, many of which he had on his crowded office shelves: bound indexes of early Louisiana censuses, Gulf and Atlantic port-entry records, state birth and death indexes, state military service lists. No dice.

Today he headed for the New Orleans Public Library.

Summer is the most popular time of the year for beginners in genealogy. Students have lots of free time, and families pile into their vans for vacations. Amateurs who have knocked their heads against bureaucratic walls of correspondence all year flock to libraries around the country for a few days of frenzied searching.

Nick could tell them that some rural county courthouses would probably be a better place to spend their summer days; and they could perhaps learn more from that aged distant cousin in the retirement home in Florida. The desire to do something, anything, drives these eager amateurs from one how-to book to the next, from one library genealogical section to another, without much to show for their labor when they get home except a much thinner wallet.

The librarians who staff the genealogical sections, usually calm and polite during the rest of the year, become testy and unhelpful during the summer. Rarely do they point out to these pesky beginners the riches of their facilities, such as wonderful old maps and manuscripts that don't appear in the general card catalogs, material which might hold in dusty, crumbling pages the crucial bit of information—say, for instance, that a state carved County X from Counties Y and Z at the end of the eighteenth century, and that Old Uncle Pierre, who seems to be nowhere around during the period in question, lived in that often overlooked county.

Nick tried to avoid searching microfilm at public libraries during this hectic time of the year. Microfilm viewers could be tied up all day during June, July, and August, or so overworked that most were out of commission, awaiting repair.

Now, here on the third floor of the library, the crush was as bad as he'd ever seen it. Full sign-up sheets hung from every viewing machine, and the fiftieth person that hour had just asked the harried librarian at the counter for copier change. A friend of Nick's, she looked at him across the crowded room and made a gun of her hand and put it to her temple.

The dozen or so round cream-colored Formica-covered tables were packed with researchers. The uncomfortable wooden chairs around the tables played hell with a hundred sacroiliacs. Nick wandered for a few minutes, half-heartedly looking for a place to light, wishing just a few of these rookies would throw in the towel and give him a crack at their family history impasse. The big room reeked with the public funk of too many people who'd sweated and cooled too many times in the New Orleans oven outside. Conversations rose to distracting levels from the stacks, as retirees droned on about who begot whom in their families.

"Excuse me, ma'am, is this seat taken?" Nick asked an overweight, bug-eyed, wheezing woman with thin hair dyed henna.

She said nothing as she raked a large mound of books and papers toward her. But she did favor him with a withering glare, as if he'd just asked her to do something extremely objectionable to her moral sense.

He worked for a few minutes in the stacks,

frustrated to find that most of the books he needed were out—probably in the possession of the ogreish woman at the table.

Nick was treating Corban's familial oral tradition with a large grain of salt—a wise course for a genealogist. Much of the time, the sort of legend the old man related only confuses and misdirects the uncritical family historian. Take for example the common one that tells of three brothers who emigrated from the Old Country. One stayed in the New World base, where they landed, one went west, and the other south. The brothers, of course, did no such thing, if the individuals even existed at all. Most families have such an innocently misleading story tucked away in their collective memory. The truth usually proved to be more complex, sometimes even unpleasant. Human lives do not follow nice and easy symmetrical patterns or unfold according to formulas.

But Nick fought another doubt about Max Corban, as well. Was he leading him somewhere for a purpose other than normal familial curiosity? He sensed something lurking within Corban's story, something dangerous in the subtle details of their meeting. Nothing definite he could put his finger on, but still, certain things about Corban bothered him . . . the old man's vehement refusal to consider probably useful overseas research; his peculiar preoccupation with blood; his failure to recall even the name of the ancestor at the end of the interview. Nick had learned to rely on his intuition to lead him through the fog of life; a faint warning was sounding somewhere in his mind.

Ah, forget it, he told himself; get back to work. Maybe he was being too hard on the old guy; maybe it was time to start trusting people again.

He'd decided to check the phone books. It was a long shot that a genealogical search like this one, so devoid of details, would have such initial success—finding the right family of the right name, such an odd one at that, in the most accessible of places: a book everybody has in a kitchen drawer. But Nick was a gambler, especially when the losses came from someone else's pocket. Genealogists have to be gamblers—the most certain clues can turn out to be nearly useless; the chance discoveries from wholly unrelated sources often point the way. You never know when you'll draw the joker or the ace.

And if you got lucky, a simple phone call could crack a difficult genealogical case, make the family tree sprout with previously unknown generations. A handful of times he'd located a living survivor of a lost lineage this way, who guarded a wealth of family lore, and who'd waited years simply for someone to ask the right questions. Nick had found few things in life as exciting as those unexpected revelations.

Genealogy is like drilling for oil: lots of dry holes, but the stuff is down there, somewhere. The cardinal rule is to start with the simple, then work up to the complex, start with the living and work back to the dead. Corban wasn't helping him do that, so Nick was improvising.

Was there a breathing bearer of the name Balazar somewhere in the state?

In dozens of Louisiana phone books he could find nothing exactly matching the name. There were plenty of Balthazars and variants, and even a couple of Belshazzars. An unfortunate surname, that one, he thought, scanning the blue plastic cards of microfiche, the transparent writing so small that to the naked eye it looked like specks of sand.

"'*Mene Mene, Tekel Upharsin,*'" he mumbled several times, enjoying the incantatory sound of the words and remembering the great story of the judgment of a king written supernaturally on a wall. *Your days are numbered, you are weighed and found wanting, your kingdom will perish*, Daniel told the terrified Belshazzar. Genealogists rediscover the truth of that prophecy each working day.

The woman at the next microfiche machine shot him a worried look and clutched her bulging purse.

He still wasn't discouraged. Finding no Balazars might simply mean that this family had no phone, or that the number was unlisted.

He tried several current and old city directories—fascinating volumes of data that aided businesses with marketing information about local citizens and other businesses. These directories can sometimes fill in the years between the decennial censuses. Nothing there, either. Not an unusual state of affairs. Many people slipped through the fingers of those who would tabulate them, especially in the days of fierce pioneering individualism, when distrust of the ever-curious government was stronger even than it is today. And there were whole classes of people who, according to the prevailing notions, simply did not count.

Next he searched the genealogical indexes for articles or existing family histories dealing with or referring to the surname Balazar. Nothing again. Even the scholars and family historians of the past were letting him down.

Nick was a resourceful researcher and had more tricks up his sleeve.

He phoned a friend, a volunteer congregant, at the local Latter-day Saints Family History Library. She made a quick search of the computer catalog of the main Salt Lake City library for anything relevant. Eight times out of ten the Mormons, who have a world-renowned commitment to genealogy as an article of their faith, came through for Nick. This, though, was one of the two times that nothing turned up.

It was time to search the federal censuses page by page, household by household, for the individuals who might have been skipped in the various indexes.

But not here, he decided.

He had a more secluded venue in mind, a secret he kept closely, knowing that popularity and crowds would irreparably damage it.

The Plutarch Foundation was only a few blocks from Freret University, filling with its thousands of books, original documents, microfilms, and exquisite antiques a superbly kept, stately Uptown "American cottage"—a cameo in a frame of ancient oaks, veteran camellias, and brick walkways worn smooth and friendly with nearly two centuries' use. Scholars dreamed of places like the Plutarch.

Seldom were there more than half-a-dozen people in the two-story building, two or three being volunteer staffers. If they liked the researcher, these staffers might personally guide him to the required source, and later offer coffee and sweets in a sitting room overlooking a lush English garden at the back of the house. Though it specialized in the Battle of New Orleans, the Plutarch was an excellent all-round genealogical facility—a fact few knew.

"Man alive, am I glad to see you," Angus Murot said to Nick, who stood in the foyer, dripping from a sudden downpour that had caught him on the walkway.

"I got this letter here from France," Angus began, without further preamble, excited as usual over his long-running genealogical project. "I can't make head nor tails of it. That French gal at my urologist's office—you know, the one that helped me write my letter—she run off with one of the doctors."

Angus had ushered Nick into a small book-lined room with a central worktable that looked like genuine Duncan Phyfe. Around the room, among other pieces of museum-quality furniture, there were shelves, stands, and cases displaying rare editions or splendid objects of historical interest.

"I dragged you in here," Angus whispered, full of awe, "because Coldbread's out there. You know how he gets when there's noise." He limped over to close the door a few more inches.

Angus had a false leg from the knee down. He had lost it fighting the Japanese on New Georgia, as he would readily tell anyone with the slightest interest. For a decade now he had been tracing an ancestor, a member of Lafitte's entourage, who was personally commended by General Andrew Jackson for bravery. Angus had a certified photocopy of this letter, along with expert opinion that the now-missing original was not a forgery. Maybe, maybe not, Nick believed but had never said. A disconcerting portion of genealogy is based on half-truths and honest errors.

The taciturn Mr. Coldbread was a cranky fixture at the Plutarch; no one knew exactly what he had been researching here for six years, but it had something to do with hidden treasure and the Duke of Wellington's brother-in-law Sir Edward Pakenham, who died with many of his men in the disastrous 1815 attack on General Jackson's defending forces.

"Says here," Nick said, struggling to translate, "that they find no trace of the guy in that *département*, or province. Who was he, anyway?"

"The second cousin of the soldier that got commended."

"There's more: you owe them a little over seven dollars."

"After all the money I already sent them, after all we did for those Frenchies in the war?! Why, they didn't even have the courtesy to write me back in my own language, like I did for them. Can you believe it?!" Angus's face was beet red. "Just look at it: like some chicken walked all over the keyboard."

"Some memories are short when gratitude's involved, Angus. Better get used to this kind of thing. Genealogical research can be like that. Tell you what you do. Read this article first." Nick wrote down the title of a brief treatment of the vicissitudes of foreign research at a distance. "I know you have a copy here. Then we'll send them a few international postal coupons, along with some other questions you and I'll come up with. I'll help you with my miserable French. And don't worry: they're proud but efficient, and probably really want to help. After all, you're their countryman. We'll get to the bottom of it."

Nick made sure to send an annual donation to the Plutarch, but it was payment of this kind that really kept his welcome warm here.

Little Mrs. Fadge, profoundly deaf but always cheerful, helped Nick find the census microfilms he needed, though he didn't really need her help. After promising her to have coffee and cookies when he finished his work, he entered the converted butler's pantry that now housed five microfilm viewers, of sixties vintage and bulk, but in perfect order.

The subject of his research today was to be the 1880 census. This date would certainly be the far end of this mysterious Balazar man's possible life span.

The government had by 1880 become aware of the vast significance of the mandated prying every ten years. It had become clear that descendants of *Mayflower* passengers and of Virginia gentry would thenceforth constitute a diminishing percentage of the country's populace. Someone in Washington decided it was time to find out who *were* these millions of new Americans Walt Whitman was singing about. Nick always found lots of good information in the 1880 census, though not as much as in the 1900. But first, he needed to check the Soundex, a phonetic index that groups names by first letter and consonants.

The Work Projects Administration during the Depression was given the task of indexing certain censuses. Social Security was starting up, and it was essential to know who might be eligible, who would be turning 65 in 1935. The census was the perfect place to look for a person's year of birth. It's the actual testimony of the person in question, or at least someone who knew him. Sometimes the only testimony.

For a country with a Babel of names from skyrocketing immigration, for vital records where clerks spelled for convenience or by whim, the Soundex is a good place to start. But one caveat is that the 1880 Soundex includes only those households with children ten years old and under.

Nick had seen many amateurs tripped up by this last arcane detail: an ancestor may in fact be in the census proper, even if he doesn't appear on the Soundex.

Keeping such knowledge to himself was job security, a way of ensuring that there would always be a need for professional genealogists, Nick reflected as he coded the surname Balazar.

In the darkened microfilm room, Nick used the Soundex code for Balazar—B426—to find the Balzar family, living in the old town of Natchitoches, Louisiana, Natchitoches Parish, 9 June 1880. He had already checked for the surname Balazar without success and reluctantly was about to call it a day.

As always happened when he made an important find, a triumphant smile of discovery spread across his face, and an unmistakable shiver hit him between the shoulders. He sat under the hood of the reader, leaning into the tunnel of light which vouchsafed him a glimpse of a century earlier, savoring the moment, but also questioning his find—as a good genealogist must do, no matter how rock-solid the evidence seems.

The spelling similarity was too close to ignore, he thought, struggling to be the rational researcher. Simply a question of a missing vowel. Worse errors on birth certificates were common, he knew. In such cases, the midwife was confused, the doctor was guessing or too busy or too drunk to care, or no certificate was ever issued because the child was born in a sharecropper's cabin with just the family around. And, of course, the enumerator wasn't a detective; he wrote down what he thought he heard.

The rush of discovery flooded through his body again as he studied the projected image of the Soundex card before him. His eyes lingered on the line indicating "Color": the head of household, Ivanhoe Balzar, was listed as a mulatto.

Either Nick's hunch was incorrect, and these were not the people he was searching for, or Corban's family tree had just become more complicated, even more interesting, and somewhat puzzling. Certainly, it was common for former slaves to take a garbled version of the slave-owning white family's name, and slavery was only fifteen years before this date; but could Ivanhoe Balzar have had a more direct relationship with the family called Balazar?

As he loaded up the appropriate reel of the actual census, which he had slipped out to get without Mrs. Fadge's helpful interference, he heard several voices near the entrance of the microfilm room. It was Angus, giving somebody a tour. Somebody important, judging from his eagerness to explain everything in the building and beyond. Angus loved to talk, but he was really cutting loose this time.

Nick was more like the cantankerous Coldbread than he would have cared to admit: he hated to be interrupted during his research. He prepared a hard face for the intruders. But turning, he was astonished.

Whoever she was, she was beautiful. A grin of adolescent delight settled on his face.

She stood in the doorway of the darkened room, the faint light of his microfilm machine on her face, the stronger light from the building's interior giving her long dark hair and her enchanting curves a sort of glowing outline. He'd seen lots of pretty female students pass through his classes, but if this woman had been in one of them, he would have been in more serious trouble much sooner.

She was taking notes on one of those digital pads Nick refused to learn anything about. Two young fellows behind her watched her every move; each was glued to a cellular phone.

She looked Nick right in the eyes; he felt absolutely transparent. It seemed to him that not only did she know him, but also that she had just read his own listing in some psychic census of character.

"Terribly sorry to disturb you," she said. "Just be a moment. We're honored that you've chosen the Plutarch Foundation for your work."

Disturb me! Baby, you can disturb me all day and all night! he wanted to shout. But she was gone already. The two young men were so busy relaying her observations into their cellulars that they missed her departure; finally realizing she was gone, they hurried off to catch up.

This woman was no ordinary tourist, Nick was sure.

Still staring at the empty doorway, he could hear Angus talking about him; he squirmed at this extravagant praise, but hoped she believed at least half of it.

He returned to the spring of 1880.

Sure, he knew he'd be more productive if he just rolled the film to the specific place under investigation; but he never could do it. He was a window shopper, lingering over interesting details and names along the way. Who was related to whom in the household, who could read and write, where the parents were born, age, birthplace, marital status, occupation . . . each elegant or rudimentary letter from the pen of the enumerator a possible saga in itself, with ramifications that might ripple through centuries.

Nick carefully transcribed the Balzar census information, forming hypotheses as he wrote. Odd thing: in the "Color" column of the "Personal

Description" section, the "W" had been overwritten with "Mu" on Ivanhoe's line. Had the enumerator made a simple clerical mistake, or had Ivanhoe been trying to pass for white under the nose of a public official who knew him and would have none of it?

Before long, Nick heard a couple of the magnificent clocks in the place chime the hour of four: quitting time. A few other clocks chimed intermittently for the next fifteen minutes.

When he emerged, red-eyed, from the microfilm room, he saw that Coldbread was packing up, making sure no one got a glimpse of his top-secret project.

Nick made his way to the wide, gracious porch, where Angus stood watching another sudden shower roar down on the steaming street. "Who was that woman?" he asked Angus.

"Oh, I figured you'd want to know, you old wolf, you!" He laughed his belly laugh. Angus considered Nick something of a playboy. On what evidence, Nick wasn't sure, unless it was his habit of helping the attractive women in their research and ignoring the others.

"That's one very important lady, let me tell you," said Angus. "Miss Zola Armiger. Big executive, manager or vice-president or something or other—I'm not sure what you call her—of the investment company that handles the Plutarch's finances. You know, the endowment and all that? I forget the name of her company. They say her family owns it. Comes by now and again to make sure everything's up to snuff, that we have everything we need to stay a first-class place. Better take this."

Angus lent Nick an umbrella, though it had quit raining for the moment. Nick loudly assured Mrs. Fadge, who had joined them, that he'd take her up on coffee and cookies next time.

Then he walked outside in the stifling late afternoon toward his car, a BMW 2002 that once, in his youthful days of hedonism, had been a hell of a vehicle. He recalled with a sigh how fast he used to drive his metallic blue baby between the empty streetcar tracks on St. Charles, at four in the morning! Highly illegal and dangerous, of course, but once he hadn't cared. Oh, the idiotic, ecstatic things he'd done in this car . . .

It wasn't exactly a collectible now, unless you were a dealer in scrap metal. He accepted total blame for its rust and general deterioration. The oil-change sticker was no longer legible, and didn't the owner's manual say to always leave the windows open in the rain?

When he'd bailed out the driver's compartment enough to navigate, he was already late for his meeting with Hawty Latimer.

Chapter 5

Nick banged the steering wheel.

St. Charles Avenue was flooded, and rush-hour traffic had him in its taffy grip.

Kids played in brown water backed up from the heavy downpour, and when a big wave came they retreated with summer squeals to the craggy sidewalks deformed by the roots of the old oaks that defined the famous street. Cops wrote tickets to hapless drivers who had stalled, or worse, tried to make a left turn—a grievous sin in this city, where murder attracts less notice. The cars looked like boats, complete with wakes.

Traffic crept on, with the occasional surprise of some urban cowboy barging through an opening in his fifty-grand SUV; the cops, of course, never saw *him*. The dark-green streetcars rocked along with their roar and clang, packed with sweltering riders, the windows raised for a speed-driven breeze in spite of the continuing drizzle. They made only slightly better time than everyone except the joggers who competed with them for the soggy "neutral ground" of grass that separated the traffic lanes.

Nick would have loved a jog about now, to ease the tensed-up muscles of his neck and shoulders, to get the blood moving in his legs.

Behind fogged windows, in the cool confines of posh bars, he noticed well-heeled patrons ignoring the unfortunate drones outside. Once or twice, he imagined he saw the blurred figure of Zola Armiger, laughing with glass raised, as in some happy Renoir party. Closer to Lee Circle, the bars and the patrons got seedier; befuddled men and women peered forlornly or belligerently from open dark doorways at the parade of those who still played the game.

Maybe, just maybe, Hawty had grown disgusted waiting and had left, Nick thought, his mood brightening. He'd used that ploy often enough with pesky or psychotic students before.

He was certain he wasn't going to like this girl, much less hire her, no matter what he'd promised Una. He'd made up his mind, and that was that!

When he finally arrived at his street, he parked in a tow-away zone.

□

"I just want you to know that I was on time for our interview. See?" she said, pointing to a machine-printed note taped to Nick's office door. "Mr. Herald, how do you do. I'm Hawty Latimer."

They shook hands. She had a plump, cheerful face, with wonderfully youthful dark-brown skin and dark eyes like black onyx set in pearl. Self-confidence emanated from her, along with a rather nice perfume. She wore understated jewelry and interview clothes, just like, like . . . a normal person. Nick figuratively bit his tongue, even though he'd only thought that. Una and Dion and their little devious plots! They had neglected to tell him one significant fact about his prospective employee: she was confined to a wheelchair.

But what a vehicle! Hawty sat in what looked to Nick like a futurist's wildest conception of a wheelchair for the next century, a cross between an all-terrain vehicle and a physics lab.

"My apologies for being late, Hawty." Nick unlocked his door and stepped aside to let her in. "Got hung up in traffic. I was just over in your neighborhood, over by school: the Plutarch Foundation."

"Sure! I've done research there, on the documents of the *Escudo*, the slave ship. I did an article for the school magazine."

"There was a revolt during the voyage, right?"

"That's the one! 1839."

"I'd like to read your article one day. I fancy myself something of a writer, too."

"I know. Professor Kern has told me *a-l-l* about you."

Just as Nick had suspected. Una had recruited Hawty as a spy and had briefed her accordingly.

"Has she?" Nick said, amused by all the hidden stratagems he sensed at play. "Well, before we talk about the job, Hawty, I'm curious. How in the world did you get up here?" As far as he knew, his building was innocent of an elevator.

"It wasn't easy," she replied "I'm going to write your landlord and request a ramp the first thing. The LIFT-bus driver helped me up the front steps—that's the city handicap bus. Then, after a while, I found the freight elevator at the end of the hall. This place is awfully lonely; hardly any tenants. Anyway, if you want to know what I did for an hour and a quarter, I read as many articles on genealogy as I could access on my computer. I was just about to call the bus back when you showed up."

She wasn't chastising Nick, he realized; hers was the tone of a determined person who often confronted the doubts of others. She had obviously seen other people's hang-ups become self-fulfilling prophecies for her. She seemed accustomed to defending herself.

The marvelous machine she rode moved with humming precision around Nick's humble daylight quarters. She directed her chair with a joystick, using her arms with the wheels for subtler movements. The car companies should hire her to light a fire under their halfhearted efforts to develop alternatively powered vehicles, Nick mused.

Her chair brushed a pile of books, manuscripts, and journals leaning against a wall; the pile collapsed, setting off a domino effect that took a few moments to run its course.

"Don't worry about that, Hawty. Happens all the time to me."

"How long have you been here, Mr. Herald?" she asked, continuing her excursion around the room. Nick got the distinct feeling that she was sizing *him* up. He heard a hint of disapproval, maybe even derision.

"Well, I, uh . . . I'm sort of still in the transitional stage. Used to work out of my apartment in the Quarter, but things got a little tight there. Been about a year, I guess."

"A whole year! And the place still looks like *this*?"

Nick was soaked; his briefcase weighed a ton; he was tired. He invited Hawty to roll over to his desk, where he dropped his briefcase, causing another minor avalanche. But she wasn't quite ready and drove around the cramped office a bit more. She even checked out the bathroom.

Gutsy, if a little too blunt, he thought, beginning to like her. He'd come from a long line of smart-asses himself; sarcasm was a second language to him. Hawty was a member of the same club. She talked fast, and obviously thought faster. As she joined him at his desk, he looked at the putty-colored computer, about the size of a thick magazine, mounted on a pivoting metal arm, like a tray table on an airliner seat.

Unbidden, she bombarded Nick with technical terms, explaining that a cellular modem hookup allowed her access to the entire world and even some other planets. At least that's what Nick thought she said. He was lost in jargon. She also said that her actual given name was Harrieta, but that she kept it secret because she hated it; she asked him not to tell anyone because her friends would probably start using it to tease her.

Guilt ambushed him as he listened. He should have been here to help her. No, he told himself, that wasn't the right attitude. He'd taught many handicapped students, some in wheelchairs, some in much worse shape than Hawty. He knew that pity usually enraged them. But he'd always found it difficult to hide the pity he felt for them. He tried to make his face a blank of expression as Hawty chattered on about her wheelchair.

Nick hadn't much bothered to keep up with the current politics of vocabulary. How was he supposed to refer to her condition? Was she "differently abled," "physically challenged," "motor-skills impaired," "special," or simply "disabled"? He would have to do his best to treat her as he would anyone else; he had a sense that that's what Hawty would want.

" . . . it's all part of a project undertaken by the computer sciences department at Freret," Hawty was saying. "We've made some pretty amazing discoveries, Mr. Herald. I predict there're going to be lots of patents, lots—maybe even a Nobel Prize—in this thing. Not to mention the doctorates on the line. Guy I'm dating is one of them; he's already had job offers from NASA and a bunch of industrial heavyweights."

"Look, Hawty, I don't want to keep you too long. I have no doubt you'll be right for the job. You come with great recommendations. So consider yourself hired. But, I'm sorry to say, the pay will be nothing to write home about."

Holding his breath, he mentioned the low figure. She didn't laugh in his face, at least.

"Oh, that's wonderful, Mr. Herald! You don't know how much this means to me." Her eyes filled momentarily with tears, but she quickly rubbed them away. "I'm having a little trouble making ends meet, and that really, really bothers me. I had some unexpected medical expenses. Another kidney infection. Going to Freret is the best thing that's ever happened to me. My education is more important than eating. I'd starve if I had to."

Moved by her gratitude and inspired by her commitment to her schooling, Nick pressed his lips together to keep himself from offering triple the figure he'd just mentioned; he knew that would be impossible.

He said, "To start, I'll ask you to handle mostly clerical tasks. As you learn more about genealogy, I hope you'll move into original research. Your, uh, electronic gizmo can type—I mean print, right?"

She pointed to Nick's massive typewriter. "Makes that old thing look like a Model T."

"Good. Tomorrow, you can do a much better job with this than I did. It's a draft of an article I'm working up on the yellow-fever epidemic of 1878, and how to use the death lists in family history research."

"No problem," she said. "Sounds interesting. Oh, there are a few other things I'd like to get started on, too—if it's okay with you. Maybe figure out some system for all this," and she made a sweeping motion with her arm to indicate the sea of paper and books around them. "I bet your files could stand some attention. There's no toilet paper. And most of the lights are burned out. I was thinking maybe I could put a desk—if I can find one—in that other room. Don't worry. I'll take care of everything. I bet there's lots of spare furniture in this building."

"Hey, chill out," Nick said, smiling, trying to show her how hip he was.

She made a comical face and covered a giggle. Oh, well, so much for being hip, Nick thought.

"Let's not rush things, okay, Hawty? Tomorrow morning, say ten, we'll get to work. I don't like time clocks, and I don't expect you to work under the tyranny of one."

"If I waited on people to help an African American woman in a wheelchair, I'd be dead of frostbite or something else already. *I'll* be here at eight. Got another key?"

Nick searched for one in several overstuffed drawers.

"Here we go," he said. "Better take one to my apartment, too. I think of it as a large filing cabinet. If I'm on the road, I may need you to go over there."

He briefly explained the most pressing current project, Max Corban, telling her the old guy might kick off at any moment. She was eager to get started.

Nick asked her to search current Natchitoches phone books and city directories for a living Balzar in Natchitoches, and to find the libraries and archives in that area that have material on local family history.

"No problem," she said, her fingers dancing over her computer's keyboard.

That must be her motto, Nick thought.

When Nick asked about her arrangements to get home, she assured him a special cab would be around in a few minutes for her, driven by a friend who didn't charge her. She would wait in the entryway downstairs.

He noticed the sun outside making one last encore through the clearing slate-colored clouds. He was glad Hawty would have good light while she waited for her taxi.

Nick was impressed. The girl was a dynamo with more contacts, schemes, and chutzpah than a crooked Louisiana legislator.

They rode the abominable freight elevator down together. In the entryway she said, "They were wrong, Mr. Herald. About the plagiarism thing."

"Call me Nick. It'll save time. Fewer syllables. Sure, I know; I didn't do it."

"No, I mean empirically. They used faulty data, a flawed program. That was a few years ago. Programming has come a long way since then. Over at Computer Sciences, we ran the two articles through our own new program—kind of a test case. I wrote a paper on it, found fifteen fewer identical phrasings. See, the first time they counted some hyphenated parts of words as whole words. That makes a big difference. Shouldn't trust those over-the-counter programs too much. Lots of bugs."

Not sure whether to be grateful or insulted that he had been a "test case" for some brainy hackers, Nick realized that what she had just told him might have made all the difference in the world.

"Hawty, you're about four years too late, but I'm damn glad you're here now. See you tomorrow—at eight."

Chapter 6

Ah, the French Quarter!

Museum, theme park, bordello, midway, haunted house, shrine; tacky in its inimitably stylish way, Paris, Hong Kong, New York City, Port-au-Prince, Rio, Heaven, and Hell, all packed into a square mile, an international heroin of beauty and dementia.

Nick had never wanted to live anywhere else in New Orleans. Other sections with an equally rich history or eccentricity seemed less interesting, even boring, by comparison.

Residents of the city invariably put down the Quarter, but where do they take a visitor first? Here, of course—what tourists flock to see, either to wallow in it or to point sanctimonious fingers.

In Nick's imagination, the Vieux Carré was a mad Old World princess in a G-string, the last of her line, still gorgeous in her bedraggled way, reeking of stale perfume, rotting teeth, and recent copulation, irresistible for the fascinating tales she told when high, tragicomic operas pregnant with danger, heartbreak, and ecstasy. For some Quarter denizens, she had attained surreal, mythic status as an androgynous demigod presiding over the bizarre transformations of the night.

Around a few corners from Nick's place was Lafitte's Blacksmith Shop; the voodoo queen Marie Laveau II killed a man a block away with a curse; down the street Confederate official Judah Benjamin hid the night he hoofed it for England as the South crumbled; Sieur de Bienville, Dickens, Twain, Faulkner, Degas,

Tennessee Williams, Anne Rice, and Mr. Bojangles all slept or did something else noteworthy nearby . . . this and more according to the narration of the mule-carriage drivers who routinely make up such stories at will for their gaping foreign passengers.

Nick's Dauphine St. apartment was on the third floor; sometimes he caught fragments of these narratives during the pleasant spring and fall days when the weather and the mosquitoes let him open his windows onto his dozen feet of balcony.

A gift shop run by two gay guys took up the first floor of the building. Coordinated place settings, European cutlery, minor and suspect antiques, soap, potpourri, scented candles . . . Nick had no use for their merchandise, but he did enjoy their fabulous complimentary shop hors d'oeuvres, which often served as his meals. For favored customers or neighbors, like Nick, most afternoons they mixed excellent drinks. They were the principals of an unofficial gay neighborhood Carnival krewe; all year they planned their outrageously obscene costumes and parade theme. Nick was told that their Mardi Gras ball at a Quarter bar was so wild it took several weeks to recover from.

The second floor, as far as Nick could tell, was abandoned. A few years back, a well-heeled family from Colorado got it into their heads that they wanted a cozy French Quarter hotel. Three gung-ho sons spent millions buying this building and the one behind it, made the second floor below Nick the office, and promptly ran the whole works into the ground. The family still owned the buildings, but seemed content now merely to collect rent and let the former hotel decay as the bankruptcy played out and the Formosan termites munched.

New Orleans will do that, rob usually sensible folks of their mother wit, anesthetize common sense so thoroughly that even a prude with a good upbringing can fall prey to an overpowering desire to bare body parts from Bourbon Street balconies in broad daylight.

The courtyard in the back of Nick's building was lushly overgrown, the fountain now quiet. Nick liked the aura of gentle decrepitude.

His apartment must have been gutted at some point in the past, maybe by the big 1788 fire that destroyed most of the original Quarter. Now there were hardly any interior walls, just eighteenth-century bricks, and beams that looked like pieces of a sailing ship. Topography is not a term often associated with human dwellings, but in this place, the elevation wasn't the same at any two points on the old oak floor. You could stub a toe standing still. Nick half expected the whole building to crumble any day like so much stale icing. Whenever he started worrying about that possibility, he said a few propitiatory words to the spirits of both Marie Laveaus.

❑

Who was Ivanhoe Balzar? Nick wondered, reviewing his notes. He'd polished off a leftover portion of a hero sandwich from his favorite Greek restaurant over by the French Market. Cheap but potent screw-top red wine was aiding him in his ruminations.

For the sake of argument, he toyed with the theory that the "a" had been dropped from the name somewhere along the line, either accidentally or deliberately. Linguistic disinheritance. The fact that Ivanhoe was mulatto might explain this—often the case during and after slavery, when even a fractional part of black heritage led to exclusion from society in general—at best. Mulatto, a word derived from the French and Spanish ones for mule, was an insulting definition to those who had to bear it. So it didn't surprise Nick that Ivanhoe had apparently attempted to pass as white on the census, perhaps to establish some baseline of evidence that he was white.

Louisiana, then as now, sinned first and asked questions later. There was a great deal of mixing, and a complex hierarchy of race was born. Even today the term "Creole" is hotly debated by whites and blacks who define it to suit their traditions and satisfy their egos.   Upper-crust customs only magnified the confusion: light-colored beauties were favored by young white French, Spanish, and American rakes as mistresses. In New Orleans, quadroon balls were big social events, where these beautiful young mulatto women were shown off by their mothers to the rich white men in masks. A few mulattoes attained high social status through such arrangements, and many prominent white men maintained separate families—white and "of color"—when mere forbidden pleasure gave way to genuine love.

In the census, Ivanhoe stated that he was born in Louisiana, but he said his father was born in France, and his mother in Mississippi. The France part got Nick's attention. He knew that boundaries had shifted frequently in Europe; this man might have been from that contested area that changed hands so often, Alsace-Lorraine. Not too far from Corban's German birthplace. Was this Corban's collateral ancestor, the surviving branch the old man so ardently hoped to find? Was Ivanhoe's father the Balazar who had emigrated, the individual who would unlock the door to old Corban's American family?

Ivanhoe was forty-one in 1880, or so he said; he seemed prosperous. His wife, Mary, was twenty-seven. Their children were Erasmus, 8; Amicus, 5; Victoria, 4, all described as mulattoes. Ivanhoe stated that he was a barber; Elizabeth occupied herself with "keeping house," the usual description of a woman's activities at the time. One or both had some education, Nick inferred from the somewhat novel names of the children. There were two others in the house, both black: Eliza Crome, 43, "servant" under the relationship column, performed the duties of "cook"; John Crome, 20, perhaps her son, was also a "servant," his occupation being "laborer."

Nick felt sure this Ivanhoe was a crucial link in the story. Since he now had a different strategy, he would need to recheck earlier censuses for Ivanhoe, fill in the picture of his youth, if possible. That could lead him to the father, who just might be the crucial Balazar individual.

But what Nick really needed to do was rummage around the local courthouse in search of birth, marriage, and death certificates, suits, wills, and deeds—the usual building blocks of the genealogical edifice. That would require a personal visit. He had severe doubts that his car was up to the drive. He'd probably make better time in Hawty's chariot!

It was past midnight, but he had an urge to revisit the early days of Louisiana, in which Natchitoches played a pivotal role. Like a bloodhound, Nick hated to let go of a good scent. Stretched out on his couch, he refreshed his memory regarding the tag-team wrestling match between the French and the Spanish and various Indian tribes before the Louisiana Purchase, until the combination of satisfying food, bad wine, and fatigue brought the curtains down on the day's performance.

❑

"Coldbread?"

"Stay where you are, Mr. Herald! I'm warning you!"

"Put that gun away," Nick said. "What are you doing in my apartment at—what is it—three in the goddamn morning? You must be crazy."

The neatly and expensively dressed, pallid, flabby little man stood in the corner of the room that served as Nick's bad excuse for a study. There was a dangerous look in his eyes, a mad glaze; a few sad strands of hair hung over his perpetually indignant face. He had been rummaging around in Nick's papers and books, ineptly and not so subtly. Nick could see he didn't know much about the small-bore revolver he held unsteadily; he didn't want to use it, obviously, despite his unconvincing threat.

"That's what my father used to tell me: crazy," said Coldbread, lowering the arm with the gun, as he returned to the old slight that apparently burned in his soul. He sighed deeply. "Oh, this. It's not loaded. I don't have the heart for this kind of thing, you know. I am but a humble scholar. My father desired ardently that I should be a lawyer, a diplomat, a statesman, as our family tradition dictates. To move in the circles of great men, to enhance the standing of the family with my Ciceronian declamations from the forum of public service. But then I discovered *it*!"

"'It'?"

"The treasure! Well, not exactly the treasure itself, but the legend of the treasure, and through the years the irrefutable evidence of its existence."

There were few words that could make Nick more skeptical than "irrefutable."

Coldbread rambled on, as if Nick were his well-paid shrink: "He cut me off without a dime, but my saintly mother supported me for many years and then restored my inheritance on her death. Now, I have the means to attain my rightful status in history. I will be the Schliemann of New Orleans!"

"That's great, Coldbread. I'm happy for you. What's all this got to do with me?"

"I found *this* in the trashcan at the Plutarch."

He held up a piece of scratch paper with Nick's scribblings on it.

"I'm flattered you think my scrawl important enough to dig for in the trash," Nick said. He would have to be more careful. Maybe he'd get more sleep. Maybe he'd live longer.

"You're looking for a man named *Balazar*. You know! You know, don't you?"

"Know what?"

Coldbread seemed to be weighing his options; he scowled at Nick from below his sparse eyebrows. "Oh,

all right! You know that Hiram Balazar fought with
Lafitte as an underage volunteer, and that he was one of
a handful of men near Pakenham when the latter fell,
mortally wounded, screaming like a madman the
whereabouts of the gold the British officers had
secreted after stealing it from a sinking U.S. gunboat in
Lake Borgne." He was on the verge of sobbing. "I've
been looking for Balazar for four years, and now you've
found him first and you're going to find the treasure and
be famous instead of me!" He broke down and
staggered over to the couch.

"No, I haven't found him, Coldbread," said Nick,
sitting beside him, at the same time wondering why he
was comforting a man who had just threatened him with
a gun.

"I don't even know the given name of my Balazar,"
Nick continued. "They might be two entirely different
individuals. You were going to shoot me over a
mistake? There, that's all right. Stop crying. Give me
that pistol. Look, I'm a genealogist, not a treasure
hunter. It's just pure coincidence that my guy may be
part of your project. I'll make a bargain with you:
anything I find out I'll share with you; in return, you
share the treasure with me. Half."

"Seventy-five, twenty-five."

"Half, Coldbread, or no deal."

"Oh, if you insist! But I get publication rights."

"Agreed," Nick said, vowing to check his lock
from now on.

Nick didn't trust him; Coldbread didn't trust Nick;
Nick didn't believe in the treasure; Coldbread didn't
believe in the coincidence. Their faces told the story.
Nick understood all this, but he had to get some sleep.

They shook on it.

After Nick had shoved the sniffling, apologetic
Coldbread out, he was too tired to go to the trouble of
going to bed. He turned out the lights and stretched out
on the couch again. Coldbread's gun poked him in the

back.   He fished it out of the cushions and tossed it across the dark room.

The gun discharged with a white flash and a sharp pop. Cursing the little incompetent bastard, Nick found the pistol on the floor, unloaded the other chambers, and searched for the bullet hole, hoping it hadn't traveled far enough to injure one of his strange neighbors. Good thing it was only a .25 caliber.

For old time's sake he kept on a bookcase shelf a casual group photograph of the English department from those happier days; he liked to remember whom he hated, whom he liked.   The bullet had shattered the glass, and shot the cigarette right out of the mouth of a younger, thinner, but no-less-smug, Frederick the Usurper.

Chapter 7

It was three days after Nick had hired Hawty Latimer.

He felt fifty, though he still had a good decade to go. A big cup of Styrofoam-tainted coffee and a sticky baked atrocity from an overpriced Quarter grocery were beginning to revive him as he maneuvered through the narrow, bustling streets. He kept his car in whining second gear and let it steer itself on the short straightaways. He wolfed his breakfast as he could, eyeing the scalding coffee sloshing between his legs, threatening to emasculate him. A juicy lawsuit waiting to happen . . . maybe, but the personal price was just too high, he decided, now holding the cup away from his vitals.

He was late, according to her new office regime. As if on cue, city crews mangled the streets he needed. Familiar one-ways were now no-ways or other-ways.

The usual assortment of governmental, financial, and legal types strode down the sidewalks near his building, dollar signs of other people's money in their eyes. The professional bums from nearby Camp Street had turned out for their cadging forays. A family of lost tourists also wandered about, the sevenish boy no doubt wishing he was back at home tormenting lizards, the mother wheeling a stroller occupied by an infant, the father scanning his guide book vainly searching for his bearings.

Nick lurched into one of his favorite tow-away zones.

He unthreateningly approached the lost family
and directed them to the Aquarium. The man tried to tip
him a couple of dollars. Had Dion been right? Did he
actually look *that* bad off? He almost took the cash.

Walking toward his building, he saw two
workmen at the front entrance. They were putting the
finishing touches on a concrete ramp. The glowering
type, they ignored his questions.

Inside, there was another young fellow, wearing
a carpenter's belt dangling dozens of tools; he was busy
widening the door. And down the hall, Nick saw two
other workers giving the freight elevator meaningful
looks.

Must be Hawty's doing; he recalled their first
meeting, and her criticisms on the issue of access for
the handicapped. Great! Her first week, and it looked
like a coup plotted by an urban renewal subcommittee.
He wondered how long it would be before the leasing
company decided he was too much trouble and booted
him out on the street. Surely no one had looked at his
lease lately; the rent was astonishingly low. He tried in
vain to remember the name of the man he'd dealt with
when he rented the place; he should call him, apologize
for all this bother, abase himself, if need be.

He rubbed his aching forehead on the way up the
stairs. Probably that last glass of superb cognac.

With his typical prodigality, he'd splurged a
couple of hundred of his recently earned thousand
dollars on a shopping spree at Martin's Wine Cellar.
With some of the rest he'd raided the fabulous "junk"
shops along Magazine Street. In one, he found a
suitcase for fifteen dollars filled with old photographs
and letters; in another—for six dollars—he acquired an
armload of turn-of-the-century Louisiana "mug books,"
collections of biographical sketches and photos, in
which one could be included for a fee. What history-
altering genealogical secrets hid among this discarded
junk? The thrill of discovery would be his, all his!

❑

Now in his office, it took him only a few seconds to realize that something had changed drastically. The place had become a functioning scene of business.

Where was the dark, dank, dusty hole he'd grown used to and fond of? Where were the piles of books and papers? He gawked at unfamiliar chairs, desks, tables, filing cabinets, rugs, plants (healthy plants, at that), all bathed in bright light. The air-conditioning seemed actually to be working as designed; it was crisply cool. The crazy girl had brought chaos to his beloved chaos, which meant order.

"Look what the cat dragged in!" Hawty said cheerily, rounding the corner from the larger room. "I hope you don't mind. I did a little redecorating. Those nice men downstairs moved a few things in from some abandoned offices and storerooms. They said no one plans to use this stuff—you know, the building's almost empty—so we might as well have it. Oh, and I bought a few plants; there was a big sale on campus."

Nick hadn't paid much attention to Hawty's quiet activities the past few days; he'd been in and out of the office, as usual preoccupied by genealogical quandaries and his own life's failures. He'd asked her to read several introductory genealogy texts. When he bothered to think about her, she seemed a diligent worker, quite willing to take advice, anxious to stay out of his way until she learned the ropes.

"What's with all that construction downstairs?" he asked, hoping it was just chance that less than a week ago he'd hired a dynamic disabled woman, and today the place was becoming a model of progressive accessible architecture.

"Well, I, um, just made a few phone calls, offered a suggestion or two, cited a handful of my favorite ordinances . . ."

Better start packing, he thought, heading for his desk. They would surely be evicted by day's end.

Hawty had converted Nick's desk into a strange place occupied by someone with good work habits. The neatness was intimidating. He made a few halfhearted efforts to restore a comforting messiness.

"I worked up a report for you, there on your desk . . . boss." She smiled broadly as she said the word. "I did find a few Balzars in Natchitoches. And three good places to look for original records: the parish library, Northcentral College, and a private collection at an old plantation."

"What about the courthouse?"

"Well, I don't have to mention that, do I? Oh, they've made the old courthouse a genealogical center and museum. But it's mostly microfilms and secondary material you can find here in New Orleans.

"I have the name of a good bed and breakfast. Natchitoches is a four hour drive at least, you know."

"Better find me the nearest cheap motel." What the hell, Nick thought. The old guy would foot the bill; he could afford it. Probably keeps a fortune hidden in his mattress. And then there was Coldbread's treasure, and Nick's share of it. *Hah!* "Belay that last order," he said.

Feeling like a big-shot CEO, he looked over Hawty's report. No extraneous information, just the facts, in outline form. Commendable.

"One of these current Balzar addresses is near the one in the 1880 census," Nick said. "Next door, or part of the original house, maybe. Wonder if there's anything left of old Ivanhoe's stuff there." He envisioned trunks of undiscovered material. This Balzar lead looked promising; he'd checked all other parishes, and this was the closest he could come to the surname Balazar.

Hawty was rolling around the office again, zealously attacking the organizational laxity that had resisted her previous efforts.

"No!" Nick shouted. She was about to trash some

disintegrating pages. "Don't throw anything away!"

"These aren't even yours. They're from someone who rented here in the forties, for Pete's sake."

"Here's your first lesson in genealogy. The impossible gap, the worst thing a genealogist can confront: that missing bridge to the past that *no* amount of research is going to repair. Someone, deliberately or inadvertently—or some force of nature, maybe—has destroyed it. The impossible gap is worse than simply a temporary obstacle, Hawty. It's more than not knowing where to search next: it's the awful certainty that there is *nowhere* left to search."

"Yeah, but . . ."

"Once you cut that vital and delicate string to the past, it's *gone*. Gone forever. Then the revisionists triumph, the victors write history. The link to the past can be as mundane as an engraved button, as bulky as that stack you have in your hand at this moment. The testimony of insignificant artifacts has shaped our conception of human existence. A fragment of a scroll, a shard of pottery, a chip of inscribed clay in a river. Destroy them, you destroy part of someone's life, part of history."

"What are you *on*, boss?"

"Please, just don't throw anything away, Hawty. Okay?"

Nick began to read a fascinating new book on Czech immigration to Louisiana, sent to him by a genealogical publishing company. That was one of the great things about being a so-called expert: lots of people sent him free books, hoping for a positive, quotable comment. Too bad they didn't also send a small donation to brighten his opinion!

Finishing up the book a couple of hours later, he stretched and looked around. Hawty was gone. He remembered mumbling affirmatively about making reservations for the coming Monday in Natchitoches. He noticed a confirming fax on his desk from Cane Pointe

Bed and Breakfast.

Time for a jog. Usually, he drove over to Audubon Park, across from the hulking neo-Romanesque buildings that occupy the St. Charles boundary of Freret University.

He went into the bathroom, where he normally kept a running outfit behind the door. The outfit had disappeared. He removed a note stuck on the door. From Hawty: "Washed your nasty old stuff. Drying outside, first window opposite."

He slid up the stubborn window to retrieve his shorts, shirt, socks, and sweatband (she'd apparently disposed of his jock strap), all of which were clipped ingeniously with paper clips to a picture wire. Down below, Nick noticed a woman chatting with the two guys who'd made the ramp. The workmen had been painting yellow and blue here and there on the railing and concrete, and hanging signs with the familiar wheelchair icon.

The woman was power-dressed, but so stylishly that she would have drawn admiring stares on the streets of Paris or Rome. The workmen listened to her every word and seemed eager to please in their responses—in contrast to the unspoken hostility with which they'd greeted Nick.

The woman's platinum hair spoke of the most expensive efforts to disguise the full effects of her sixty-or-so years. When she looked up at Nick staring down at her, he saw a wide angular face with understated makeup, striking narrow chevrons for eyebrows, and a long horizontal zipper of a mouth. She might have been a model, of effortless beauty, four or more decades back, or a silver-screen femme fatale in the Lauren Bacall-Joan Crawford mold.

Face was character, Nick had always believed; read properly, faces don't lie. And this one scared the daylights out of him.

He instinctively shrank from the woman's

penetrating gaze, even though four floors separated them. Slowly he began to move back inside, hoping she had somehow missed him. That mouth! What internal hate, fear, or grief kept it that shape, like a Ziploc fault line in Hell's outer shell? What poor slob had she eaten sliced up on her cereal that morning? A face like that sent Nick disconcerting vibes of cabals in ancient castles deciding the future of millions of serfs and soldiers—and he was no soldier.

Just when he thought he was getting a little carried away by his gothic imaginings, she addressed him.

"Mr. Herald?" she called out. "You are Mr. Herald, are you not?"

Caught. He poked his head out again. Sheepishly he answered, "Yes, that's right. What can I do for you?"

"Invite me up. I'm here particularly to see you."

❏

"Natalie Armiger," she said, extending a well-manicured, tastefully but expensively bejeweled hand. She sat down. Nick, suddenly feeling out of place in his own office, resumed his chair behind his desk.

"I'll get right to the point," she said. "I am engaging you to commit a crime."

"Hey, lady . . . uh, Mrs. Armiger, you've got the wrong office, maybe. I'm a genealogist. I do things like pedigree charts, family trees, inheritance traces, applications for lineage societies—"

"I know who you are. And what you've done. I *have* come to the right place, I'm sure. My company is Artemis Holdings. I own this building."

Sweat broke out on Nick's forehead. She was here to draw-and-quarter him about Hawty's architectural activism. Had to be. But what was this "crime" stuff? Artemis, Armiger . . . they had a familiar ring. *Yes.* Una had spoken of Artemis the other day, at the Folio. *This* Artemis, unlike the Greek original, made rich people richer, the powerful even more powerful. Nick didn't want to know what it did to people like him.

"Oh, have no concern about your employee's persistence in requesting the alterations to the structure. Hawty Latimer," she said, referring to a small notepad in a plush-looking leather case. "I admire that young woman. We share a certain, how shall I put it, intellectual impatience. In fact, I offered her a position with my company. She turned me down; she was concerned a full-time job would interfere with her schooling. And her work for you. Admirable.

"These things—cosmetic, really—should have been done long ago by the former owners. We acquired the building recently. Many such details have been on my list. I find that in business, as in life, the simple things are often put off until circumstances demand action. What one must always keep in the forefront is survival."

"I suppose that's one way of looking at it," Nick said, carefully noncommittal. At the moment, Nick was interested in his own survival. He knew he wasn't exhibiting an exceptional amount of Hemingway's grace under pressure. When the bull charged, Nick preferred to be behind the protective fence. Ernest would have thrown his drink on him in disgust.

"You are currently employed by a man named Maximilian Corban. You are investigating the history and possible descendants of a man named Balazar. Max Corban is a liar. This is not his family. It is mine."

"What? Sorry, you lost me. Are you two related?"

"Not remotely."

"Why would Max pay me to do genealogical research on a family that isn't even his own?" Though he wasn't sure he believed her, her words seemed to explain that pebble of doubt he'd had in his boot about Corban. "And how do you know what I'm doing for him, anyway? That's confidential."

"A few innocent questions at the public library

and the Plutarch. You see, I have been conducting my own research. I'll take up the story where I believe he left off. He was indeed unfortunate enough to be a victim of the Nazis. That much is true. I have heard his story, and I sympathize deeply with him. He has even told you the truth up to the time of his arrival and subsequent moderate success here in New Orleans. But in 1987, his story begins to involve me, and my family."

There was that ominous tone again under the words "my family."

"One of the many divisions of Artemis Holdings is an investment group. We have a public brokerage service, but we do more work with private clients of considerable means who seek specialized investment services. We have just opened, as a matter of fact, a new mutual fund managed by my daughter, that specializes in what is known today as 'socially conscious' companies."

She gave what Nick supposed was, for her, a chuckle.

"A fad of political correctness married to the age-old blind altruism of youth. But the demand among my daughter's generation seems to be there. Soon, they will learn that money and conscience cannot coexist in the same boardroom. Inevitably, when there is a choice to be made, it will be conscience that yields. My daughter seems to believe the pious claims of company officers . . . forgive me this little digression. I am proud of my daughter, even though she has much to learn.

"Now, Max Corban. I'll refrain from going into the details of his complaints. I can see you are not at home discussing financial matters of these kinds."

Right she was. Nick was usually searching for spare change in old coats, not pondering interest rates and the Dow.

"Artemis was found blameless by the appropriate regulatory entities. So, I will simply say that Mr. Corban, like many investors, suffered severe paper losses in the crash of '87. Unnerving, yes; irreversible, no. He had consistently chosen the riskiest portfolio allocation. His downfall was primarily his own doing.

"But Max—I call him that, because at one time we were on cordial terms—Max would not listen to me and my staff. He blamed us, and sold. As you may know, the markets enjoyed substantial subsequent gains, with intermittent losses."

"Of course," Nick said. "Who doesn't?"

She knew he was lying. "In fact, we did very well in 1990, considering the extent of that pullback; we had learned a great deal from '87. I believe that Max could have recouped all his losses and made a handsome profit in a very short time, if he had listened to us. A historic bull market appears to be taking shape even as we speak.

"My opinion, however, is not what Max wants now. He wants revenge. He is a sick, paranoid man, bent on destroying me. You are helping him do that. He intends to blackmail me with certain information about this ancestor of mine, this Balazar. Specifically, that he was born into the Jewish faith."

She waved a hand in the air, as if shooing away a mosquito that had become a hornet.

"Why don't you file a complaint, take him to court? I'm sure it's not for lack of lawyers on your staff," Nick said.

"Max would like that, I'm certain. No. Such steps would not bring to this dilemma the thoroughness, expertise, and—as you mentioned—confidentiality I expect from you."

It sounded more like a warning than a tribute.

"What do you need me for? You already know more about this ancestor than I do," Nick said.

She smiled faintly, as if she had just witnessed her opponent make a stupid chess move.

"Knowledge is not enough. What I do know is this. My ancestor came to this country, he prospered, he sired heirs, he made more powerful friends than he made enemies, he died. Not such a remarkable story, in this land of opportunity, even for a Jew, hounded as he was by the ancient Christian animus that required him to share guilt for the alleged murder of Christ. Jealousy, competition, avarice, economic and doctrinal, of course, were and are the driving forces behind anti-Semitism, though the common man still sees it as a conflict played out on the Sistine Chapel ceiling. A comforting theology, wouldn't you say?"

"Yeah," Nick replied, "if you're Christian."

He still smarted from the word "Jew"; his father always heard it as a slur on the lips of a non-Jew, no matter the context. As if he didn't have enough hang-ups of his own, he had to carry around his father's, as well.

"Quite so," the woman said. "I'm sure you are well versed in the fascinating story of Jewish immigration to the South, the pivotal role Jewish merchants played in the development of the region? This ancestor of mine surpassed historical precedent and laid the foundation for my family's present wealth."

"You speak like someone proud of her Jewish heritage, though, obviously, you're not a practicing Jew. And even if you were, what would be so terrifying about Corban's revealing that fact? I still don't see the 'dilemma' you mentioned."

"I am Episcopalian. As far back as most people care to go, my family has embraced one of the mainstream Christian sects. Balazar converted; he was Catholic, finally, I believe. Religion for him was a matter of indifference, as indeed heretofore it has been for me. Max would have it otherwise."

"I will relate an anecdote about Jews and New Orleans society: it is said by one of the old-line Carnival clubs that no Jew has ever peeked past the foyer; they're proud of this fact and intend to keep it that way. My late husband was a member of that club;

I, as a debutante, was a queen. At the upper reaches of New Orleans society, all is not sweetness and light, certainly, but the hallowed custom of exclusionary chauvinism often produces strange bedfellows. The French and Spanish Creole elite—both white and of color—sneer at the Anglo-Saxon elite, but they unite in their distaste for Jews. Unspoken for the most part, but no less powerful. You know of the recent demands by blacks, Jews, and women for inclusion in the musty traditions of this city? Several old-line krewes ceased their public involvement in Mardi Gras, their very reason for existence, rather than admit the *ancien régime* has breathed its last."

"Let the plebeians eat king cake, eh?" Nick said, still a bit stunned by this woman's candor.

"You joke, like those who say this masked power structure is now irrelevant. But I assure you, this is deadly serious business. I have excellent Jewish clients, but Christians outnumber them five to one. Surely you've heard of 'old money.' Here, that is the polite term for white Christian social and economic snobbery and hegemony. Pleasure and prejudice are New Orleans delicacies; we savor and guard them as a chef protects his recipes. We coined the idea of separate *to remain* unequal; *that* should be on our Carnival doubloons, in Latin. You do not understand this city, Nick, if you believe that I would be in business, in any meaningful way, a week after the news broke that I am of Jewish extraction, even at this remove."

Nick wanted to argue that this was the 1990s, that the Nazis had been bombed to oblivion, that the *Protocols of the Elders of Zion* had been forever discredited as the political ruse of a czar's secret police, that even Henry Ford had apologized . . . but he realized he was pretty damn naive. She was right. Teenagers wear the swastika and burn the Klan's cross proudly these days in just about every state; the reality of the

Holocaust is questioned by straight-faced hucksters on talk shows and online (despite Hawty's tutorials, he still wasn't sure where "online" was); and that undying canard, the *Protocols*, and worse are best-sellers in certain New Orleans suburbs. History doesn't repeat itself; mankind does.

Nick recalled his father drilling this into his memory: "No matter what you do or where you go or how you pray, when your back is turned you're Nick the Jew." His father had helped liberate the concentration camps during the war. Nick had always thought his dad was talking rubbish, forever scarred by that experience; who listens to his father, anyway? Now people probably whispered: "There goes Nick the Word-Thief." He'd needed no help to earn his own personal infamy.

"Why did Corban come to me?" Nick asked.

"He has lost his mental balance, undoubtedly. Perhaps he believed that you, as a writer on genealogical subjects would broach this discovery to the world. He needs the credibility of scholarship. He has already tried rumor and innuendo, to no very great effect. Fortunately, he does not belong to the class of people with whom Artemis usually deals."

"Mrs. Armiger, as far as I can see, it's your word against a disturbed little man's screwball ravings. Who's going to believe him? I'm sure you've had worse crises in your business. Call your public relations experts. Get some spin control. Your clients will understand the situation when you explain the truth to them. I think you're overreacting."

"Truth is a mask one wears for the evening's ball. I am not concerned with the truth. Controversy must be avoided at all costs; the slightest scandal could foster a desire to doubt the mask, to seek the homely face beneath. That would be fatal for the romance that keeps the whole affair whirling into the dawn." She seemed to be envisioning some Mardi Gras gala from her youth. "Stop your work for Max Corban. I propose another assignment for you: track down my link to Balazar, and when you have found the evidence, steal it."

Nick had had enough of this designer dictator.

"Wait a minute, lady! Who the hell do you think you are, coming in here, ordering me around like some flunky? I'm not one of your cringing minions."

One of her eyebrows assumed a more acute angle.

"Do you know that I am on the Permanent Endowment Board of Freret University? Years ago, I was instrumental in the hiring of Dr. Herman Newtic, who, as you may know, was the first Jewish member of the English department. I squelched all objections to your own Jewish background. Oh, don't bother asking how they knew that your grandfather had changed his name from Herzwald. Prejudice in this city is a many-eyed beast."

"Can you blame him?" Nick said, remembering how strange the name had sounded to him as a kid. He hadn't thought about that buried family secret for thirty years. *Genealogist, know thyself!*

"No, I cannot say that I do." Her gash of mouth seemed tickled into the suggestion of a smile. "Being such an advocate for inclusion is my way of beating the bigots at their own game, by working within their system, until I can change it. It is all the more rewarding to know that I myself am one who would be excluded from the highest circles under the old rules. I *cannot* allow my past to interfere."

"I'm sorry, Mrs. Armiger, this is your crusade. I've got my own problems. And by the way, it's not *your* past; it belongs to everybody. Now, if you'll excuse me . . ."

"You may also be interested to know that I was the single dissenter in the vote to fire you. As a result, in deference to my substantial influence, a quieter settlement was arranged. Was I wrong? It is not too late, however, to rectify my error. I can discredit you in this business. I can make you unemployable in this city, in this state, in this country. Do you begin to understand? Accept my proposal. Perhaps, later, I'll have other work for you. What is your price? You name it."

Talk about spin control. Nick felt she could spin him out of this galaxy.

"Your instincts have been correct so far," she said. "I believe you will find something in Natchitoches, though I haven't any certain idea what. Isn't that where you had intended to start?" She checked her notebook. "Yes, that was my information. As you might guess, my family has avoided discussing this man—my great-great-grandfather. A form of self-hatred, I suppose; that is perhaps the most pernicious byproduct of bigotry. Hyam Balazar was his name. There. Now I have told you all I know."

She held her fat, expensive black pen poised to fill in the amount on a check.

Nick wanted to explain that you couldn't just erase someone from history these days. Records have been microfilmed, copied, disseminated, even written in stone, in the case of grave markers. But the challenge piqued his perverse spirit. His bombastic performance for Hawty earlier in the day had been only partly serious; but now he wondered: if one anchoring strand were cut, might not the whole web collapse? It was hard enough finding records that do exist; one forgery, one deliberate theft, one malicious act of destruction, could cause a perpetuation of error lasting centuries—or forever. It could be done.

"Is twenty thousand fair for your services?" she asked.

"Do you have any idea of the difficulty, maybe the impossibility, of what you're asking me to do?" Nick said, standing up in desperation. This was all too much. He walked to the windows, trying to rub the reality of this woman out of his eyes. But when he turned around, she was still there. "I could go to jail for this!"

"Forty?" Armiger said "More? Very well, fifty, then."

"Fifty thousand . . . dollars!?" The words didn't make sense to him, suddenly.

"You drive a hard bargain, Nick."

She filled in the check with the incredible figure, which represented to him the earnings of a couple of good years.

"This is a credit card for your expenses. Please try not to be too extravagant. When you have something to report, call this number."

He watched her place the check, the credit card, and a business card on his desk.

Pick the check up, rip it to pieces, Nick thought, again flaring briefly into anger.

But he didn't.

"You just bought yourself a cringing minion," he said, a bit out of breath with visions of beautiful women and the south of France. He could buy enough wine to float in, purchase whole junkshops whenever he pleased, research and write to his heart's content . . . for a while, anyway.

Natalie Armiger's face was a portrait of conquest; she might have just triumphed in a successful hostile corporate raid.

❏

It was dusk before Nick realized how many times around the Audubon Park track he must have jogged. He had been trying to run away from the concentration camps tattooed on Corban's soul, from the fiendish Nazi doctors, from the Queen of Artemis Holdings, from Balazar, Hiram and Hyam—but most of all, from his shame.

Chapter 8

Saturday afternoon Nick was finally able to summon the courage to call Corban, to break the news that their deal was off.

On the phone, Corban threatened, pleaded, and bribed. It seemed to Nick that discrediting Armiger had become the only thing in his life. Did he even care any longer for the money he'd lost? Nick was no psychologist, but he sensed that somehow, in the old man's crumbling mind, Armiger had come to represent all of the relentless terror he had seen striding across Europe, casting its deadly shadow on his life.

She might be an unpleasant woman who used questionable means, but did she deserve such hatred? Maybe Armiger was right after all: the old guy just might be bonkers.

For all of his skillful rationalization, Nick couldn't fight the feeling that he had become a genealogical gigolo, a mind and a conscience for hire to the highest bidder.

"I have something for you," Corban said on the phone. "There is more that you must tell the world. I am too ill to come downtown . . . yes, yes, I lied to you! Big deal. What is my lie next to hers? A flea!"

Nick tried to interrupt with Armiger's side of the story. But the old man became even more agitated and cut him off with a volley of impenetrable Yiddishisms that didn't fail to express vehement disdain.

"God forbid she should be one of us! But once upon a time, yes, there was a *landsman* in her family.

Oh, I could hurt her real bad with that." He whispered confidentially: "Her rich goys, they hate Jews. But that's not the whole *schmeer*. I got something better to fight with. I show you what I mean. You don't understand. She has *got* to be stopped, before she does more evil! She is one of *them*, with blood on her hands. Come! I have no one else, except the *yentes* from the community center. You must come!"

Nick's kind heart—and his curiosity—got the best of him. He agreed to see Max Corban the next morning.

❑

That afternoon, though, as he worked alone at his office, he began to feel less sorry for Corban. Wasn't it the old man's fault that he had become involved in this mess?

From now on, he decided, no more weirdos for clients.

Chapter 9

Max Corban wept over the scrapbook, as he had done so often.

Darkness still cloaked the morning outside. Lately, sleep had become more difficult for him. The aches and pains of his damaged life tormented him. But worse: each night he awoke terrified, exhausted, lost. The body could be dealt with; but the mind . . . he had seen many people go mad in the concentration camps; they were the lucky ones, remaining unaware of the inevitable, ultimate horrors to come. He knew what his mental turmoil meant. It was how the final madness started.

He had put water on to boil, in the kitchen of his house. His life now was no more than a teaspoon of instant coffee, sere and bitter. Only another scalding inundation could offer peace, the peace of death.

It was their fault. Her fault. No difference.

The scrapbook on his kitchen table held the story of his return from the grave. Liberating soldiers had snapped photos of the stick figures that had once been human beings. Corban moved his fingers over the image of one such figure in a crowd, as if feeling the bones beneath the stretched skin. Even now, when he looked in the mirror, that is what he saw staring blankly back at him, below the flesh.

He turned pages. There were happier pictures of the years after the war. Of other survivors, new friends, and his future wife; of relief workers and Allied soldiers who had taken a fancy to him; of simple pleasures like card games, picnics, reading . . . that, after the war, had been so precious to him.

Further on, the scrapbook documented his and his

wife's journey to America, from the first applications for emigration, to the final papers of his naturalization. He read again, for the thousandth time, some of the letters from the people who had helped him. He had kept in contact with a few of them for many years; now, most were gone. And one of them, on his recent death, had finally sent what Max most needed—a weapon of information.

It had been thirty-five years since the sad day he opened the letter on the next yellowed scrapbook page. His friends, the letter informed him, Maurice and Erna Balazar, had been murdered. Thirteen years after the war, they were killed in their own hometown in Germany, in an act of local terrorism, leaving an orphaned child.

The four of them—Corban and Mignon, Maurice and Erna—had been through a lot together, in those many months in the displaced-persons camps. That is where they had met and nursed each other back to health.

Corban shook his head. The war had changed nothing. Would they always win?

After the war, the Balazars eventually decided to go to New Orleans. They asked relatives there for sponsorship; but difficulties arose. The Corbans, after leaving Europe, had tried New Jersey first as a residence; they had not hit it off with his distant relatives there. Having caught some of Maurice's enthusiasm for New Orleans, Corban and Mignon wanted a taste of the exotic city themselves. They made it their home.

For many years, Corban did not know exactly what went wrong for the Balazars, even though his friends in the relief agencies had solicited his help after the deaths in 1958 and had sent him copies of some documents relating to the lives and families of Maurice and Erna. But the *name* of the New Orleans relatives went unmentioned; nor had he any recollection that the Balazars had told him, back in the DP camps or in the few letters from them that very soon trickled to a stop. Maybe these relatives had died or moved away from New Orleans in the intervening years; he presumed the agencies were doing the best they could.

In 1958 the Corbans knew only that there was an orphaned child, and that the agencies needed their help in trying to place her with other American cousins. They knew of no others, but Corban and his wife immediately volunteered to adopt the girl. Suddenly, however, their communication with their friends in the agencies ceased . . . until several months ago.

He had memorialized it all in his scrapbook. And the scrapbook must be saved. It was his mission. Like Job, he had been chosen to do God's bidding. There were no coincidences; his suffering now had meaning. God had brought him here, He had thrown him back into the clutches of the beast. The beast that had killed a people, the beast that had killed his family and friends.

The beast was hungry again, hunting, on the move. He knew he did not have much time.

The water boiled, but Corban did not notice it.

He took a large tan envelope from the back of the scrapbook, dumped the contents on the table, and tore page after page from the book, until there were more than two dozen before him. He worked them into the envelope; pieces of the old pages crumbled like brittle bones to the floor.

Soon it would be light. He made his way through his neat house, located tape to seal the envelope, and some stray stamps he did not bother to add up. He licked and stuck them onto the thick package, over the older stamps. In the Yellow Pages, he found Nick's name and address and hurriedly wrote the words and numbers with a pen that was running out of ink.

Corban opened his front door. Outside, it was quiet; nothing moved on the fog-blurred street. He wore pajamas, and though the night was warm, he shivered as he scurried the few feet to the mailbox.

❏

In the last moments of darkness before daylight, Corban stood in the middle of his kitchen, listening. He had heard the goose-steps of doom before; he heard them now. Again the insatiable beast galloped toward him.

He turned slowly to face the evil that was rumbling through the utility room, even now at the kitchen door. Vividly he remembered how, in the camps, such moments of horror took mere seconds, but stretched into infinity as his lagging mind struggled to process them.

The kitchen door flew open, kicked by a strong foot.

Like a match in a tornado, Corban rose from the floor in the grip of the intruders.

He could not be sure how many there were—two, as there had been a few days before, a hundred, a million? . . . He felt himself rapidly, roughly carried down the hall, into his bedroom. Then there was utter darkness, stifling closeness. He could not breathe.

Yet he was not afraid.

Come then, death. His mind formed the words, but his mouth could not speak them. *I am ready. I have won.*

Chapter 10

Nick knew well the area where Corban lived; Uptown, but not in one of the sections being rejuvenated by Yuppies from other states. There was a world-famous jazz club a block away. He had frequented the several quirky neighborhood bars that served boiled crabs and raw oysters weekends during games on television. And students from Freret University were fond of bringing parents to the nearby ramshackle family restaurant that made probably the best poboys in the city, and therefore in the world.

Neighborhoods evolve in seesaw cycles in the old sections of New Orleans. The peeling, dilapidated shanty or battleship of a house becomes the pink, olive-green, or slate-blue showcase, gleaming with brass fixtures and etched glass, the kind of place that ends up in home-and-garden magazines between the recipes and ads. Odds are Artemis Holdings would have something to do with most of these transactions and remodelings.

The Irish Channel, it's called. The train tracks are close, and the river, too, which meant, a century ago, a good supply of backbreaking jobs for the starving immigrants, who were the cheap labor that in part helped build many coffee, sugar, and produce fortunes. The neighborhood is still working class suspicious of "foreigners" (who isn't a foreigner, Nick often wondered, on a hundred-year scale?); but today there seems to be room for just about every other ethnicity in the human jambalaya of this city.

Though predominantly Irish and Catholic around

here, there is nevertheless a Jewish cemetery right in
the middle; and in March, when the green beer flows,
the festive noises of the St. Patrick's Day parade echo
over the bones and tombstones of Russian, Prussian,
and Alsatian Jews who came over in the waves of 1848,
the 1860s, and the 1880s—each time the pogroms heated
up or cooked shoes started appearing on the dinner
table.

    Corban lived across an alley from the cemetery.
Nick, reading the address, guessed Corban had brought
his memories here to rest, a new surrogate urn for the
scattered ashes of his dead. This cemetery must have
served as a palpable memorial for his placeless
mourning, a symbol to grieve over every day when he
stepped onto his porch with his coffee, or cough syrup.
Nick understood; he too was a man who cherished his
tragedies.

    Nick knocked, rang the doorbell, knocked, and
knocked again, until his knuckles hurt. He leaned on
the doorbell button for a full minute. He knew it
worked; he could hear it. He went around the back, to
a scruffy yard full of cast-off household items and
automotive parts, all the while feeling that it was
happening again, that his cogwheel train of fate had
just taken a sharp, unpleasant turn, or entered a tunnel.
The interesting thing about such moments, he reflected,
is that you have no doubts, and you act with unusual
determination; that was pure stupidity in his book, but
others wiser than he had become rich and famous
calling it heroism.

    A screen door hung off the hinges. Beyond the
door, Nick entered what must have been the former back
porch; crammed into it were a washer and a dryer that
had to be older than he was. Forgotten shirts, yellowed
by the elements, hung from nails and wire hangers on
the walls. The door to the kitchen was more rot than
wood, but there was also some recent damage. It was
open a few inches. Nick eased it back with a toe of his

sale Nikes.

Inside, at the range, a gas burner blazed blue under a blistered, red-hot pot, which seemed about to splinter into shrapnel. Corban had been boiling water for coffee; Nick saw the dry grains of instant still in the cup.

The narrow house was of undistinguished "shotgun" design. The lights were on in the kitchen, but the rest of the house seemed illuminated only by daylight. That made sense, Nick thought; Corban, like most Depression-era seniors, was habitually frugal, and, like just about everyone, probably spent most of his waking hours in the kitchen.

"Max?" he called out. "Max, it's Nick Herald." Louisiana had a shoot-the-burglar law, and Nick didn't want to become a legal footnote to it.

He walked down the hallway, past the bathroom, a bedroom, another one, and then into the dining area.

Corban hung by an electrical extension cord from a rather nice crystal chandelier. The motion in the air caused by Nick's entrance made a few pendants chime.

The large expandable dining table had been picked up and moved, not shoved, out of the way; the threadbare oriental rug underneath was not bunched up. Corban didn't have that strength.

His face was waxy, a pale blue. The eyes were closed. Nick was glad about that. The expression was defiant; maybe that was just the growing stiffness of death. Nick touched a pitiful bony ankle, exposed above a fallen thin black sock, the kind only elderly men seem to favor. The skin there was purplish, but whitened to Nick's touch. The poor guy had not been dead long enough to turn cold.

There was a vaguely familiar, offensive, animal odor. Was decay already attacking the corpse in the hot apartment? No. Nick realized that Corban had lost bladder and bowel control at the last. The body twirled slightly, and Nick saw that the pajama pants still dribbled into unpleasant puddles on the rug.

Nick stepped back, appalled.

His stomach briefly threatened to revolt. All the actual death he'd seen so far was in the flowered decorousness of funeral homes—aunts and uncles he hardly knew, friends' parents he'd never liked. But he forced himself to pay attention.

Nick had a talent for storing useless information; his mother always bragged to her friends that he had a photographic memory. He wasn't *that* good; but it was true that his friends Dion and Una would not play *Trivial Pursuit* with him anymore.

A few years before, he'd read in the school paper a graphic analysis of a Freret student's suicide. The boy—not one of Nick's students, he was glad to see—had hanged himself out of his dorm window. The zealous student journalist had gone into gross detail about rigor mortis, lividity, and the telltale dark-red color of a hanging victim's head and neck. Nick recalled a good bit of that article now, enough to realize Corban must have been dead when he was strung up. This was a murder, not a suicide.

Could he have prevented it, two or three hours earlier? He had a sinking feeling in his gut, and it wasn't nausea now.

Was this the work of a burglar? Not likely in daylight. It would have been obvious that Corban was home; a look through a window would have proved that. Confrontation with the homeowner was the last thing a burglar wanted, and if that happened, he would get away as quickly as possible. A burglar, generally not a Phi Beta Kappa anyway, wouldn't hang around to create such an elaborate subterfuge.

Nick began to look around for anything that might indicate what Corban had wanted so desperately to tell him. He was careful not to touch anything else.

The house, furnished with some taste and maintained with an old widower's care, had been ransacked. It might appear to someone unacquainted with the dangerous details of this case that the old guy had lost his mind, then trashed his place in rage before offing himself. If Nick knew his New Orleans police department aright, suicide would be the convenient verdict here. They had bigger fish to fry, with cops killing cops over drug deals and graft.

What had the killer been looking for? And who was it?

The people he'd encountered lately all paraded through his mind, each a suspect until eliminated. Una, Dion, or Hawty? He knew them well enough to rule them out. Coldbread? Well, he was certainly pathological, and there was that strange business of "his" Balazar; but he was a milquetoast, basically harmless, incapable of murder. He'd proved that at Nick's apartment. Besides, where was the connection?

Frederick the Usurper Tawpie? He hated Nick, that was for sure. They'd almost come to blows at the Folio. Maybe his victory in the plagiarism affair wasn't enough for him. Could he now be trying to frame Nick for murder, put him once and for all out of the picture, this time in prison?

Nick's thoughts then turned to Natalie Armiger, his new employer? Had she sent some of her corporate thugs to do the dirty deed of snuffing out a blackmailer? She seemed to Nick like a woman capable of such a thing.

But why? The documents Armiger wanted were awaiting discovery. They weren't here. She already knew that. In fact, she'd urged Nick to go to Natchitoches to recover them. And when Nick had accomplished his job, Corban's proof would have been gone; his allegations would have been dismissed as sheer lunacy. Killing him was unnecessary, unbusinesslike, a useless courting of danger.

Unless there was another reason, one Armiger didn't want Nick to know. Hadn't Corban denied on the

phone that he was blackmailing Armiger about her
Jewish ancestry? If that was so, if her impassioned
explanation was indeed a lie, what else had Corban held
over Natalie Armiger's head?

The answers were locked away in the old man's
inert brain.

Nick suddenly wondered if he himself was safe.
Armiger needed him to burn the books, to purge the
records of the offending facts—whatever they were—so
no new Corban could come along and make threats,
sneaking up on her through her family's past. Didn't
she? And when Nick was no longer useful? If she was
the killer, was there a noose waiting for him, too?

Whatever it was Corban had on her, it just didn't
seem to him worth the life of a man. Or two.

He returned to the kitchen. Making coffee didn't
seem to Nick the action of a man about to do himself in.
He covered his hand with his shirttail to shut off the gas
at the range. No sense imperiling the whole
neighborhood with a fire. The kitchen itself was a
contrast to the disorder of the rest of the place. Nick
noted Corban even had two places set for the next meal
at a folding card table in a windowed alcove. There
were bits of yellowed paper on the floor, below the
table.

He remembered what Corban had said on the
phone about volunteers from the Jewish community
center. He had been expecting a visitor to bring lunch,
not death.

Car doors slammed out front. Footsteps thudded
on the porch. Heavy, official footsteps, vibrating
through the house and clinking the chandelier pendants.

Nick peeked down the hall. Two policemen were
nosing around the front door, peering in the windows.
Probably, someone at the community center had called
to remind the old fellow and, getting no answer, had
asked the police to check on him. Maybe that phone call
had scared off the killer.

Time to leave. Authority and Nick never had been on cordial terms, and now there was the difficult question of what he was doing in the house of an unreported suicide or a murder victim. The back door seemed clear still. The alley leading off the back yard offered an escape route.

At a fast walk Nick followed the alley, exiting on a street around the corner. Then, heading back toward the scene, he made for his car, which was parked a few houses down from Corban's place, beside a pair of mailboxes.

Nobody seemed to notice him. He felt that his every pore shouted with the sweat of near panic. An ambulance had arrived; a few neighbors congregated in the street around it, quizzing one another for information.

Nick drove slowly away from the growing commotion.

Chapter 11

The straitjacket of guilt paralyzed Nick. He didn't know what to do. He spent much of Monday morning fishing the paper clips out of the rubber bands in an old tarnished silver box on his office desk. He was alone in his morass of guilt; Hawty was on campus attending to her own projects.

He tried to convince himself that, despite motive and ability, as well as his own strong intuitive suspicions, Natalie Armiger did not have Corban killed. Surely it was the suicide of a man who had endured the most horrible episode of human history, a man whose grief finally had overpowered him. Nick desperately needed to believe he wasn't working for a murderer.

But the dead face of Max Corban accused him; and the words that had seemed to float in the foul air of Max's apartment still echoed through Nick's memory: *I fought them to the very end. You are a coward if you do not fight back. You are as guilty.*

He called Artemis Holdings seven times throughout the morning, only to be told that his previous messages had been noted—in other words, bug off. Then he thought better of trying to get through to her. What if she told him she'd had no hand in the old guy's death? Would that satisfy him? No. What if she said, "Yes, I killed him"? That would be even worse! He decided to leave things to the police. Ignorance was not only bliss but possibly life—his own, in this case. And no matter what happened, nothing he could do would bring Corban back to life.

Thus chained to a rock of moral catalepsy, he did nothing—nothing more, that is, than what he had been hired to do.

❑

He sped west on I-10 across the postcard-view spillways and swamps toward Lafayette. At a suitably desolate stretch, somewhere in St. Martin Parish, he hurled his tennis shoes through the sunroof, into the water. He'd watched enough television mysteries to know about shoe-sole evidence.

At Lafayette he headed north on I-49 toward Natchitoches, mouthing as he drove what he remembered of the Jewish prayer of mourning, the Kaddish, for poor Corban.

It was over ninety degrees already, and his air conditioner was blowing heat; he rolled down the windows. Mountainous clouds boiled up from the hot farmland planted with corn, cotton, cane, and soybeans. Every few miles he'd lean forward to let the air peel his shirt off his back.

❑

Natchitoches is a beautiful little town on the Cane River—now more a lake than a river, and called one, officially. Though La Salle and the Le Moyne brothers, Sieurs d'Iberville and Bienville, had for some years been dodging hurricanes and swatting malarial mosquitoes farther south, along the Gulf coast, a French soldier named Louis Juchereau de St. Denis, under Bienville's command, claimed his paragraph in history as the founder of the oldest permanent settlement in the vast French Louisiana territory. It was 1714, and Fort St. Jean Baptiste was supposed to stand as a sentry to the expansionist dreams of the Spanish. Like Natchez, founded soon after by Bienville, Natchitoches bears the name of the Indians it displaced. When locals say it today, the name comes out "NAK-ah-tish."

Exiting the interstate, Nick saw first the ugly, contemporary side of the town's dual personality. He drove by the typical American mixture of gas stations, chain restaurants, convenience stores, and strip shopping centers clustered competitively within sight of I-49. Next he passed through suburban neighborhoods that had once fronted a sleepy state road and that now hung on along this busy artery between interstate and city. Many of the furry patches on the pavement must have been family pets, Nick thought with a shiver.

The road became two way where the federal dollars had stopped. On either side Nick saw buildings which had been built cheaply and quickly, probably in the fifties and sixties, to house small businesses. A profusion of letter signs, fast-food joints, washaterias, copy shops, computer stores, religious centers, and bookstores told him he was now in the vicinity of Northcentral State College, the local branch of the state higher educational system. And there it was, to his right.

Northcentral had done its best to conform to the French-Spanish-Old South look, but Nick noticed that a few past administrators had favored concrete-and-steel boxes rather than constructions of red brick and white columns. He knew he would be visiting one of these buildings soon.

He arrived in the old section of town, and felt as if he'd come home. The accretion of centuries of human striving and failure calmed him. The streets narrowed further and bent unpredictably, as if, like New Orleans streets, they'd given up trying to follow the best-laid plans from the Age of Reason. He could almost believe he was threading his way through the car-choked Garden District or Faubourg Marigny. But it was hilly—unusual for Louisiana. He craned his neck to see old cemeteries jumbled together on shoulders of ground. He was sorely tempted to stroll through them, reading the genealogical tales written there.

Another day, maybe, when he was here on good faith, when his communing with the dead wouldn't include stealing their lives.

Some of the old houses he drove by were modest buildings dating from the founding, with crude walls of cypress posts and the clay-and-moss mixture called *bousillage*; others were multistoried, elegant structures of the prosperous early nineteenth-century period, when cotton was king, lumber cheap, slaves plentiful, and the Red River cooperative. The river later changed course and cut off the town's main transportation route, Cane River, leaving Natchitoches in a state of charming arrested development.

Driving along the becalmed, tree-shaded river, Nick remembered some of his students begging him to understand that they needed a few days off to travel here for the filming of *Steel Magnolias*; they had landed parts as extras. Fiction had nourished fact ever since: the popularity of the movie had revitalized the setting, giving tourists from around the world all the more reason to visit.

A huge gleaming tourist bus lumbered in front of Nick's car for a few blocks. It leaned from one side to the other as the tourists inside shifted in unison for a better view.

Nick had been to Natchitoches once before, with Una. They and two other couples drove to Arkansas for a canoeing trip, and on the way they detoured for a day to amble along the downtown Natchitoches streets, admire the old riverfront buildings, and stroll through the quiet, oak-lined neighborhoods.

As he searched for his temporary base of operations, he yearned for those carefree, youthful days, when his life had been merely an academic exercise.

❑

Cane Pointe Bed and Breakfast occupied a two-story building of the West Indies/French Creole style, circa 1823, according to a plaque in the lobby. The establishment was on Front Street, with a nice view of the sleepy river and the surprisingly busy old brick street, along which the early settlers had built their exchanges, banks, and stores.

Rebecca Barclay, an outgoing fortyish woman of robust complexion, ample flesh, and seemingly boundless energy, greeted Nick in a booming voice.

"Welcome to Cane Pointe, Mr. Herald! Oh, excuse me a sec. Darlene, honey, carry some more towels to twelve. Sam, here, take this money and go buy some more *Shreveport Times*—now, how was your trip, Mr. Herald? We have a lovely room waiting for you, with a complimentary basket of fruit and a bottle of champagne—well, sparkling wine." She laughed at her small gaffe. "Got in beaucoup trouble last year when some French wine merchants heard me say that. Sharla, Sharla! Where is that girl? My daughter will show you up. Sharla!"

A woman who gets up before the alarm clock rings, Nick suspected, standing at the desk as she checked him in. Her unfussy appearance bolstered that idea: she wore a peasant blouse and Mexican skirt, and had obviously devoted no more than five minutes to her makeup and curly permed brown hair.

Filling out the necessary forms and waiting for Sharla, Nick explained that he was a free-lance writer doing an article on genealogical resources in the area. Inside of five minutes he knew just about everything about Rebecca Barclay and Natchitoches, including many local legends; purported illustrious ancestors; her husband, Bob, who "moonlights as a lawyer when I don't need him to hammer something"; the awkward youths mangling his duffle bag and scrambling his account, who were "hospitality-industry interns" from the state scholars high school located on the college campus; the menu for supper and breakfast; and possibly dangerous eccentricities of the hot water flow in his room. And then came Sharla.

She was a creamy-skinned girl of about twenty-three, with lustrous auburn hair in bangs; freckles bridged her meringue-flip of a nose. Her lips were ripe strawberries. Her eyes were rock-like jewels of speckled green, yellow, and black. Nick had seen cockatiels with beautiful feral eyes like that, eyes that said, *Yeah, I'll come perch on your arm, but it's going to really, really hurt.* She wore demure shorts that were anything but, a prim embroidered cotton blouse that somehow looked lewd on her, sandals, and a straw boater with a red silk ribbon.

While a young fellow sprinted madly with Nick's bag and briefcase up the several flights of stairs to his room, Sharla and Nick walked at a more leisurely pace. The young fellow soon sprinted past them on the way down.

"You're from New Orleenz, I hear tell," she said, looking back at him under the brim of her hat, proudly showing off her white teeth.

Real New Orleanians analyzed pronunciation like a code to determine who you were, and who your family

wasn't. "Orleenz" was something of a desecration; only
tourists and singers were allowed to get away with it. Even
though Nick was a relative newcomer to New Orleans, he felt
an urge to correct her.

Sharla dawdled on each step. "I just *love* New
Orleenz. I been to the Jazz Festival, once. You ever go to
that? Good*ness*! I was wild, let me tell you. Me and a bunch
of my girlfriends. I drank a lot of tequila, and got up on the
stage and . . ." she stopped abruptly in front of Nick and
moved closer to whisper in his ear, "took my top off in front
of the whole crowd! Thousands and thousands."

"Sorry I missed that. Did you get arrested?"

"Arrested?!" She grinned and her eyes sparkled in the
sunlight streaming through the louvered shutters. "Shoot,
no! The cops all asked me out and the crowd loved it. I got
all of us into a party at the band's hotel afterwards, too."

They arrived at the room and Sharla conducted him
inside.

"Well, here we are. You staying a while, Mr. Herald?
I bet your wife doesn't want a man like *you* away too long."

"Oh, I'm not married," Nick said, startled that he'd
made such a personal admission. This woman had some
strange siren-like power. He liked it. "Just here for a few
days of business."

"That's nice, I guess. Well, you just call me if there's
anything I can do for you, okay? Anything at all."

She took a proprietary stroll around the room, making
one last check of the accommodations. Then, waving in her
girlish way, she backed out of the door, gently closing it.

Nick was eager to get started. His list of tasks jeered
at him like a bully as he reviewed it. But he couldn't help
admiring the room. Rebecca Barclay and her handyman-
lawyer husband had done a remarkable job converting the old
building into a world-class inn. So what if the service was
somewhat provincial. The place oozed character and history.

An armoire dominated one wall. A splendid keyhole
desk nestled against another. The four-poster, testered bed
made Nick feel like a Lilliputian. These were not repros. The

plush ivory carpet was surmounted in half-a-dozen places by wonderful oriental rugs, each with a couple of centuries of tales in their elaborate weave. There was wainscoting enough for a wing at Versailles, period wallpaper and light fixtures, ceiling fans nearly as big as windmills, and a lavish fireplace Nick regretted not being able to enjoy in the summer heat. He felt already in the midst of the nineteenth century—despite the modern appurtenances like the fax-phone, the television, and the hair dryer in the tastefully refurbished bathroom. He toyed momentarily with the idea of faxing Hawty to compliment her on her choice, but he didn't know how to work the damn fax machine.

Maybe he should call Sharla? *Bad idea; you've got work to do*, he reminded himself with a sigh.

First, he needed to learn as much as possible about Hyam Balazar.

Downstairs again, he asked Rebecca about the name, but she drew a blank. She admitted that she, unlike her husband, was not a lifelong resident of Natchitoches, and did not know all of the oldest families. But she knew of a structure called the Balzar Building.

"Balzar," Nick said. "That may be it. I've probably got the spelling wrong."

"The building is a historical landmark, like everything else in this town. Even me," she said with a mirthful snort. "Empty now, about to fall to pieces. City can't tear it down, and nobody seems to have the cash to renovate. My Bob and I are thinking of buying it and opening another B&B, if we can line up some investors. Interested?"

"Not me," Nick said. "What I know about real estate you can't dip an oyster in. The Balzar Building. Yes, yes, I remember reading somewhere that it once housed a title company. If there's something left—old deeds and such—I really should put it in my article as a resource. Important material like that ought to be gathered and safeguarded." A complete crock, but he hoped he was convincing enough in his preachiness to cover his real intention—stealing all the Balazar genealogical material he could get his criminal hands on.

Rebecca suggested checking with the Chamber of Commerce office to find out how to get in the building. Then she offered to guide him there herself. It was a few streets back from the river. He persuaded her that he was capable of finding the place on his own.

Nick stepped out of the cool lobby and into the prostrating midday heat. He navigated through knots of window-gawking tourists from many nations. Down on the river, packed party boats greeted each other in passing with a few pre-recorded bars of "Dixie."

He felt the proximity of important discoveries. Here was the family name that had drawn him to this town in the first place. Had it been mere coincidence that he'd focused on the surname Balzar, and that it so closely resembled his original target subject, Hyam Balazar? His intuition was leading him again, and he knew better than to ignore it. He wasn't particularly a believer in the paranormal, but sometimes he couldn't figure out any other way to explain a wild inspiration that paid off.

He would certainly want to find the living Balzars before he left Natchitoches, as he'd intended to do before Natalie Armiger started calling the shots. And he would also like to explore the building bearing the Balzar surname—a waste of time, maybe, but he was feeling uncommonly lucky.

❑

At the parish courthouse, his story was that he was in town doing amateur family-history research. Just an ordinary guy, with a harmless hobby. Clerks got nervous and snippy if they thought you were researching their records for nefarious reasons, like trying to make a buck.

Nick proceeded to search through probate, deed, and tax books, and other public records beloved of genealogists. Two hours later, he had found no mention of Balazar. Weird. Frustrating. The records were misfiled or missing, or this was the wrong locality altogether.

There had been a fire at this courthouse, and a flood, for good measure; so the woman at the clerk of court's office curtly told Nick when he asked for assistance. She was filling in for a regular worker who was sick, and was clearly impatient to get back to whatever she'd been doing before he disturbed her. Her coffee break, he assumed.

Some old records had been destroyed, or damaged probably beyond reclamation, she said, drumming her fingers on the counter. Nick suspected she was making up the story as she went along. A good liar can always spot a bad one.

"But most of it was just those St. Denis Parish records. Nobody gives a hoot about those," she said. "Ancient history. We got us a parish government to operate, hon."

Nick recognized the blind arrogance public office could bestow on certain people.

Stubbornly quizzing the woman further, he knew he was onto something.

Once there had been a small parish named St. Denis, very French and anti-American, just a few large landowning families. St. Denis Parish declared its ethnic pride by seceding from larger Natchitoches Parish in 1816; the old boundary was just a few miles outside of town. During the fifty years it claimed to be an independent parish, plucky St. Denis squirmed out of conducting decennial federal censuses—but it did conduct local ones. Natchitoches Parish never recognized the split. Thus the obscurity of the junior parish to all but specialists in the area. No map or reference book Nick had checked in New Orleans so much as mentioned the ephemeral offshoot.

Even the experienced researcher is humbled every day; and so he learns.

The two parishes decided to reunite in 1866. Over the years, less-determined researchers had swallowed the story that the records no longer existed, that they had been destroyed in the Civil War or later, after the two parishes had consolidated, in the fire and the flood at this courthouse.

It seems that many courthouses have suffered such disasters. Nick was ever skeptical of this excuse for missing records. He knew that often this was the way apathetic or overworked local bureaucrats handled pesky genealogists.

The dirty little secret of this courthouse was that much

of the St. Denis Parish records had indeed survived, and it was rudely piled in boxes on bowed steel shelves in a large dank subbasement just off the stairway, where Nick's reluctant guide now took him, after he had persisted beyond her endurance.

"Microfilmed? You got to be kidding!" she responded to Nick's question. At certain moments, she reminded Nick of his seventh grade teacher, for whom he still held an abiding antipathy. "'Course they haven't been microfilmed. Reagan blew out the candle on that project, and Bush took away the cake, hon. We don't get funds to keep the place from leaking, these days. I don't even know what all's in here; nobody does, since old Juanita died; and if you ask me, we ought to have us a nice big bonfire and throw it all in. We close at four o'clock."

She turned her lumpy backside to him and bounced toward the door, but paused to deliver one final warning: "Sharp." And then she left.

Her gruffness didn't affect Nick's glee, which he had struggled to disguise. The room was crammed with undiscovered material—and not just from St. Denis Parish, either! A substantial cache of early Natchitoches records was here, as well.

Oh, Juanita, Juanita! He could have kissed her. Had she inherited this mess or caused it? Nick was grateful to her for at least saving it from oblivion.

He felt like one of the colonial adventurers who had wandered these lands two hundred and fifty years ago. How many bridges across how many impossible gaps could he find here, in these heavy volumes and moldy record packets? How much permanent damage a person of sordid motives could cause. Nick was such a person, and he had just under three hours to do it.

He worked quickly below naked epileptic fluorescents. Initially, he lingered over a few loose fascinating documents he found in unlikely places. But he knew the clock was ticking, and after a while, he was running frantically from box to box, shelf section to section, like a junkie looking for a misplaced fix or someone who's won a five-minute shopping spree in a jewelry store. Fortunately, it was cool down here; but chunks of the concrete floor shifted under his feet and gurgled with smelly liquid; pipes wrapped in tape drooled on him. Did he imagine rats eyeing him warily or hungrily from dark corners? He didn't have time to worry about that.

The Swiss Army Knife people really ought to advertise the wonderfully precise way their blade cuts fragile old pages out of ledgers and court minute books, Nick thought. His fourteen excisions were masterful and would certainly be the envy of any surgeon.

Hyam Balazar and his descendants didn't feel a thing as Nick separated them.

Chapter 13

At sunset Nick sat in a wicker rocker on the balcony of his room, overlooking Cane River. He was studying the documents he had stolen a few hours before, and working on a third glass of sparkling wine. There were other important records of other individuals on some of the pages; he felt bad about that, as he sipped. But his crime was in the interest of one of his favorite causes—keeping himself alive.

He learned as he read that the life of Hyam Balazar would have interested him, whether he was being paid fifty thousand or nothing.

From court proceedings, tax rolls, marriage records, newspaper stories (he'd found a stack of old brittle issues of defunct local newspapers), and a few partial parish censuses, Nick was able to see the outlines of Hyam's life.

His birthplace appeared variously as France, Martinique, St. Lucia, and St.-Domingue, today's Haiti. He apparently used whatever factual invention benefited him most at the time. Nick guessed that he was born between 1780 and 1792. Definitely in Louisiana by the time of the Purchase, Hyam thus instantly became a citizen of the United States. Nick found no evidence to back up Coldbread's identification of him with Hiram, he of the Packenham Five treasure; but the time frame was right.

Early on, records referred to Hyam as a "Hebrew itinerant peddler." From his wagon he sold pots and pans, cloth, spices, newly mass-produced sundries, whatever the country folk and the Indians needed and couldn't readily provide for themselves. He teamed up with a Natchitoches shop owner, one Isaac Makher. Hyam became the traveling salesman for Isaac. Their enterprise was lucrative, their territory broad. They sued frequently over contractual disputes, and from court documents Nick inferred the large amounts of capital involved in their growing enterprise. They were making money hand over fist.

Hyam made the leap to landowner in a very few years. Nick wasn't sure how he had obtained the land, whether from a Spanish land patent or through purchase during the early American period. He had not come across records that would help on that question. Had he missed them? Maybe Hiram and Hyam Balazar were one and the same, as Coldbread thought. Could the lost treasure have financed Hyam's land purchase?

Nick shook his head. He was slipping into Coldbread's fantasy world, where verifiable facts and convincing evidence were no better than dream visions between sleeping and waking. He took a deep breath and forced himself to reason like the professional genealogist he was.

Local land records are vastly important in genealogy. Often they mention birth and death dates, relationships, neighbors, and other crucial family information. Before he left New Orleans, Nick had already checked the *American State Papers* and other relevant references that might have mentioned Hyam making a private land claim to establish a first-title deed to his land. But this lack of primary evidence wasn't unusual. Title to land from the colonial period was sometimes established a hundred years later for lack of contemporary documentation. In the South, land records are complicated and incomplete; add frequent fraud to the mixture, and it's enough to give any genealogist indigestion.

Nick was glad he couldn't locate a patent or a deed: that meant no one else had found one either, and his scavenger hunt for Mrs. Armiger was that much closer to being complete.

All Nick knew was what he could piece together from the records he'd found. In the mid-1830s Hyam owned a large tract of land in a remote area of St. Denis Parish. He bought slaves and started farming in a big way. Corn first, then indigo, then wood for barrels, then cane, which was certainly familiar to him from his childhood on the island—whichever it was—and finally, cotton. He was involved in a few court cases with buyers of his commodities, but these records provided Nick with little personal information.

Hyam's financial successes were blighted by family tragedies. Life was perilous, then as now—though Nick didn't need reminding. He'd found two marriage-license returns (1817 and 1826), which the ministers presented as proof that they had performed the legal ceremonies. There was a death listing only for the second wife (1840). The cause: "fever in consequence of childbirth." Nick found no birth registration for surviving children of these marriages; but that wasn't unusual, even in Louisiana, which began such civil record keeping relatively early.

Nick thought of Hyam's descendant, Natalie Armiger, when he saw the planter's willingness to change religious overcoats. His first wife, Sarah Whortleberry, was Methodist; his second, Mary Debuis, was Catholic. On both marriage documents, there was peculiar reference by the minister to Hyam's conversion; such a prominent man must have been a catch. Hyam was playing the roulette game of life with obvious skill, and was determined to have enough chips to cash out and enter Heaven. On his next trip to Natchitoches, Nick would need to visit the churches, if they still existed, and attempt to gain access to congregational records.

If he could continue to silence his conscience.

His prize discovery was a clerk's transcript of Hyam's nuncupative will, a type of dictated testament, in a batch of district criminal court records with singed page edges. There *had* been a fire, after all.

A genealogist is never surprised where he finds wills. Judges heard cases when and where it pleased them, and clerks sometimes recorded proceedings in the wrong register books through convenience, incompetence, or laziness. Sometimes multiple copies were made, sometimes only the original can be found, sometimes nothing. This clerk was plain messy, or maybe drunk or nervous, in making his blotted copy. Was he the last person to touch the actual document that was Hyam's will and know its fate? It wasn't in the courthouse basement now; Nick had been rushed, but thorough.

Strange. Hyam, a man of business, dying without a formalized written will to dispose of his considerable property. It didn't seem in character for him to leave such loose ends, to treat succession as a mere afterthought. He waited until his final illness before assembling witnesses to make his last wishes known. What if he'd died a moment earlier?

At any rate, the heirs would have come out all right, valid will or no will, thanks to Louisiana's civil law, founded on French and Spanish legal traditions stretching back to Roman times. When there was a valid will, the state's unique law of forced heirship then in effect guaranteed legitimate children a portion of the estate; after 1870, illegitimate children, also, could inherit from the natural parent. Without a will, the children inherited a parent's *entire* estate; and in Hyam's case, there was no surviving wife's community property to consider.

In terms of spontaneity, the nuncupative will is as close to an oral last will and testament as Louisiana's Civil Code allows. Was Hyam replacing an earlier written will because of some final changes of mind? Or had he indeed been content to let state law divvy up his property, giving in finally to someone's persuasion to make a formal record?

Hyam's deathbed statement of his wishes for his estate may not have been the tidiest, most prudent way to do it, but it was binding nonetheless.

Memorandum.

That on the Eighteenth Day of May, 1859, these Declarants do solemnly affirm that Hayam Balazare was Sick upon his bed unto Death, and instructed us to write this Will with respect to his Estate. He being, in the best of our determination, of Sound Mind to direct and dictate such Disposition. Said

Hayam did desire that his Immovables, along with his Movables, be given and bequeathed to his Son, one Jacob Balazare, and to his unmarried daughter, Euphrozine Balazare. To wit, his Immovable Property, set down in the books of this Parish, St. Denis; and his Movable Property, to wit, his gold, his silver, his crops in field, his 43 slaves, his furnishings and clothing, his animals, and all chattels inclusive which are not herein set forth.

Further, that his son Jacob Balazare be made his executor. This Will being read back to him by these Declarants, and being too weak but to make his mark with some aid, the said Hayam Balazare then did declare and affirm that this Will was true. We bear witness, or words to that effect, accordingly.

Ransom Coulton

HB   John Swett X (his mark)

(mark of said Hayam Balazare)   Wlm. Nason

A true gem of genealogical information! Here, Nick had learned of two of Hyam's children, and three men who were perhaps business associates, lawyers or notaries (not Swett, who was unlettered), friends, or relatives. He had a certain death date, and he'd also seen important details of Hyam's elevated financial circumstances.

More questions to answer, but a good day's work.

Dusk had given way to gentle evening, and the lamplights on the street below had switched on, giving a distinctly nostalgic glow to the smooth river-lake and the New Orleans-like section of buildings that faced it. Nick was hungry and tired. He shuffled his pilfered documents back into his tatty briefcase and stood up for a stretch before going downstairs to investigate the possibilities of dinner. He was thinking he was actually earning the obscene fee Armiger had paid him. Noises from his darkened room stopped him cold.

Ah, so this was Natalie Armiger's plan: let him

stumble across the important facts, like an unwitting retriever, and then knock him off. She'd taken care of Corban; now it was his turn. Was the assassin waiting in his room?

His paranoia had shifted into overdrive.

"I knocked . . . a little," Sharla said, coyly penitent, when Nick confronted her in his room. "I thought you might be in the shower or something, so I just came on in. I brought you a club sandwich. And another bottle of wine. On me." She gave the last two words a sultry intonation.

There were two wineglasses. Nick recognized the expensive California chardonnay. Sharla wore a very fetching flowery cotton dress, which showed her otherwise unadorned young figure to delightful advantage.

"Guess I'm nuts," Nick said, "or old-fashioned, but that would seem a reason *not* to come in." He switched on a bedside lamp and put down the nearly empty bottle of bubbly he'd grasped as a possible weapon.

"Oh, you don't have to worry about me. My mother teaches all us hotel staff to be the soul of discretion. Don't you want to tell me some of your deepest, darkest secrets?" She giggled.

In spite of his scruples to the contrary, Nick smiled.

He was a slut and he knew it. Why should he fight his nature? Nature with a big "N"? He was just a man, fallible and helpless, ultimately, in the big scheme of things.

He uncorked the new bottle. "How old are you, by the way? Somehow I get the feeling you're trouble in a pretty package. But a very pretty package, I have to say." He poured wine into the two glasses.

Sharla gave a throaty chuckle that did to Nick exactly what it was no doubt supposed to do. "Why thank you kindly." She moved closer, almost touching him.

He saw the pulse jumping at the base of her neck, felt the warmth of her body, and learned in an instant her distinctive combination of scents.

She kissed him.

And when she was through, running a finger around

Nick's lips, she said, "How old do you have to be to have fun, Mr. Nick Herald from New Orleenz? Maybe you should unwrap me and find out."

She saved him the trouble, and flicked off the straps of her dress; it fell to the floor.

Nick switched off the lamp. In the final blush of twilight, she helped him out of his clothes.

Chapter 12

Nick ate breakfast in an airy sun-filled room downstairs, in the company of ficuses, palms, and about thirty Japanese tourists videotaping each other eating such unfamiliar Louisiana fare as grits and grillades, eggs Benedict, and beignets. Sharla, fortunately, was absent.

I shouldn't have, but I did anyway . . . words for his tombstone. One of these days, he would have to pay for his libidinous lapses; the avenger waiting for him might be some dread disease or a jealous husband. He also worried that maybe he'd shared too much with Sharla the night before, in the way of words; he foggily remembered opening a second bottle of chardonnay, which Sharla just happened to have iced down and handy.

A couple of bagels, some fresh fruit, and two pots of steaming coffee and chicory were getting the better of his hangover. He had a lot of work to do. Moping over indiscretions he might have made, but couldn't now change, wasn't on his schedule. He had to be back in New Orleans for *As You Like It* at eight, with Una.

Una . . . she would definitely not approve of his fall to temptation. And he cared about her approval. The weight of dishonesty he was lugging around was becoming very heavy indeed.

❑

Rebecca was just a little colder toward him at first, as he checked out. She obviously sensed what had happened between her daughter and him. Maybe, Nick thought, she hadn't been much different when she was Sharla's age, and this was just peevishness at the creeping of years, at having to admit to herself that attention of the opposite sex had shifted to the younger generation. He wanted to tell her he understood, and in fact found her attractive, too—but decided she might take his empathy the wrong way.

Soon, though, her irrepressible good nature shone once again, and she was insisting on having one of her workers take him to the Balzar building. Finally, he escaped on his own.

❑

The Balzar building was a post-Civil War beauty, sadly neglected. It sat at the lesser-traveled end of a side street perpendicular to the river. Four floors, herringbone-patterned brown and cream bricks, classical masonry details. The bottom floor once housed other small businesses besides—possibly—Ivanhoe's barber shop; Nick studied the old torn posters and faded painted signs that remained in the windows or had merged with the brick.

Did Ivanhoe, the mulatto barber, own this prime piece of real estate? Perhaps the building just became identified with him, as the long-time, popular tenant; perhaps he was a more influential citizen than was usual for a man in his position in the rigidly stratified society of those bygone days. What bygone days, Nick thought; nothing much had changed since.

The block had the forlorn look of past bankruptcies and sheriffs' sales, of Louisiana's casino-mentality business environment—bet it all and throw the dice! A car rolled by, but the driver took no notice of him. Now he was alone on the quiet street. He slid his Freret University laminated library card through the simple door latch.

"Oh, the manifold uses of the tools of a liberal education!" he said to the silent room he entered.

Any barbershop once in existence had been succeeded ultimately by an insurance agency, Nick judged from the calendars on the peeling walls, and from the scattered stationery and brochures on Sherman tank-like metal desks. The place had been cleared out in a hurry, unceremoniously, and no one had looked back. February 1963 was when the ax fell for Triple-V Insurance. In places where the green-speckled linoleum squares were missing, he could still see the holes in the floor where the barber chairs had once been. This was Ivanhoe's place, all right.

He walked into the back hallway, stirring up dust and breaking cobwebs. There wasn't much here except dozens of paint cans and jugs of pesticide, a regular toxic waste dump. He hoped the stuff had evaporated years before. He hurried upstairs, holding his breath.

His ascent was a journey back in time, each floor a quarter-century, it seemed. Flashlight in hand, he rummaged awhile among a multitude of boxes in hallways and dry-rotted black holes of rooms. He learned a little about the other businesses that had been here, but nothing relevant for his project.

He made his way to the fourth floor, in increasing heat. Was it just a wild-goose chase? That seemed more and more likely with every step.

The fourth floor consisted of one large, long room; it would have made a good indoor basketball court, in more temperate months. The naked walls and floor were a primer on the construction methods of the mid- to late-nineteenth century. It seemed this floor had always been the dumping ground for the major debris of decades, and Nick now found himself amid a beckoning archaeological site. Something was here, something crucial. He could feel it.

Feeble light from the street windows illuminated in colorless relief a blanket of dust covering everything. His slightest movement created minuscule tornadoes that sent galaxies of dust motes swirling up his nose and into his eyes. He poked around several piles of stuff, until a random swing of his fading flashlight found in the far corner of the room the barber chairs.

Or what was left of three or four chairs. The good ones had long ago been commandeered, and now no doubt served as decor in some Americana-theme eatery. There was other detritus of the barber's trade: drawers with Ivanhoe's scissors and combs, razors, brushes, and other implements that he must have used for the minor surgery barbers performed in those days; some bottles of whimsical and ornate design, that probably once held the rainbow array of tonics and scents Ivanhoe splashed on his customers' faces and scalps; striped poles, and signs advertising the many grooming services available at "Balzar's Tonsorial Emporium"; an oak file cabinet, which stood sentinel over rat-eaten piles of account ledgers.

And there, atop the file cabinet, inconspicuous below similarly mildewed volumes, was Ivanhoe's diary, the most momentous impossible gap Nick would ever be likely to discover in a long life of genealogical research, if such were to be his fortune.

Chapter 14

Pacing around downstairs, in what once was Balzar's Tonsorial Emporium, Nick eagerly plowed into the diary. He couldn't resist.

It was a meticulously kept, almost-daily journal of Ivanhoe's life and dreams. A priceless find for a historian, and no mean discovery, either, when viewed from a strictly monetary angle, Nick thought.

Ivanhoe's handwriting was self-assured, his spelling reasonably good, his attitude proud. From the very first words, Nick sensed that he was a man with a clear-eyed view of what was right, and a man who had always striven to keep his conscience clean.

Nick began to carefully turn the pages, pausing at entries that grabbed him. He knew the journal would require months, years of close study; even the first few passages gave him tantalizing hints of what lay deeper within.

❖

From *The Diary of Ivanhoe Balzar: Mulatto Barber of Natchitoches*

We buried my beloved Mother in Natchez, her Bible on her chest, this day of our Lord April 14th 1869. She told me before she died,— Son, you are as good as your brother Jacob, and don't let him take nothing away from you, because your Father, may he rest in Peace, wanted it that way. The law of the land is on your side, now— she said. She been keeping my Father's letter,ever since he passed, near ten years ago. Just before she passed to her Reward, she gave me the letter, and I have hid it so that Mister Jacob can't find it, and I won't show it, no! not for my own life. Some day Providence will make all things right. And til that glorious time I am going to make this rekord so my Children and their Children after them will know Hard Work, Clean Living, and Faith in the Almitey is worth more than the riches of this sinful world, that only causes hatefulnis, pain, and sorow, the which you can see in the way Mister Jacob and his half-sister treat all us others. Remember, my Children, when you are born, to trust in the Good Book, and in your Grandmother's Eternal Love.

....

November 3rd 1870. Jacob, my half-brother, came in to my shop this afternoon. It was not a plezant meeting, though I cannot say that such meetings ever been so, and espeshly since dear Mother died and I bought my place with the money she left me. Jacob— I don't call him Mister anymore, or even Captain, like some folks do, because he carry himself so high. I don't like to give him the plezure of such titles. Sometime I call him Brother, and that makes him madder than a rattler. Jacob, he marches on in and everything just stops. Mister Fabergas from the hat store was in my chair and he just gets up real quick and pays and leaves, and don't even wait for his change. James was doing Mister Flaneur's fine English boots and he just slip out the back door. There were some other men sitting inside and outside, smoking cigars and spitting and jawing about this and that, like they always do, and they all tucked tail and left the two of us alone. Everybody knows Jacob carries a sord in his cane, and a gold and pearl litel pistol, because he has used it twice since the War. Once on Blane Paternoster when he blamed Jacob for losing that fite outside of town with the Yanks back in '64 (shot him through the throat and he died in a most awful way, I seen it). And once on my half-brother Jeremiah, when Jacob said— Your mother, Mulatta Belle, wasn't nothing but a common whore and a nigger!— and Jeremiah lit into him like a hericane. But I was not around for that one, or I might have stopped them. Poor Brother Jeremiah. He is alive, but he don't know his name. Lost an eye, too. After all he been through, to come to this! Jeremiah is the son of my Mother and a slave called Putnam on my Father Hyam Balazar's plantation, Mitzvah. After my Father died and before the War, Jacob sold Jeremiah

to a planter in Missippi! The hardhearted scowndrel!
Selling my half-brother to spite me! Father wanted
Jeremiah to be free, and said so in his own will and
testament. Such paper don't mean nothing to Jacob.
He tore that will in peeces, rite there at my Father's
deathbed! My Mother never spoke a kind word to
Jacob after he did that and sold Jeremiah. Father took
care of all of us while he lived. He made sure we got
some learning. Me espeshly, cause he liked me and let
me read many a time in the library out at Mitzvah. He
taught me to speak French. He even had a fine portrait
of the two of us painted, and it used to hang in the
library where he taught me. But Jacob he slashed it up
with his sord. Just like he do to anything he don't
like. He kill it. So, Father promised Dear Mother on
his deathbed that my Mother's children would be free
and get our Portion after he died, no matter what
happened in the war he could see coming. I was there,
I remember. He talked to her in French, that nobody
else in the family but her and me, a little bit, could
understand. Course, lots of folks around here talk
French, still, and Spanish, too. He told her, I
think,— My dear, I have loved you more than the two
white wives who gave me Jacob and Euphrozine.— And
then he said some words in a langage I could not
understand. I guess he was raving by that time, for he
was very old. But Mother said he was praying. Then
Jacob, he said— Bout damn time the old Jew
died.— Well, I don't know what he meant by that, cept
he always hated Father, because Father was a good
Christian man and never missed a Sunday, at one
church or another. Father was a man of Honour and
Compassion and Charity and Christian Love. Jacob
and Euphrozine call theirselves Christian. Make me
want to laugh out loud! But Jacob didn't know rite off
about those three letters Father gave to Mother. One
for me, one for Jeremiah, and one for my other half-
brother Chapman Winn. He was born a free man, like
me. Chapman is the son of a white gambler and my
Mother, and almost white himself. They say his father
had Choctaw in him. Around here, we all mixed up
like Missippi mud. I hope the Good Lord keep it

strate! Father left me 1000 acres of good land, Jeremiah got his freedom & 500, and Chapman got 250. Jacob has never rested since my Father died. He got poor Jeremiah's, and he paid a little for Chapman's. Chapman just want money to gamble. He is no good, like his father before him. That one don't care about what's rite. Don't like me, neither. Now, my Father loved my Mother very much, seeing as how he gave the three of us what he did. Jacob near lost his mind when he heard. He do what he like around here.

But my birthrite is safe and I don't care how long it takes, I will have Justice! I will set the story strate without help from nobody, and my children will know the truth about who they are. Now, Jacob says— Got a mitey nice place here, Ivanhoe.— He takes his cane and swings it down my counter. Broke eleven dollars worth of tonics and French colone. Bent my best two dollar German razor. I just about jumped on him, but he looks so pitiful and thin, with that hole in his chest you can hear like boiling gumbo. I think he was drunk, like usual, because they say he spits blood and drinks whiskey all nite and never eats and never sleeps. He wanted a fite, I reckon, cause he has his hand inside his coat just itching to pull out that mean litel gun. Lucky there was some men looking in the window from across the street. Jacob may be crazy, but he ain't dumb. He says— Lots of folks don't appreciate you putting on airs, Ivanhoe. Figure you must have stolen that money you got all of a sudden. Lots of powerful people, who can take action when it is necessary. They don't like you setting yourself up white, they don't like you calling yourself by my Father's name, or almost, they don't like you thretning to go to those traitor tirants in the Yankee Legislachure in New Orleans.— Times have changed— I say— You can't do like you did before. The War is over, Brother.— He come rite up close to me. His breath put me in mind of those breezes we used to smell coming from the east after Vicksburg, carrying the odor of dead men. He says— Give me that letter nigger because you sure won't live to benefit from it.— I just stare, don't move a musel. He wanted to

shoot me rite then and there, but something stayed his
hand thank the Good Lord. I suspect I'll be having
trouble from the Thanes of the Gardenia soon. They a
bunch of white nightriders who look to Jacob for their
money. They do their drilling out on Mitzvah, I hear.
....

December 10th, 1870. Today I bought 30 acres
from the old Chirke place. Chirke, he think he was
being foxie telling me how good the land is, when I
know it is full of rocks and mostly scrub and bog. Five
dollars an acre, too much by half, but I have a desire
to be a farmer one of these days, and have something
my children can feel beneeth their feet. My children's
Portion is safe, but it don't put food on the table yet.
I hear that Mrs. Devlin died, on account of a bad
midwife. They say the collera is breaking out again in
the south, round New Orleans. Loaned Newman Judd
eight dollars for three months at four percent, for him
to buy some milk cows. I get as much milk as I need,
too. Business is good, and I mite hire another barber.
Know of a young colored boy working at the Stable, of
good carriage and manners, if I can get him for the
rite wage. Guess if he can groom a horse, he can a
man, just as easy. They say Jacob getting more crazy
every day. He chase the sheriff off the place with a
shotgun, who just come to see how he was, like he
chase Mr. Roberts off last spring when he come to do
the census taking. Jacob think everybody out to cheet
him, so he cheet everybody else first.

Nick couldn't tear himself away, though he was
aware he didn't have time just now to be enjoying
Ivanhoe's account of his family's bloody drama.
Skimming, he saw that it wasn't long after this
1870 entry that Ivanhoe married; then, the first child,
Erasmus, arrived. Ivanhoe wrote lovingly of his land
and his hopes for his children. Eventually he moved his
family out to the old Chirke place. This, Nick guessed,
was where the Balzars lived today. Clearly, he'd bought

the building in which Nick now sat, and the Chirke
place, with money Mulatta Belle, his mother, had left
him.   He had gotten nothing from Hyam—except a
father's love.

The evidence was there in the diary: Jacob had
stolen Ivanhoe's rightful legacy. He obviously suborned
the three witnesses to swear to a bogus nuncupative
will.   Ivanhoe, in the room as his father lay dying, saw
Jacob rip apart the legitimate written will, the will that
really expressed Hyam's intentions, the will that dealt
generously with Ivanhoe and the sons of Mulatta Belle's
other unions.

Had Jacob acted alone?   As yet, Nick knew
nothing of the personality of Euphrozine Balazar.

Ivanhoe was about thirty when he started his
journal; he reserved a few pages at the back for some
vital statistics on family births and deaths, which Nick
knew would be invaluable later in his investigations. It
seemed to Nick that Ivanhoe had an intuitive
understanding of the meaning of genealogy that most
people lack in these times.   Ivanhoe was facing the
stark possibility of the destruction of his past, having
already seen the hijacking of his present. He realized
that knowledge of his ancestry, and especially the
transmission of that knowledge, was of life-and-death
importance to the generations that would follow him.

How many impossible gaps had Jacob created?
His father's dalliance with Mullata Belle was a
humiliation for him. Thus the real will had to go. What
else had he eliminated?   Was this why there were no
further courthouse records showing Hyam's estate
moving through the probate process?   Jacob was a
powerful man, who brooked no opposition.

And what of the letters to Ivanhoe, Jeremiah, and
Chapman?   As mini-wills, they posed a threat; they
could cost Jacob a lot of land—and more, in the case of
Ivanhoe. If, with his letter, Ivanhoe could prove he was
Hyam's son, could he have taken Jacob to court to claim

some portion of Hyam's estate? Maybe a thousand acres wasn't all Ivanhoe would have been due if the issue had been adjudicated properly. Jacob might have faced coughing up more than his ravaged lungs.

Nick surmised that the letters to Mulatta Belle's three sons were identical, each setting out Hyam's bequests to the three of them, as insurance. That would explain why Jacob would want them all, why he would kill for those letters, and why Mulatta Belle was so careful with them.

For Jacob, it was a question of twisted honor, not merely land: he could not live with Ivanhoe as his acknowledged brother.

The letters were probably long gone now; but in this diary, written by his own hand, Ivanhoe had made his own immortality, attained his own silent victory.

Nick noticed a change in the style and content of the diary. Ivanhoe started with the noble intention of presenting his side of the story, of instructing his children; but as the years passed, his affairs become more complicated, and he seemed to reach a level of relative affluence and considerable respect in the community. His attention shifted to his business and civic affairs. Town gossip, only momentous family news, and balance-sheet concerns persisted, without much of the humanizing spirit of the first entries, until an abrupt cutoff in 1881.

Isn't that the way of the world? Nick thought, taking a last look at the room that had once housed Ivanhoe's shop. We start with the grand visions of overconfident youth, with a simplistic lust for radical accomplishments, and soon we lapse into a belittling obsession with minutiae, like an old man on a park bench picking lint from his sweater.

❑

Ivanhoe wrote his diary to preserve the truth; now it was Nick's task to continue its destruction. He didn't like the role he was playing. Ivanhoe's testament should not remain silent forever. He should edit and annotate the volume, get it published. It would become an instant classic of the field, stocked in libraries around the U.S. and the world, translated into a dozen languages.

Nick would be famous. Posthumously.

He walked to his car, hearing Ivanhoe's voice as if he'd spent an hour with the barber. Nick understood that Ivanhoe had intended his diary to shake the rotten fruit from his family tree, no matter how long it took.

A dangerous place for a genealogist to be sitting, under that tree, more than a hundred years later, Nick was thinking as he tried to get his car to turn over.

Chapter 15

Nick knew he should be concentrating on further sundering the thread from Hyam Balazar to Natalie Armiger. But wasn't it possible that Ivanhoe had a place in the *direct* line of her ancestry, that the Ivanhoe-Jacob conflict wasn't just a fascinating sideshow? The likelihood of surprises multiplies geometrically the further you go back. No, Ivanhoe shouldn't be relegated to a ghetto of collateral unimportance just yet.

Wouldn't *that* be a kick in the pants for Madame Armiger, finding that her blue blood had black *and* Jewish tributaries! She wouldn't have a client left—even in the city of which Huey Long once said that a cup of red beans and rice could feed all its "pure" white people, with some to spare.

Besides, Nick was willing to bet that Jacob Balazar, because he hated his father and his father's origins and was so concerned with creating his own version of his family's history, probably had done a lot of the work for him; a few dollars or threats from Jacob might have caused the damage of a dozen fires or floods . . . or of one Nick Herald. No wonder so few traces of Hyam existed.

Nick felt entitled to a little genealogical diversion. He was, as usual, curious: did Ivanhoe ever get his "portion"?

Ivanhoe had been right about the old Chirke place: he'd overpaid for it. The terrain didn't look at all like the rest of mostly flat, fertile Louisiana; Nick drove up and down scrub-pine-covered hills that had some pretensions of being mountainous. The distinctive red dirt gave the area a rusty, disused appearance. The property was about five miles from Natchitoches, real estate that must have been undesirable even to developers. But the highway department apparently had liked the desolate location: cars zipped along I-49, half a mile away.

He drove into the dirt driveway of a small wood-frame house with a lean-to carport and a screened front porch. Country silence and red dust enveloped his car when he killed the engine. He knocked on a vertical piece of screen-door frame that had needed painting a long time ago.

"Morning. My name's Edmund Spenser," Nick said to the woman who answered his knocks. "I'm a research associate at Freret University, in New Orleans. Are you Mrs. Balzar?"

"Why, yessir, I am. I'm Dora Balzar." She was cherry-wood brown, with purple pouches under her eyes; thick around the middle, in her late fifties. She wore a blue polka dot skirt and a polyester white blouse with lots of ruffles. She didn't seem to be the pants-wearing type.

"Oh, good. Well, Mrs. Balzar, I'm working on a book, a book about . . . ," Nick stammered, realizing he hadn't fabricated the details of his deception on the drive over. "A book on the African American role, uh, in the expansion of the frontier to the West. I have reason to believe that an ancestor of your husband's might have been a buffalo soldier."

"A *what* kind of soldier? You best talk to my husband, Erasmus. I don't know nothing about buffaloes, and don't want to, either. Come on in. I'll go get him." She opened the screen door and let Nick in, looking back with some suspicion, he thought, at this white stranger who might very well be the taxman or some other figure of authority who would bring hassles.

Nick heard a television from another part of the

house. A talk show. The audience erupted in laughter, then groaned in disapproval, then applauded and hooted. The living room was as comfortable as straitened circumstances allowed—lots of discount store furniture and the kind of damaged antiques and knickknacks well-to-do white people discard when aged relatives die. Clearly, the Balzars were proud of this room, and it was reserved for company, though there probably wasn't much of that.

There was no air-conditioning, but several lethargic oscillating fans kept the place remarkably cool. Nick inhaled the aroma of some wonderful meat dish emanating from the kitchen, and decided that Dora Balzar was one of those great Louisiana cooks who could put any New Orleans chef to shame, but whose artistry was known only to their families.

As he waited, Nick studied family snapshots and Wal-Mart portraits in cheap frames hanging on the walls and dotting every table. Three attractive, happy brown youths, frozen at various stages of life. *The newest generation of Balzars.* One son looked very much like Dora—probably the eldest, Nick judged. The most recent photo of this young man showed him stone-faced, in some kind of military uniform. Another frame enclosed a lighter, slighter young man, no doubt the younger son; he beamed with pride in a college cap and gown. Following a progression of pictures, Nick jumped through the daughter's life, each shot a stepping stone in the stream of time. The laughing, gap-toothed girl became the starry-eyed bride in the space of seconds.

Erasmus Balzar had entered the room before Nick noticed him. He asked his guest to have a seat. Dora brought him a Dr. Pepper and some freshly baked cookies. Erasmus was lighter skinned than his wife, considerably overweight for his five-eight frame, and in poor health. He explained, in short breaths, that he'd worked at the local poultry plant until it closed without warning five years ago, and since then the family had

lived on his small Army disability pay, his wife's meager
earnings as a seamstress at a store in town and as a
freelancer for certain wealthy white women, and on
various other government benefits.   A heart attack,
diabetes, a lifetime of smoking, and high blood pressure
had taken a toll on his activities. The worry showed in
the hollow bewilderment of his eyes, and echoed in the
pensive silences between his sentences.

"Now, my grandpa in there, watching the TV.
Erasmus the Second—we just call him 'Twice,' you
know, because of the two after his name. Sometime we
call him three times." He laughed up some phlegm at
this old family witticism.

"Rasmus," Dora Balzar said, "Lord have mercy,
don't be talking about Twice that way. It's shameful."
She left the room shaking her head, but smiling
nevertheless.

Erasmus the Third continued: "He don't have
nothing wrong with him, 'cept he can't all the time
remember things too good. But he's ninety-two. Yes
indeed. Ninety-two." He seemed to lose his way, but
then added, "Don't guess I'll make that."

"Do you know anything about your ancestor,
Ivanhoe Balzar?" Nick asked.

"He was my great-great-grandpa, I think. They
say he cut hair way back when, over in a shop
downtown. Somehow the building got named after him,
so he must have been a pretty good barber. I used to
hear that a white man shot him down over the price of a
shave. They did that in them days, the white folks, you
know. What's this book you workin' on? It gonna be a
movie of the week, or what?"

Nick searched his small stock of frontier lore and
came up with some convincing questions, making a
show of writing down Erasmus's answers. Erasmus
gradually grew to like the idea that his great-great-
grand might have lived an exciting life in the Wild West.

"Come on in here and let's try and get Twice to

remember something," wheezed Erasmus with sudden enthusiasm.

Twice sat on a slipcovered couch before a large, rather new television. He gripped the changer tightly in one bony hand and rested the other limply beside him. They couldn't get cable out here, and there was no money for a satellite dish, so they had to make do with the grainy over-the-air signals from Shreveport, Alexandria, and Monroe.

Looking at Twice, Nick thought he could see Ivanhoe himself, and beyond him, Hyam and Mulatta Belle. Just a few pinches of the human clay, just a layer or two more or less of watery beige tint, would do the trick. He was strikingly thin and bent into angles like a grasshopper, though he was probably six-and-a-half feet stretched out. His skin was vitreous, like a piece of glazed china, relatively unwrinkled and surprisingly youthful looking, with a sandy darkness deep down. Nick imagined he would shatter into a million pieces if touched too hard. His eyes were milky with cataract; Nick doubted he could see much of the show he watched, or even understand it. There were a few curlicues of gray hair around his sunken temples. He was dressed neatly, by Dora certainly, in a light-blue button-down shirt and a crisp pair of work jeans.

Nick rapidly figured the relationships: if Ivanhoe was Erasmus III's great-great-grandfather, and Twice is his grandfather, then . . .

"Twice, can you tell me about your grandfather, the man named Ivanhoe Balzar?" Nick began, sitting down next to the old man on the sofa. "Did your grandmother or your father ever speak of him? Maybe tell you if there were any important family papers put away somewhere?"

Nick was thinking of that letter Ivanhoe had mentioned, all the while feeling guilty because the diary really belonged to these people.

Well, I'll share the royalties when I get the thing

published . . . don't kid yourself, Nicky boy; Armiger will never let it happen. Nick struggled to banish those thoughts.

Twice stared straight ahead at the television. His face twitched with the effort of recollection. "Chocolate! Vanilla! Fresh, fresh berries! Half-price! Hurry, hurry!" he screamed, startling them all. Here was a man who had heard too many commercials.

"He likes his ice cream, he sure do," Dora said, smiling patiently at her antediluvian in-law. "Let me just go get him some. Maybe that'll calm him down."

"Twice, Twice. Think, now," Nick began again, feeling like a hypnotist. "I'm trying to learn all I can about your grandfather. He might have been a hero, and we want to tell his story to the world." Nick was convinced about the hero part, though not sure that he was exactly sincere about telling the world.

"The Good Book," Twice said solemnly, holding up an index finger, in a credible impersonation of the Grim Reaper. "First shall be last, and last shall be first. Time to reap and sow. Rejoice, leap for joy, for your reward. Happy are the mild-tempered; lo, they inherit the earth. Make your peace with your brother and offer up your gift. Yes mean yes, no mean no. Store up treasures, where moth and rust do not consume, thieves break not in and steal. There your heart will be also. Keep on asking, and it shall be given; seeking, you shall find. No rotten tree brings forth fine fruit. Fresh, fresh! Hurry while they last! In the Good Book, look to the Good Book!"

Dora brought his ice cream, and he was pacified.

More than eighty years of Ecclesiastes and the Sermon on the Mount had left plenty of echoes in old Twice's brain. Nick didn't detect anything useful in the old man's muddled oration. Too bad. Family secrets often were hidden away in the memories of old ones like Twice.

"We always been a family that keeps our

important dates and such in the Bible," Erasmus said. "That's probably what he jabbering on about. It's right over here. But there ain't nothing older than Twice written down. Guess the one before this got lost somewhere."

Erasmus showed Nick the family Bible, which was nothing special—the branching out of the family from Twice's generation. He jotted down the information recorded between the testaments, out of habit. At least now he could attach names to the faces in the photos hanging in the Balzar living room: Shelvin, Ronald, and Winfred . . . for all the good it would do him.

After promising to send a copy of the book on buffalo soldiers to the Balzars, Nick preceded Dora to the door, eager to move on to his next stop. He had only about two hours left; and even leaving at four, he'd have to burn rubber and any remaining oil getting back to New Orleans by eight.

He walked out to his car in the searing heat. The trunk and passenger door were open. His bag, in the trunk, had been ransacked. Fortunately, he had hidden the diary and other documents in the spare-tire well, and that seemed undisturbed.

He looked around, but saw no one. Puzzled and pissed-off, he started stuffing his things back into the bag.

A pair of strong hands grabbed his shoulders and spun him around, slamming him against the side of the car.

"What the fuck you doing out here, whitey?" said the big guy who was using a forearm to do a professional job of stopping the flow of air through Nick's windpipe. "I been hearing about you in town. Asking questions about my family. Friend of mine works over at that hotel you stayed at. So, who are you and what you want?"

"Shelvin! Leave him alone, you hear me! Shelvin! Let the man go. *Now!*" Dora shouted from the porch.

"You all right, Mr. Spenser? My Shelvin, he don't mean nothing. That Army training and the Gulf War plum ruined my boy's manners. Shelvin, tell Mr. Spenser you sorry."

"That's not his real name, Mama. He's up to something no good, like all the white devils. Ain't that right, Mr. Nick Herald from New Orleans?"

When a guy introduces himself with the etiquette of a commando and the ecumenism of a religious zealot, small talk is moot. Nick merely coughed in reply, feeling lucky to be alive.

Shelvin was six-six of lean muscle topped by a shaved head that looked like the old football helmets from Knute Rockne's day. He wore knee-length black biking shorts, a black muscle shirt with a gold *X* front and back, and black Converse high tops—all of which made Nick hotter just looking at them.

"I don't care what he call himself. You just leave him alone and let him be on his way," Dora said firmly. She went back inside, confident of being obeyed.

"You a lawyer, huh?"

Nick continued stowing his belongings. "No, I'm not a lawyer. I'm a genealogist, someone who researches family histories. I'm in Natchitoches trying to learn all I can about a certain family that lived here during the nineteenth century. Some of the descendants now live in New Orleans, and I'm working for them."

"What's that got to do with us?" Shelvin asked, showing interest in hearing something besides gagging from Nick's throat.

"That's what I'm here to find out."

Shelvin stared off into the distance. "I always wanted to know what it was like to live in Africa, before slavery days."

"I'd be glad to help you get started in genealogy, Shelvin. No charge. Hey, I'm not such a bad guy. Really."

Nick wanted to come clean. He felt he owed it to

Ivanhoe. But he couldn't. Not yet, anyway, if ever.

Shelvin looked Nick up and down and seemed to come to a decision.

"Sure, I heard of them Balazar people just about all my life. They the ones you interested in, right?"

"Right."

This guy was quite the detective. But he apparently didn't see a connection between his family and that one, any more than a Smith would assume a relation to a Smythe.

"Since the mayor always telling us to be nice to tourists, I guess I better be," Shelvin said. "There's an old plantation outside of town once belonged to Balazar folks, people say. Used to be St. Denis Parish, way back. Me and my women go out there, and, you know ..." He demonstrated with fingers what carnal choreography he and his lady friends performed. "Come on. I'll take you there."

Nick followed Shelvin, who drove at a maddeningly slow 20mph in his low-riding matte-black 1953 Ford pickup. Nick could feel the thumping of his audio system from thirty feet behind him.

After a succession of potholed parish roads, they ended up on a meandering, grassy lane bordered by ancient oaks. Through the trees Nick glimpsed vast fields, producing now only stands of immigrant shrubs and trees; now and then he saw a weathered, disintegrating tin-roofed sharecropper's house.

The manse itself was nothing more than seven columns and remnants of two brick walls. Hyam had planned the approach with drama: the house once towered over the carriage roundabout that the grassy road unexpectedly led into; it must have been a breathtaking event to pull up in front of Mitzvah Plantation. Within the round enclosure stood a lichen-gray classical water nymph, her head missing, petrified in the act of emptying giant seashells into a dry pool. A new "For Sale" sign was nailed to one hoary tree.

Artemis Realty, it read.

Figures, Nick thought. Natalie Armiger was systematic, he had to give her that. She was pursuing her own track to destroy evidence linking her to the Balazars. And she knew a lot more than she'd admitted.

Nick felt awash in a confluence of paradoxes flowing from the nymph's empty shells. This place that Shelvin used as a sexual playground had been the setting for Hyam and Mulatta Belle's unconquerable love, a relationship so far beyond mere physicality that it had stretched into the succeeding century; and even though, unwittingly, Shelvin represented the line of disinherited Balzars, robbed of part of their heritage and their "Portion," he considered himself the master of this rotting kingdom.

"They say it burnt down about a hundred years ago," Shelvin said, as they walked amid the steamy shadows.

Cicadas wailed, and then suddenly ceased as if strangled; but others took up the mournful antiphonal song.

"Was anything saved? Business records, books, letters?"

"Can't say as I heard anything like that. How come I get the feeling you not telling all you know? You ain't playing fair with me. I think there's something going on here more than just this genealogical bullshit, man. I'm in New Orleans a lot. In the Army Reserve, and we got our summer exercises just across the river in southern Mississippi this year. I be looking you up one day and ask you again . . . where my mama can't interrupt us."

"Suit yourself. But I'll tell you one thing: I'm not your enemy, Shelvin. One day, I may turn out to be the best friend your family ever had."

"I heard that before, fool, from lots of white folks, and still got fucked over. When you prove I *can* trust you, then I *will*."

❑

Nick followed Shelvin back through the maze of deteriorating roads to a convenience store Nick recognized as a reference point from his earlier navigation of the town. Shelvin pulled his thumping truck into a parking place that seemed reserved for him, in front of the ice machine and the pay telephone. He got out of the truck and just stared at Nick, cross-armed, refusing to acknowledge his farewell wave.

Chapter 16

The librarian explained to Nick in numbing detail, while her phone warbled annoyingly, that the most recent parish library tax issue had failed, and that workers were being cut right and left, so that even if the genealogical collection had not been transferred to Northcentral College last year, the library wouldn't be able to serve the public in that area as it should, for the library *is* a servant of the public, dedicated to the ideals of furthering knowledge and improving the quality of life for— . . . Nick thanked her over his shoulder as he headed for Northcentral College, and the Naomi Gascoin Widdershins Collection.

Because it was summer, there were only a few students on the campus of Northcentral. Tanned and supremely narcissistic, they slouched around in shorts, flip-flops, and T-shirts sporting images of the latest counterculture poseurs.

The overcooled interior of the Gardner P. Singletoe Memorial Library had the smell of air in most public buildings. It seemed to Nick to have been recycled for thirty years, and suggested industrial-strength cleaners, hidden mold and mildew, countless trapped airborne viruses, and undiscovered carcinogenic materials hidden in the janitorial quarters and embedded in ceiling tiles. Nick stood for a moment in the ground-level lobby, a standard-issue Herman Miller seating area, wondering why anyone would still refer to the sixtyish terrazzo-aluminum-wood style of the decor as modern.

Up a flight of stairs, through several membranes

of glass doors, past copiers, bad sculpture, water
fountains, and a nasty-looking electronic theft gate,
Nick found himself before the desk of Fabian Bunting,
M.L.S.

As Nick introduced himself, Bunting looked up
from his stamping. Bunting's body had the delicate
insignificance of a small, nervous dog; his head seemed
larger than normal because of his scrawniness. Nick
detected a tendency toward monkish asceticism in the
man's weary but rapturous blue eyes.

"What a pleasure to have you here, Mr.
Underwood," Bunting said to Nick, in a barely audible
voice, as if he were praying in his cell before sunrise.
"My favorite time of year. I have the library all to
myself, for weeks." Apologizing for asking, he checked
two of Nick's fake scholarly cards.

"Oh, our Widdershins Collection is quite a
triumph for the library and the college, indeed it is, Mr.
Underwood. I shall have the honor this coming
semester of conducting a seminar for our library-science
undergraduates, during which we shall undertake to
catalog the material that has so recently been entrusted
to us. You are doing research, I believe you said, on..."

He had something of the stealthy inquisitor in his
monk's demeanor; Nick hadn't yet mentioned why he
was here.

"I'm doing an article on the Southern culinary
tradition, and I'm looking for authentic plantation
recipes in collections like this one."

"How thoroughly appetizing," Bunting said, with
unconvincing interest. He probably subsists on water
and stale bread crusts, Nick thought. "If you'll follow
me, Mr. Underwood, I shall direct you to the section
holding the Widdershins Collection."

Bunting walked like a balloon in a breeze, not
quite sure where he would go next. Twice he returned
to his desk before they had gone ten feet, once to close
his inkpad, then to line up his four extremely sharp

pencils. As they continued, he darted to a stack to adjust a book slightly protruding, then to a card file to close a drawer some thoughtless patron had left open. On the stairs to the third floor, he pounced on a crumpled piece of paper, shaking his head, apologizing, lamenting that the children simply would not obey the rules.

He gave Nick a quick description of what he might find in the several dozen lawyer's cabinets that held the papers and books of the collection. There was a volume on hand, supposedly an index of the material, but Bunting confessed his doubt that it was complete, though it might possibly be useful as a starting place. With some self-effacing words and bows, he left Nick to his work.

Naomi Gascoin Widdershins had been the clerk of court in a neighboring parish from 1931 to 1970. Being of plutocratic background herself, she made a point of rescuing whatever was left when crumbling plantations were boarded up or torn down, as the old families died off or scattered. But then old Naomi went too far: when she retired, she took her precious collection with her, out of the public domain.

Nick knew this was not unusual; he'd run into such situations before, in other parts of the country. Clerks sometimes were unwilling to relinquish control of their beloved documents, or to allow profane hands to touch them. After their deaths, these irreplaceable hoards of information might end up in a historical collection, with luck; or, less fortunately, they might be piled in garbage bags at the curb, mistaken for run-of-the-mill personal papers of the deceased clerk.

Free of the solicitousness of the emaciated Mr. Bunting, Nick quickly located a promising case of bundled papers, and lifted the glass door. The bundles seemed to have been kept separated according to plantation. For Nick, the names were evocative of the juleped euphemisms that finally could not sweeten the

bitter reality of the antebellum South. Bonneheure,
Montclair, Shadowick, Heatherdowns, Canebreeze . . .
ah, Mitzvah! Finding it did indeed feel like a good deed,
a commandment to do the right thing, as Nick knew the
word connoted in Jewish tradition.

Now there was no time to linger over the
tantalizing items—letters, bills of sale, household
papers, most slightly charred. He checked around for
surveillance cameras. Finding none, he smoothly slid
his discoveries into his briefcase.

❑

"Well, Mr. Underwood . . ."
"Ralph, please," Nick said, standing again before
Fabian Bunting's desk.
"Very well, Ralph . . . you aren't leaving already?"
"I'm afraid I can't work up there, Fabian. The
conditions, positively deplorable. You see, there's a
fluorescent light that's incredibly noisy. If there's one
thing I *cannot* tolerate it's a noisy place of research. No
offense to you personally, Fabian, but as a fellow
academician, I am shocked. Shocked, that your fine
facility would be marred by such . . . such . . . well, such
gross incompetence!"

He was devastated. "Oh, my! Please, Ralph, have
a seat for a moment. I am going to summon
maintenance immediately. But it's summer. Oh, dear
me!" He put a hand to his temple, as if some throbbing
pain had just erupted there. "There is only one
maintenance man on duty. Not our best, I'm afraid.
Well, I'll just make the call anyway, and go up myself to
investigate."

"Thank you, Fabian. You are most kind. I knew
you would understand."

"Oh, completely, completely. I am the same way.
The least little noise or . . . disorder can make me lose
my concentration."

Fabian stood up, looking as though he didn't know
exactly what to do; then he caught a breeze and was off,

stepping softly as if on eggshells toward the stairway, his concentration apparently back.

When he was safely out of sight, Nick walked over to the electronic theft device, slid his briefcase through the narrow gap between one of the posts and the wall, and left.

Chapter 17

Gwen was a retired paralegal from a small north Louisiana town. "Nine months," she said, affectionately patting the stacks and stacks of notecards in her briefcase. "Nine months to compile this stuff, and I'm only halfway through my survey of northwest Louisiana. It's my baby; it's all right here. Can't bear to be separated from it." She tittered apologetically.

"My publishers in Little Rock are always on me to speed up, but I want it to be right, you know?"

In retirement, she'd finally devoted herself to her lifelong interest: the study of family Bibles and small cemeteries throughout Louisiana, those often overlooked places where the passages of life were lovingly, and usually accurately, recorded. Gwen asked Nick if he'd read her article on the headstone inscriptions of Claiborne Parish in *ArkLaTex Memories*?

"As a matter of fact I did," Nick said, wishing he actually had. "Loved it."

This was his last stop on Hawty's list: Shady Dell Plantation, home of the archives of the Daughters of the Glorious Gray. A fiercely unfriendly woman watched over the shelf-lined reading room, formerly the grand ballroom of the three-story, square-columned, white Italianate mansion. The woman on duty eyed Nick and Gwen with obvious suspicion, as she dusted one of the Confederate-soldier mannequins.

This wasn't going to be easy, Nick warned himself.

With the possessive pride of the frequent visitor,

Gwen showed him the splendid collection of family Bibles, forty-six of them, she explained. From Antwyn to Zimmer. Some of the books were bragging statements of conspicuous piety and wealth, with ornately tooled leather and gaudy clasps; others were unassuming, utilitarian objects of daily devotion. For some months Gwen had been laboriously transcribing the handwritten family chronologies and notations scattered throughout these books. Now working among the Js, she'd already passed the richly decorated quarto Bible of the Balazar family.

She was a sweet, pudgy woman, as likable as a stuffed toy. Nick was already sorry for what he was going to do to her.

He grabbed several Bibles, seemingly at random, the Balazar one among them. Then, he took a seat at a separate library table.

Thumbing through the Bible, he quickly decided there were three pages in the front he wanted: "Births," "Marriages," and "Deaths." He kept his knife ready. Ten minutes, twenty minutes went by.

Nick squirmed in the too soft, crushed-velvet Victorian chair. He was getting desperate.

But just as he was about to do something rash like grab the book and dash out, Gwen said, "God! I just *have* to have a cigarette. You smoke? No. Well, I've tried to quit. I'm chewing that nicotine gum." She removed a wad and wrapped it in a piece of paper. "Doesn't do a bit of good. Watch my stuff will you? I have to go outside. The old bat won't let me smoke in here."

Innocent as baby Nero, Nick commiserated.

The old bat followed Gwen out of the room, not so discreetly indicating her disapproval of Gwen smoking even exiled to the wide front gallery, where the soaring square white columns had endured the breath of cannons. Gwen's briefcase was the kind lawyers and accountants use, a deep box-like affair. In a pocket inside the lid Nick noticed an extra pack of cigarettes and a book of matches. He took the matches, lit one, and dropped it and the matchbook in the briefcase. A brief, violent flare erupted. In a few seconds, smoke and flames roiled up from the crib of Gwen's "baby."

Poor Gwen. The world will just have to wait for your book . . . lacking, alas, the Balazar Bible details.

By the time the first of the smoke detectors started to blare, Nick had removed the pages he needed from the Balazar Bible and made it to the lobby, where he shouted, "Fire!"

The old bat ran past him, followed a moment later by Gwen. Several other Daughters of the Glorious Gray appeared on the curved stairway, pausing melodramatically before a mammoth triumphal painting of the First Battle of Bull Run, their faces mimicking the expressions of the snorting war-horses in the picture.

At least that's the image Nick had as he left the building, nearly colliding with a black woman in a maid's uniform, who ran in from somewhere with a fire extinguisher.

❑

He drove toward the highway, gunning through every yellow light, consoling himself with the thought that maybe he'd helped Gwen kick the habit.

❑

"Oh, hell! Just what I need!"

Blue lights flashed in his rearview mirror.

Nick wasn't sure how fast he'd been going. The vision of Corban's dead face again had commanded most of his attention.

For an interstate, I-49 was little traveled; Nick had become accustomed to the clear field. If need wasn't the justification, some legislators, contractors, and their cronies must have made a killing on this thing. The Louisiana way. He figured he was about to find out firsthand about one of the new revenue sources the highway had brought.

Nick could see the officer gesturing with his arm,

toward an exit. Why not just pull over on the shoulder? he wondered. Great! He would have to go in front of some judicial bumpkin to pay a fine. He had little cash on him, and he doubted any trustworthy person would take one his checks.

The two cars pulled into the dirt lot of a boarded-up convenience store on the verge of being reclaimed by the pine forest behind it.

The officer got out of his car and began walking toward Nick. Nick didn't have insurance, as required by state law, so there was no reason to go through the charade of searching his glove compartment for the papers. The guy might think he was reaching for a gun, anyway. Maybe he could talk his way out of this.

"Afternoon, officer. Was I speeding?"

"No sir. Problem is, you wasn't going fast enough." The man drew his pistol, which to Nick looked like more gun than rural duty required. "Get out of your car, Mr. Genealogist."

"What's this all about?"

"You good at asking questions, ain't you? Les us take a stroll on over behind that there building. Careful, now: I get nervous when people look at me like that."

The young man, slightly taller than Nick, had short blonde hair, a thin fair face, and a paunch that strained at the khaki uniform he wore. The patches on his short-sleeve shirt told Nick he was a deputy with the sheriff's department of a nearby, otherwise unremarkable parish. His nametag read "Chirke."

Chirke? Sounds familiar. Nick tried to find the name in his overcrowded memory. Thinking helped keep the panic at bay.

They walked through piles of old garbage and a graveyard of refrigerators. The squawk of the patrol-car radio faded into the hiss of unseen life as they entered the dense pine forest. A breeze now and then disturbed the canopy of needles far above them but didn't do anything for the oppressive heat.

They descended a slope to a small bayou running through fallen trees and clay banks. On level ground now, beside the bayou, they stopped on Chirke's command.

A good place for a shooting, Nick realized. That slope will block much of the noise of the shot, and no one from the highway can see. He had always hoped to have a glorious epiphany before death; instead, his mind was now merely a camera.

"Okay, Mr. Genealogist. Turn around. I got to shoot you in the front 'cause you went for my gun. That's after I done found the drugs in your car and you took out runnin' for the woods, you understand."

"You're a descendant of Gershom Chirke, aren't you?" Nick said. Gershom Chirke sold Ivanhoe Balzar the inferior land.

For a moment the man was rigid in astonishment; then his eyes narrowed.

"Well, what my cousin Sharla been sayin' 'bout you ain't far wrong, I guess."

Ah, Sharla, the Mata Hari of Cane River country.

"You been pokin' your nose in *everybody's* business. You even been pokin' Sharla. There's some folks 'round here don't like any of that kind of bizness. My family's some of 'em."

"Got a lot to hide, don't you, Chirke? Like, for instance, the fact that the land you sold to the state for the highway wasn't really yours. What did you do, forge a phony deed from Ivanhoe Balzar selling the land back, giving your family title again? That's how I would've done it, maybe." He was guessing, but he'd hit a raw nerve.

"Them Balzars don't know how to work land! Never did. They just lazy niggers, thas all. My great-great-granddaddy gave one of 'em a chance, and look at 'em today." Chirke had said more than he'd intended. "Well, it don't matter, anyhow, 'cause you ain't gonna tell nobody. I'm gonna shut you up, but good."

A mound of forest carpet above them exploded, and what looked like some huge, winged animal pounced on Chirke. Nick went for the gun. It fired twice, as loud as a cannon. A large black hand covered Chirke's face. In the ensuing frenzy, Nick gave a few punches and took a few. Then he had the gun.

The owner of the black hand used Chirke's eye sockets as if they were bowling-ball holes and dragged the deputy down to the ground. This man—or bear, as it seemed to Nick—draped in a camouflage cape, was now on top of Chirke, pummeling him. After a rapid series of head blows delivered by Nick's rescuer, Chirke was still.

Shelvin stood up, winded, and looked at the bloodied deputy on the ground. "He ain't dead."

"Do you know him?" Nick asked.

"Uh-huh. We live on his uncle's land for next to nothing, 'cept our votes whenever somebody in his family hereabouts runs for something or other, and they always do. Gerald here thinks he tough shit. But he ain't much out from under his white sheet, if you know what I mean. I been looking for a chance to do that."

"Thanks, Shelvin."

"Ain't no big thing. Enemy of my enemy must be my friend. Right, Mr. Genealogist?"

"The name's Nick. What were you doing up there, covered up with pine needles and leaves? How did you—"

"On my way to see one of my women; she live close by. Seen your cars over there, decided to look into it. I know how Gerald and his kind operate. When I seen what was going down, tried a little trick from my field training. Neither one of you saw me moving closer," Shelvin said with evident pride. "Used the wind and the crow calls to cover the noise, and my poncho to blend into the woods."

"Did you hear what Chirke said? That's probably your land."

"Uh-huh, I heard him," Shelvin replied.

"I believe there's much more to the story of injustice done to your family. I might need your help."

"That's cool. Now, go on back to New Orleans, Nick. Me and Gerald here got some things to discuss." Nick handed the gun to Shelvin, who then crouched down next to Chirke.

"Smith and Wesson 10mm. Not the FBI model; must be the ten-oh-six. Well, well, don't got one of these," he said, admiring the pistol.

❏

Five minutes later, Nick was back on the highway, heading for New Orleans, scrupulously obeying the speed limit.

Chapter 18

His ticket was waiting for him at the box office, along with an attached note from Una: "You're late—I'm angry!" The student working the ticket window told him that Una had paced around outside, expecting him; she confirmed that Una was in an ugly mood.

He'd put on a wrinkled, nearly clean white shirt in his car; now he tried to make his squashed tie and coat look somewhat more presentable. Ready as he ever would be to face Una's ire, he walked through the Art Nouveau lobby of Fortescue Auditorium, through double swinging doors, and then down the aisle into the dimmed light of the intimate theater. Sadie Fortescue College was the traditionally women's, fine arts-centered branch of Freret University.

Nick immediately recognized the wrestling scene of *As You Like It*. Dion served in one of his several roles as Charles, the boasting wrestler. His tall frame was padded out to make him a formidable match for the smaller, scrappy Orlando, who was about to vanquish him in an upset.

For late summer, not a bad crowd. A heartening number of students. Must be bad weather in the Florida panhandle.

Una had excellent seats in the middle section; but he'd have to scurry over a dozen people to get there. During a wonderfully overacted raucous moment in the onstage action, Nick plunged down the row, trailing his briefcase and copious apologies after him.

"Puh-lease! Do you mind! Watch where you're stepping," a familiar voice protested. *The Usurper.* In the dimness, he hadn't yet recognized Nick.

"Frederick, doing a little thesis advising tonight? Oh, it's you, Hilda." Mrs. Tawpie stiffened at Nick's sarcasm and shrank away from the armrest she shared with her husband. Nick gave Frederick's famously expensive shoes some good stomps.

"Where have you *been*?" Una snarled in his ear. He could see she didn't really want an answer; he shrugged a plea for understanding. She gave him a quick glare of disappointment and returned her attention to the play. After a few moments, her hand found his in the darkness. *Ah, sweet forgiveness!*

And so they settled back in their seats and entered the timeless world of the feuding dukes and the band of worthy exiles wandering in the forest of Arden, engaging in philosophical fencing and amorous feints. Whenever the pompous Duke Frederick strutted upon the stage, Nick made sure to laugh with inappropriate volume in the real Frederick's direction.

"A fool, a fool! I met a fool i' the forest, a motley fool. A miserable world!" said Dion as Jaques, beginning the splendid "thereby hangs a tale" passage. He was magnificent, topping even his most outlandish classroom performances, some of which Nick had been privileged to see. Just about every time Dion delivered his lines, the actors after him had to wait for the audience's applause to die down before continuing with the play.

Something Jaques had said, Nick wasn't sure what, made him "deep contemplative" in the protective darkness. He replayed the events of the last few days in his mind; suddenly, the characters he had met and read about moved on a bright stage . . .

He saw Hyam Balazar, a boy of seven or eight, standing at a ship's railing, searching the Atlantic horizon to the west for his new island home which his mother, behind him, assures him is near. Then Hyam, *growing up in lush, tropical Caribbean surroundings, working in some kind of exchange with his father, speaking French publicly, maybe refusing to speak Yiddish at home. Nick saw beautiful dark women, naked and beckoning, through Hyam's young man's eyes. And then the exciting European cosmopolitanism and urban evils of New Orleans; the lonely years of travel in his wagon as a peddler; the land, the beautiful spread of acres he falls in love with as he rides through it by chance, vowing to acquire it; the shop in Natchitoches and the drudgery of merchandising; the incremental financial and social successes; the slave auctions; the building of Mitzvah; the planting; the marriages, the deaths, the births; Mulatta Belle, leaning on Hyam's arm as they stroll through Natchez, as he gambles on a riverboat—he too rich and powerful to suffer reproach for loving her, she too beautiful and defiant to care what society thinks.*

And there is young Ivanhoe, in the study of Mitzvah, being taught by Hyam himself, to the measured ticking of a clock. Young Jacob taunting younger Ivanhoe, calling him names, fighting with him, not bold enough yet, and too afraid of his father, to cast out his half-brother. Euphrozine, whispering plots to Jacob, urging him on in their gambit for complete control when their ailing father would finally die. An old man's hand grasping a quill pen as it scratches out three letters promising land. The death of Hyam. The cruel reign of Jacob and Euphrozine. The war, Jacob's horrible injuries, which drive him nearly mad; his humiliation, which finishes the job. The death of Mulatta Belle. Ivanhoe, writing his diary at the end of each day in his barbershop, wondering if anyone will ever read it, hoping that his carefully crafted testament will somehow secure the future for his descendants—

"Nick? *Nicholas Herald!* Are you asleep? You can't be; your eyes are open."

Una tugged forcefully at his coat sleeve. The house lights were up, the curtain closed. It was intermission, thrown in by the drama department as a ploy to entice people to buy tickets in the lobby for the upcoming season.

Nick came to. *Damn!* He'd missed Jaques' great hymn to melancholy, his favorite part. But something just as wonderful had come to him in his reverie.

"'From hour to hour, we rot and rot, and thereby hangs a tale,'" he mumbled from memory toward the curtained stage. Thoughts of Ivanhoe's first diary entry, of what Erasmus III had said about keeping important papers in the family Bible, of Twice's demented oration on mortality and eternity . . . all swirled around in Nick's consciousness.

I know! I know where to find Ivanhoe's letter! He jumped up, just stopping himself from dashing to the nearest exit.

"What happened to your face?" Una asked. "If you're drunk, Nicholas Herald!" She wagged a warning index finger. When extremely put out with him, Una lapsed into frigid formality. One of his grandmothers used to do the same thing; he thought it was cute.

"Drunk? Not yet, my dear. Not yet. Come on, let's get some champagne before these artsy-fartsy types suck the bottles dry."

❏

In the urbane chatter of the lobby, second champagne in hand, he explained to Una why he hadn't phoned her for the past few days—leaving out any mention, of course, of his barbaric butchery and borrowing of irreplaceable documents.

"While I was gone, did you notice anything in the news about an old guy who committed suicide over in the Irish Channel?"

"Yes, I believe . . . I'm certain I did. It was in the *Times-Picayune*. A small article. I didn't know him, so I didn't really give it a second thought. Why do you ask? What did that unfortunate man have to do with you?"

"He was my client, Una. He didn't kill himself. I think there was foul play involved."

"You mean he was . . . murdered?" She stumbled over the unfamiliar word.

"I'm not sure. Another client of mine might be responsible."

"Oh no!" she blurted out; and then, in a lower, conspiratorial whisper, "It just occurred to me: a tourist was fished out of Lake Pontchartrain."

"So," Nick said, "that's par for New Orleans. What makes you think it has anything to do with the old man or me?"

"She was from Poland and worked in her state's archives. She was the equivalent of a genealogist!"

"Ah," said Nick, massaging his neck. Being scared shitless was tiring work. "I see what you mean."

"I don't like this. Are you in any trouble, Nick? Please, please don't get caught up in something that might . . . might lead to any harm."

"The harm's been done, long ago, and I have no choice anymore about whether I'm caught up in it or not. Someone's already made that decision for me. But you can help."

"*Of course* I'll help, Nick. You know that."

"You have a safe-deposit box, don't you?"

"Yes."

"Good. Later, I want to give you some documents to keep for a while."

"I've been wondering why you're carrying that horrible briefcase around. How old is that thing?"

Nick ignored her question. "As soon as you can, put the documents in the box. Don't tell anyone, *anyone* what they are or that I have anything to do with them. Better yet, don't even read them. Una, I can't deny that there might be some—"

"Trouble? That word again. This *is* serious. More

than harmless genealogical research. Nick, what's going on?"

"Maybe I'm like old Adam in the play; Orlando says he's pruning a rotten tree that can't yield a blossom. But I think I can right some old wrongs—and some newer ones, from what you've just told me."

Una shook her head and put her hand on his arm. "I wish you were back in the boring old English department, living the life of quiet desperation you'd grown to despise. All the *violent* plots there were merely literary."

A friend of Una's from the history department came up to chat with them; but the conversation soon turned to university politics, endangered funding, backstabbing, and toadyism.

"I'll get us another drink," Nick said, making his escape.

The table holding the champagne glasses and little masterpieces of hors d'oeuvres with a decidedly New Orleans zing was off to one side of the lobby, beneath an impressive stained glass window somewhat in the Tiffany style, except with recognizable Louisiana motifs. Fortescue students in the early part of the century made these windows, as well as Fortescue Pottery, ceramics that have gained deservedly high regard.

Nick waited in a competitive wave of bodies to get to the table; New Orleanians get testy when deprived of their pleasures.

He was admiring the big backlit window above the bar when a woman said, "'Persephone's Return to the Marsh,' it's called. A gift from Artemis Holdings." She was standing beside him, as beautiful as Persephone herself, Nick thought. "Zola Armiger," she said, re-introducing herself. "We met briefly at—"

"The Plutarch. Sure. You're not easy to forget. A gift, huh?" said Nick, pointing at the window. "Yeah, I see the tasteful donor plaque there. Tell me, does

Artemis Holdings have a weekly quota of good deeds? Like a minimum daily requirement that keeps your public relations department happy? I'm halfway expecting you to tell me your company gave Shakespeare a stipend."

"I wish we'd been able to, but I'm not quite that old. We're still searching for our modern bard." She seemed to be considering him for the position. "You wear your skepticism on your sleeve, which I suppose makes you the good scholar you're reputed to be. Tell me, do you see an ulterior motive in everything?"

"Descartes is one of my heroes: doubt everything," Nick said. The crush of people carried them a few inches closer to the bar. "Or almost everything," he added, taking in her beauty.

"I assure you, we are what we appear to be."

"You mean Artemis is a company full of great-looking women? Where do I sign up?"

Zola couldn't suppress a smile at his flagrant flirting. Her dark eyebrows, Nick noticed, were perfect sonnets of expression. Shakespeare wouldn't have needed her money as a spur for inspiration.

Finally with new glasses in hand, they walked to a grouping of pedestals topped by some choice Fortescue vases.

"A quota?" she asked. "Why should there be any limit to the good one is able to do? Artemis and the Samaritan Fund—which I manage—do good when the opportunity arises; we know this enriches us spiritually and teaches good corporate citizenship to others."

"Three cheers for benevolent capitalism."

She was determined to make her point. "We believe that the companies which treat their customers and employees with respect are the ones that will endure. Our quota of good deeds, as you call it, is our vote of confidence in such organizations. This philosophy might make enemies for us, might cause people to ridicule us—"

"Like me, for instance."

"I don't think you were being serious, were you? No, your sarcasm is a shield. You seem to me the kind of man who avoids seriousness whenever he can, who doesn't like to show the depth of his feelings."

"Take my skepticism as interest, then."

"In me or my company?"

"Oh, definitely," Nick said, intentionally vague. She smiled brilliantly, without pretense. Her eyes lingered on his face and then darted off to scan the crowd, as if Nick could read her thoughts through her pupils.

Ah, if only I could . . .

"I've always admired teachers," she said. "A friend of mine took a course with you a few years ago. He said it was a wonderful experience. Have you ever thought of giving courses in genealogy? Maybe I could arrange another grant from Artemis Holdings."

"Another grant?" Nick asked, taken by surprise.

"Have you forgotten so quickly? That smacks of ingratitude."

She thinks I'm teasing.

"Oh, of course. What grant?" she teased back, biting her bottom lip as if she'd been caught at something naughty.

His heart raced at the sight of her wet white teeth depressing her luscious red lip.

"I know all about it," she said. "No sense being coy. Mother has told me about the one you're receiving now. She has her pet projects, her own enthusiastic, perhaps impulsive, way of doing things, which sometimes I don't find out about until the machinery is already in motion. I understand: she's obviously asked you to keep the grant quiet. So many worthy projects out there."

Nick decided to nod. Mrs. Armiger was lying to her own daughter about him. Why? He hated backing up lies not his own.

"You know how older people can be about passing on control to the next generation?" Zola said. "So, when will the book be ready?"

You ought to hear about some of your mother's other special projects, Nick wanted to say. She didn't know about the sordid foundations of Artemis Holdings, the company and family history of treachery, bigotry, and who-knows-what-else. She was completely innocent. The playful look in her eyes, devoid of any double-meaning, the bantering, childlike tone of her conversation, convinced him that in life, as in her stock-picking, this beautiful woman yet saw the world as she wanted it to be.

"The book. Oh, sure," he said, playing along. "Well, you know how these things are. Lots of research, travel, that sort of thing. Maybe in a year, year and a half . . ."

The lights dimmed a few times, signaling the dawdlers to return to their seats.

"I'd enjoy hearing more about it, Nick. Angus said your friends call you that. I hope you don't mind. Listen, some of my friends and I are going out after the play, to hit some bars over on Magazine. There's just so much culture I can take in one night. Why not come with us? I've always been interested in genealogy and would love to hear your thoughts. And bring Professor Kern. The Rotting Fish-heads from Pluto are playing at the Gumbo Club. You've heard of them, haven't you?"

Though he hadn't, he said, "Got all their 45s."

Zola caught on immediately to his jesting insincerity. "Well, find me after the play if you're interested. Keith Richards is supposed to sit in." She let her hand rest in Nick's for an electric moment that felt to him like a lifetime. "Hope to see you soon."

Shaking himself free of the gorgeous woman's spell, he searched the lobby for Una, but she was gone.

❑

"I thought you were bringing me a champagne." Una was pouting. "You forgot me. The story of our friendship."

"Damn, I'm sorry," said Nick. "I got mired in a conversation with a bigwig on the board or something at the Plutarch. Time just got away from me."

"I *know* who she is. Rather pretty, isn't she?"

"If you like that sort of look, I guess."

Two or three people hissed them into silence. There was a definite chill coming from Una's vicinity as they watched the play resolve itself into dancing and marriages—a happy ending that depressed Nick terribly.

❑

In the shadows of the parking lot, Nick gave Una the spoils of his two-day Natchitoches rampage.

A sporty red Volvo pulled up beside them.

"Nick, Una! Come with us, please. There's plenty of room," Zola, in the front passenger seat, shouted out to them over the car stereo and the engine noise. Two other women and a man in the back seat clapped, sang to the music, and in general acted silly. The driver impatiently revved the engine.

"What do you say, Una?" Nick asked.

"I think not," she answered, giving the crowded car a look of extreme disapproval.

"No 'I have to do my nails, hair, whatever'? No 'I have to get up early tomorrow'? Just 'I think not'?"

"I think not!" She stalked off toward her own car, with his bundle of pilfered papers under a sweater she didn't need in the humid warmth.

Nick watched her for a moment. *Go with her you idiot. That's what you need: a good woman, loyal to a fault; a settled life; intellectual companionship for a change—hey, marriage, even. She probably has a simple but scrumptious midnight repast and some excellent wine waiting for the two of you, hoping to take up where you both left off years ago. It will be on your head, Jonathan Nicholas Herald, if she turns into a Miss Haversham . . .*

Nah!

He piled into the back seat of the red Volvo.

"Don't worry," Zola said, indicating the young guy at the wheel, "Donny's Muslim. Can't drink alcohol. He's always our designated driver."

Donny, however, inhaled deeply from a large joint as they zipped down quiet, narrow Uptown streets lined with parked cars and petrified yellow-eyed cats.

❏

Nick's couch felt like heaven. It didn't hurt, either, that Zola was next to him. They were mechanically kissing and pawing each other, both dead tired but too stubborn to admit it. They reeked of bar vapors from the Gumbo Club—where Keith Richards had indeed jammed with the band—and the four or five other dives they had crawled through.

He vaguely remembered the last place, a blue-collar bar, all the latest rage among students and the hip crowd. The regulars, old men with grizzled faces, union caps, and unfiltered cigarettes, whose fathers and grandfathers had imbibed there, had huddled at one end of the bar under the television and watched them with bewildered and resentful eyes. The itinerant rakehells were thrown out when Zola and several others, including Nick, started dancing on the pool table.

During their hours together, he and Zola had discovered much to talk about, much to laugh about. They found that they shared a fondness for things unusual, as well as the typical New Orleanian's obsession with food and drink. Nick had genuinely enjoyed the evening, and he believed she had, too.

Zola drew back and looked around Nick's cramped apartment. "I shouldn't be here. We're not twenty years old anymore. We adults are supposed to know better than to get involved on the first date."

"It wasn't even a date." He kissed her. "And we're not as involved as I'd like, yet."

"Well, I just want you to know that I don't always do this. I mean, go to a man's apartment. But I feel I *know* you. After what Angus told me, and what Mother has said. Your life has been so, I don't know, so colorful, exciting, unpredictable. A lot different from mine. I've always been sure where I came from, where I am, where I'm going. I see in you an antidote to that, that predictability. Do you know I even called up the newspaper articles on your dismissal from Freret? . . . Oh, I'm babbling like a teenager with a crush. How embarrassing."

"A tired teenager. I'll get you a cab in a few minutes. But I want to tell you a secret of my own, now: I felt something click, too, that day at the Plutarch. I've been thinking about you a lot since then."

"You could call me sometime. We could . . . go out for dinner."

"I'd like that." He kissed her again and stood up. "Now, that cab."

"Water!" Zola croaked in an exaggeratedly raspy voice as Nick weaved toward the kitchen to call a cab. "Cold water."

When he returned five minutes later, she was passed out on the couch. He corrected her twisted posture so she would be able to walk later in the day, and went back to the kitchen to cancel the cab. Then he began to trudge toward his bedroom.

He glanced blearily at his desk, surrounded by cliff walls of books and folders threatening an avalanche. He noticed that the mail for the last few days had been stacked neatly, the junk catalogs and sweepstakes offers off to one side of the important-looking stuff. Hawty strikes again!

Through an old pair of glasses mended with Band-Aids, he perused his mail. Bill, bill, credit-card statement, bill, bill, collection agency, last notice, another one . . . and a thick tan envelope that had seen several previous mailings. A note taped to it read: "Came postage due at the office. You owe me $4.50. Hawty." The envelope had lots of small-denomination stamps, the kind that fall victim to rate hikes and are rarely used afterward. No return address.

Nick had a vague sense of familiarity with the scrawled handwriting that had directed the package to him. The most recent postmark was Monday—the day after Max Corban had been murdered!

Yes, he remembered now: he had seen this handwriting that day in his office, when the old man had written down his address and phone number, and the name Balazar.

Nick ripped into the envelope.

It was from the poor old guy, all right, probably mailed just before whoever it was got to him. He must have known something awful was about to happen, and wanted the information safe; probably didn't expect Nick to get there in time. Nick now recalled the urgent tone during their telephone conversation.

He pictured Corban's street in his mind: wasn't there a mailbox just outside the house? Yes, of course; two, actually. The old man had cheated the murderer of ultimate victory. His envelope was in one of the mailboxes as Nick walked just a few inches beside it. That was Sunday; the next day, the envelope was picked up.

What Nick found inside was a leftover, deadly bombshell, a long-buried remnant of old hates, like those being dug up in French and German gardens even today.

Looking at the beautiful woman sleeping on his couch, he understood.

"This is all about you, Zola, isn't it?" he whispered. "About keeping you from ever knowing what she did."

Chapter 19

Nick held in his hands—trembling from excitement—a mass of photocopied evidence proving that Zola was indeed of the Balazar family, but the daughter of concentration-camp survivors. They had been part of one of Hyam's collateral lines—from an uncle who never emigrated—and thus distant cousins of Natalie Armiger. *Had been*, because Natalie Armiger let them die. She had refused to sponsor them in their petition to immigrate to America, in those years of anguish and confusion after the war.

Nick wondered how Corban had come to possess the documents he found in the thick envelope. There were communications from resettlement and repatriation groups Nick had never heard of, along with the expected ones. The story these copied documents told was vivid and moving. Nick came to understand the motives of the broken old man a little better, too. It wasn't merely his stock-market losses that had driven him to confront Armiger, though that might have pushed him over the edge: with a single-minded determination and bravery, he was one man fighting an immortal dragon. Nick thought of his own moral waffling and felt a new pang of self-revulsion.

While Zola slept peacefully in the dim light of his desk lamp, he sat down and pondered the material Corban had died to transmit.

❑

Among the millions of displaced persons throughout Europe in 1946, there were three sick, emaciated young Jews, standing together in a line for food at a refugee camp in Germany. Max Corban, meet Maurice and Erna Balazar. Teenagers, who had seen things adults shouldn't. All three were from the southwestern part of the country, Maurice and Erna having lived near Baden-Baden. Maurice and Erna had just been married.

Nick learned that Maurice Balazar was descended from Hyam's uncle, who had remained in Europe; a copy of Maurice's Nazi-issued *ahnenpass* proved the link.

That love should survive in a human being after that descent into Hell; that before their bodies and minds had begun to heal, before their thoughts could readily go beyond the next bowl of gruel, these shaved skeletons held hands and were able to love—strange and wonderful!

What a paradoxical species we human beings are, Nick thought: capable of such intense cruelty and such beauty of spirit.

The three refugees became close friends as they slowly recovered their health, more or less, and got a modicum of sanity back. Their confusion and grief began to give way to an awareness of their new freedom—and new dilemma. Should they go to their old homes? To Israel, where there was renewed talk of statehood? The United States? Where?

Corban had wanted Nick to know everything, and he'd included personal letters to flesh out the story. Nick felt closer to the old man than ever, as he read far into the morning.

Maurice and Erna missed the ancient towns and the mountains, but, following the lead of the rough-and-ready Corban, they decided to try for sponsorship from relatives they vaguely knew of from family legend, a branch of the Balazar family in New Orleans.

Corban had long before made up his mind; he'd lined up firm support from relatives in New Jersey. Alone, he must have been willing to wait for his friends, but soon he met and married a young woman, and their future called as the months passed and their own cases inched along through the labyrinthine process of getting into the United States. Corban and his bride were transferred to another camp and eventually made it to the promised land of America; they had their own lives to worry about and were unaware of the growing troubles for the Balazars.

Almost every family brags about a relation who's made it big, no matter how distant. At first, the Balazars had only a rough approximation of their American relatives' surname from garbled stories passed down through the generations of Maurice's family. The ultimate discovery of the prominent and wealthy Armigers of the swanky Garden District of New Orleans must have made Maurice Balazar proud and hopeful.

But the problems for Maurice and Erna multiplied after the Corbans left: the New Orleans family would have nothing to do with them. The State Department and the Review Committees turned down four subsequent willing sponsors in other parts of America; the Board of Appeals reinstated one. The red tape got worse and worse.

According to the documents, the Balazars would endure a succession of camps until 1951, when they finally returned to their war-damaged town. They entered a protracted legal battle to reclaim Maurice's family house and property, which had been taken over by Christian neighbors who naturally thought—and seem to have hoped—that the Balazars had gone up in smoke in the concentration camps. A daughter was born in 1958, the same year someone threw a grenade into Maurice and Erna's rented room, killing them. The daughter miraculously survived the blast. Zola, that daughter, became a ward of the American Jewish Joint Distribution Committee. And things began moving much faster.

There were urgent requests from a New Orleans couple, Jock and Natalie Armiger, to adopt the child.

The agency put up a fight, claiming they had refused to shelter the family in the first place. Several angry letters were exchanged. Finally, Armiger found the right price, as she had done with Nick and her other pawns. Had she bought off the right senator or representative? Whatever the reason, with her power and wealth she was able to cut through the deliberate visa and immigration difficulties the State Department and Congress had erected to keep Jewish refugees out of the country—before, during, and after the war. Had she only done so while Maurice and Erna still lived. The adoption was accomplished after just a few more weeks of further wrangling.

Awhile back, Nick had "borrowed" from Freret's Hichborn Library *The Abandonment of the Jews*, by David Wyman. Quietly, he checked that book now, to make sure Corban's material seemed genuine. It did.

Nick finally understood what was really driving Natalie Armiger. She had chosen him to tidy up the local past because these records of her European cousins were beyond even her reach. She couldn't waltz into the State Department, the Red Cross, the U.N., and the Jewish and Christian refugee agencies, to scissor the existence of three people—Maurice, Erna, and Zola Balazar. Three people who, having survived the darkest evil of human nature, were now part of probably the most exhaustively documented group in human history. Armiger could do nothing directly about this damning evidence.

Yes, it was indeed damning. Nick read nothing that implicated her in the deadly grenade attack; but her refusal to be one of the required two sponsors for Maurice and Erna branded her as complicit in their deaths. How would Zola react to that? Any parent who loved her child would fear such knowledge; and the Natalie Armiger Nick knew would do anything—anything—to stop her from finding out.

Armiger dealt in the possible. As an entrepreneur of extraordinary abilities, she was good at expending the least amount of energy to resolve a problem. Thus Nick's little scavenger hunt; and probably a similar one on the part of the unfortunate Polish librarian whose life ended in the brackish water of Lake Pontchartrain. No troop of private investigators, no team of hotshot lawyers; way too public. But if an opportunity arose to collect the governmental and agency evidence she lacked, quietly and anonymously, like a cat removing the choice morsels from the garbage at midnight, she would take it.

Armiger was destroying her Balazar past, brushing over the tracks of history so that no one—especially Zola—could accuse her of consigning her own flesh and blood to a tragic death. Everything else was secondary. With a chill Nick recalled what she had said about survival.

When the paradigm shifted, as it did when Corban threatened her with something she couldn't buy or steal, calling into question the authenticity of her role as beloved mother of beloved daughter, her response was commensurately more drastic.

Which explained to Nick why he was alive, and why Corban and the Polish librarian weren't.

❑

The next morning, Zola had left by the time he woke. She must have had a terrific hangover, too: her "Thanks" written on the back of her business card was very shaky. A society girl to the core.

After a breakfast of three-day-old McKenzie's donuts and four cups of scalding coffee, Nick threw on some clothes, and, following Corban's example, mailed the Zola papers to his P.O. box.

Chapter 20

Summer drew to a close, at least according to the calendar. The days still blistered with heat. As usual, the murder rate in the city peaked, as people cracked under the strain of living in a sauna. It was shaping up to be another record year. The last of the horde of summer tourists went home, and the smarter travelers began to show up, shopping in the less-crowded Quarter when the thundershowers allowed. Classes resumed at Freret.

Out of long habit, Nick still divided the year into school-related segments. Even now, he felt a certain quickening of body and mind, an indefinable anticipation at this time of year. The vagaries of vacation scatter in fall's gusts of decision; he had made a big one.

❑

"Think I'll become a C.G., or at least a genealogical record specialist," Hawty said. She was typing into her computer the charts for a client who had no inkling he was a descendant of four presidents. Sometimes, he'd already told Hawty, there are pleasant surprises in genealogy.

"You know, boss," she continued, "I've been paying attention to those ads for courses at the Family History Library in Salt Lake City. That might be a good investment for the firm, to send me out there."

"The firm has a cash flow problem at the moment," Nick replied, still immersed in the latest issue of the *National Genealogical Society Quarterly.*

"So what else is new? When are we getting paid by that old guy you've been working on for months now?"

Nick had kept the real story from Hawty, as much as he could; he didn't want her endangered. She did not know Corban was dead.

"Well, Hawty, you'll learn that in genealogy, money isn't as important as truth."

"Whatever you say, Saint Nicholas."

Nick looked up. "Funny you should say that. I was born on Christmas Eve."

"Yeah, I know. A firecracker stand blew up and a train derailed the same night, and the nurses had to deliver you because all the doctors were in the emergency room."

"How did you know all that? Have you been talking to my mother?"

Hawty smiled, and patted her computer. "She's online."

"You got to be kidding." But he saw she wasn't. His own mother, a fallen woman!

Hawty had been indispensable throughout the summer. Nick had actually pleaded with her not to drop him, as he expected she would need to, considering her course and teaching load for the fall. Una had indeed lined up complete funding for her; Nick hoped it didn't have anything to do with a grant from Artemis Holdings. Genealogy was catching on, apparently. A local TV station had done a story on the growing nationwide interest in family history; a reporter interviewed Nick. The ten-second sound bite that resulted was enough to improve his business to a bothersome level. Hawty claimed her cleverly disguised plug on an Internet genealogy chatroom deserved the credit.

Whatever the cause, Nick and Hawty had done an amazing amount of work, tracing lineages of Mayflower passengers, signers of the Declaration of Independence, Revolutionary War soldiers, Seminole Wars soldiers,

Mexican War soldiers, Civil War widows, territorial land grantees, and just ordinary folks who'd neglected to do anything historic except to sail from Bremen or Liverpool to Boston, Philadelphia, Galveston, or New Orleans. Hawty's technology stunned and pleased Nick; he felt a grudging fascination with the tools of the Information Age—even though his own mother had succumbed to digital seduction!

Yet, as good as business was, Nick felt that he was living on borrowed time. He was a pessimist at heart, and good times made him nervous. There had been no word from Natalie Armiger. Did she somehow know he had been reasonably successful in Natchitoches? Had Corban's murder ended her worries about the Zola problem? She'd accomplished what she wanted for the moment, right?

He hoped so, because he'd developed an overpowering possessiveness for the documents he'd stolen from Natchitoches. He felt responsible for their fate, responsible for the history they represented. The Natchitoches material was secure in Una's safe-deposit box, and Corban's envelope was slumbering in Nick's P.O. box. The diary of Ivanhoe Balzar he kept with him at all times, even sleeping with it under his pillow. When he was out and about, he placed it in his favorite hiding place—in the office, below a loose floorboard, under an old, threadbare, extremely valuable rug Hawty had bought for nine dollars on Magazine Street.

New Orleans is a psychotic city, where seemingly normal people do strange things for no apparent reason. Such behavior could land you in Angola, the state prison; or, if it's a benign weirdness of some note, you might earn a place in local lore, so that tourists evermore leave flowers at your burial vault. Nick had a new appreciation of what it meant to live here: a compulsion like a voodoo spell chanted in his ear, commanding him to save the past from unclean hands. Armiger's hands.

Then again, maybe he'd gained some immunity for

another reason: his relationship with Zola had developed into something more than a mutual crush.

New Orleans hides dozens of small, exquisite restaurants for those who know to look beneath the gaudy glare and blare, each one a wonderful vintage bottle of epicurean delight. Nick thought he knew them all, but Zola surprised him with new ones.

At such establishments the two of them had spent many hours during that late summer, exploring each other's souls in words and whispers, in touches over and under tables.

And finally, in bed, they had discovered a new country, full of wonders.

Chapter 21

Zola lived near Freret University in one of those whimsical turreted Victorian-era houses, a fine and lovingly kept example of the style known as Queen Anne.

The glow of the dashboard cast freakish shadows on her lovely face; each inquisitorial streetlight exposed her in white flashes of raw vulnerability. He thought that finally, after many fruitless years of trying, he could see what the Cubists had meant about form and perception.

More likely, his sudden insight was just a reaction to wine better than he was used to drinking. He and Zola had enjoyed a long and vinous meal at an excellent new restaurant in the Riverbend area, where St. Charles meets Carrollton.

"For dessert, we'll have . . ."

"You," Nick said.

"I mean before that." She turned her head briefly toward him; her smile shone through the shadows. "I have some wonderful chocolate thingies from the French bakery on Maple."

He reached over and brushed her dark hair over her right shoulder. "I'll have to jog an extra mile tomorrow."

She turned left from St. Charles and onto her street, where big pampered houses slept behind wrought-iron, stucco, or brick fences festooned with alarm-company shields.

Students of Freret and Fortescue get beautiful Uptown in their blood and yearn to abandon their cold northern native lands for the seductive dank decadence of this wealthy section.

Zola had graduated from Fortescue, and from Freret's M.B.A. program. A double dose of the Uptown drug. But she was in a sense inoculated, having grown up in her parents' home, another landmark known as the Fulke-Bruine Mansion, a few blocks away across St. Charles.

"Nick, have you ever considered going back into teaching?"

"Never."

"I've heard that fair-minded people think there was something fishy about your case. We could get your name cleared, if we try. And Mother could certainly land you a post somewhere. Somewhere close, I hope."

"Zola, I'm off that hamster wheel for good. It's not as if I'm unemployed, you know. I guess because it's so popular, just behind stamp and coin collecting, people see genealogy as an exercise in social climbing for the unexceptional masses. But isn't the field of education crowded, too? Aren't most students and teachers boring and insignificant? Oh, no! Teaching is perceived as a *noble* vocation, a calling on a plane with holy orders. I say, bullshit! You've never seen backbiting, jealous, petty, lying egomaniacs until you've spent a day in a college English department!"

She'd driven into her driveway and killed the engine. Now she laughed at his rage of self-justification.

"Yes, professor. And after I've done my homework, will you make love to me all night?"

"Well . . . I suppose that can be arranged."

"I never really meant to put down genealogy. I just hate to see someone as talented as you wasting—"

"Who's wasting? What about the guy who teaches for thirty years and realizes he hated every repetitious moment, every know-it-all spoiled brat trying to show-off, every kiss-ass faculty meeting . . .

hasn't he wasted his life?"

"I see what you mean," she said, reasonably. "Do what you like, and don't accept just liking what you do. Not something everyone can accomplish, but it's nice to remember." She was silent a few moments. "Nick, I'd like to know more about my own family."

"Well, uh, sure, one of these days, maybe we'll look into that."

"That's about what you say every time I ask you," she said.

"It's just that you're so busy, and you have such little leisure time. I don't want to share any of it with anyone or anything."

He pulled her close and kissed her until they both simultaneously pushed each other away.

He took a deep breath. "That settles it. We're skipping the chocolate."

Zola removed from her purse a gizmo that looked to Nick like a television channel changer. She pressed a succession of buttons. Lights came on in the house. "There. Pretty neat, huh? I just deactivated the alarm, switched the percolator and the stereo on, even turned down the bed. Come on, lazy. This remote can't do everything for you."

She was out of her door and crossing the timed headlight beams before Nick realized she was probably kidding about the bed.

"Be right in," he said, as she opened the front door of her house. "Forgot something in my car."

The air was softly humid and warm, the fragrance of sweet olive tinged with the usual New Orleans hint of rot and age. He heard a quiver of distant thunder and the deep thrumming of tugs pushing barges up and down the nearby river. Wishing he smoked, he strolled down the sidewalk toward his car; he'd brought along a former student's novel, which he intended to enjoy in bed the next morning after Zola left for work. He was adapting quite well to being the lover of a very rich woman.

A gray Ford sedan silently lurched to a stop in the street, wedging his car in—not that he had the wits about him at the moment to attempt a vehicular escape. Two very large men in West Coast-hip clothes flowed gracefully out of the car in a hurry that somehow didn't seem rushed.

They grabbed Nick and threw him back hard against the neighbors' tall stucco-over-brick fence topped with broken bottles set in cement.

Have I lived for years in the scuzzy Quarter only to get snuffed in the dignified Garden District? That's not fair!

"Listen, asshole, she wants to know what's taking so fuckin' long." He had an outdoorsy tan and cold blue eyes; his jaws and neck rippled with thick cords of muscle; his buzz-cut yellow-blond hair bristled straight up as if he'd just looked in a mirror and scared the hell out of himself. The man was so close Nick could smell dinner on his breath: burger, fries, and beer. The other man, standing back a few steps, had short black hair, toasted skin, and a black mustache.

Nick's observational powers had suddenly become very keen, even in the anemic light.

"She says she hopes you're not trying to do something stupid, like the old man," the yellow-haired man continued. "She wants to see you. Tomorrow morning, ten o'clock." He told Nick where to go. "You got that? Be there, asshole."

"Couldn't she have just called?" Nick asked.

"She likes the personal touch." The guy carefully straightened Nick's tie, and slapped him on either side of his face, forehand, then backhand. He grinned ferociously as if this were the high point of his day.

"Say, you've done that before, haven't you?" Nick said, wiping blood from his lips and checking his teeth with his tongue.

"Fuckin' smartass," said the blond over his shoulder to his partner.

Nick heard a single snort of amusement.

"What do you think you're doing!" Zola shrieked from her front walkway. She was still too far away to see exactly what was happening, but she'd obviously realized Nick was in trouble. "Leave him alone, you bastards! I've got pepper mace. Stand back!"

Nick's messenger released him.

The dark-featured guy moved toward Zola. He spoke to her with what seemed to Nick like practiced composure: "Hey, lady, you gonna hurt somebody with that, okay."

"Nuh-uh," said the blond. "Let's go."

The dark-featured guy swiftly retreated. The two men flowed back into their car and roared off without a backward glance.

Zola was next to him now. "Oh my God! Nick, are you okay? Oh my God. Somebody call the police. *I'll* call the police," she said, as reason replaced shock. In the hand that wasn't clutching the mace canister, she held a cell phone.

"No, don't," Nick said. "I'm all right. Nothing broken . . . I don't think." He moved his shoulders around just to be sure.

"What was *that* all about, Nick? Those terrible men. I thought . . . oh, I thought they were going to kill you. Did you get the license number?"

Must not be Artemis Holdings regulars, Nick figured, or she would have recognized them. *Boy, that Armiger sure does have a knack for keeping secrets, especially from her daughter!* Zola was his bulletproof vest; as long as she was near, he was safe, he thought, cursing himself for the ignoble realization.

"No, I didn't get the number," he said. "Don't worry about it. Just a slight financial misunderstanding, that's all. I guess I'm a bit behind in my rent." He put his arm around her, and they turned toward her house. Both of them trembled from fear, relief, and anger. "So, is your bed really turned down?"

Chapter 22

The next morning, Nick checked a map in Zola's tome-lined study and saw that his appointment would take him to an area off Lakeshore Drive. Metairie and the shore of Lake Pontchartrain were not his territory. Zola had left at about seven-thirty, he sketchily remembered. Off to do good deeds and make zillions. Last night, he'd evaded most of her questions about the assault he'd undergone. She didn't like that, but she knew him well enough to realize he was as stubborn as a stone.

Nick was in the care of the household staff: a Vietnamese woman with little proficiency in English, a young Mexican boy with even less, and a jolly dark woman named Claire who was in charge, and who spoke with a mellifluous Caribbean-British accent. One of them had seen to the freshening up of his clothes. He had used a man's electric razor to shave, and a toothbrush still in the wrapper, both of which were waiting for him on a tray by the bedroom door.

❑

At 10:20, after an hour of searching along Lakeshore Drive, Nick stopped cursing long enough to notice an arched stone gateway without an address number. He'd probably passed it five times already. He jerked his car into a short driveway that ended before a massive wrought-iron gate. On either side of him, a twenty-foot-high weathered brick wall curved out of his line of sight. The gate opened, and a security guard in a little brick house waved him forward.

The grounds might have contained four of five good-sized golf courses—or as many cemeteries. Nick marveled at the probable value of this real estate, so oddly isolated and serene in the midst of all the nearby development. The cobblestone road meandered through extensive, meticulously kept rose beds. Now and then there was a classical folly; belvederes and pergolas invited quiet contemplation. The place seemed ancient, strangely suspended in time, eerily deserted.

In the distance, on a slope, he saw what looked like a large and beautiful seventeenth-century French chateau. As he got closer, he realized that the distance was not as great as he had at first thought. The building had been constructed on a miniature scale, with illusion in mind.

He parked amid potted orange and lemon trees, and abundant topiary, and walked toward the front door in the heavy green silence of the rose-fragrant air. Inside, he found himself in a spacious high-ceilinged room; above him, a balustraded gallery on the two sides and back of the building suggested a second story.

Amazed, he turned in a circle where he stood: dozens of paintings hung from the walls and freestanding display flats; bronze, marble, and stone sculpture competed for space.

He moved around the room. His shoes squeaked on the polished marble floor, which was inlaid with black-and-white geometric designs. Outside, a dove cooed sedately. Nick supposed that the collection was worth a fortune; but this strange museum he'd entered as if by a magic door sent a shiver down his spine.

The art was exclusively twentieth century; not the pleasant visual discourses of the Impressionists, the severe calm of Constructivism, or the sardonic kitsch of American Pop Art, but the violent nightmares of a sick world that had lost its center, from the time of World War I, when artists no longer believed in old verities slaughtered in muddy trenches. Nick thought of Yeats's "The Second Coming," of a world circling self-destructively out of control like a falcon ignoring its master. He recognized only a few of the canvases, a handful by Franz Marc and George Grosz.

A profusion of French doors let in bleached light from outside. The place might have been a conservatory once; but now, the lighthearted spirit of the architecture nourished only this poisonous depression.   If these artworks gave any clue of Natalie Armiger's state of mind, this wasn't going to be fun.

A narrow flight of stairs led to the gallery. Nick went up, still not sure he was in the right place. Upstairs, he saw lighted glass cases, like transparent coffins, standing against the three walls of the gallery, which was otherwise illuminated only by small oeil-de-boeuf windows.   The cases contained many books, documents, and scrolls.

He walked up to one case, and his breath caught. The writing on the centuries-old documents was old Provençal, and Hebrew. That much he could tell.

"I was beginning to doubt your reputation as a skilled genealogical investigator, but I see your instincts have led you correctly once again."

Armiger was standing at double doors that gave access to a room behind her. She wore a less severe outfit than the one Nick remembered from their meeting in his office. A white silk caftan with paisley designs and a chiffon scarf for accent around her neck replaced the impenetrable carapace of couture.

"Allow me to be your tour guide," she said.
He listened as she led him by each glass case, describing the genealogical riches inside.

In impassioned detail she told him about the medieval Jewish-burial-society books; the royal permission for Jewish merchants to conduct business with Christians; guild complaints about Jewish competition; synagogue records; petitions, judgments, and proclamations; lists of deaths and property destruction from pogroms; documents relating to the final 1394 expulsion of Jews from France. In other display cases, Nick saw more nearly contemporary German, Polish, and Yiddish writing, possibly mid-nineteenth century.

Nick had come across such artifacts of the Jewish semi-autonomous communities only in reference books. He knew, though, that each item here was a marvelous priceless source of genealogical information, the disappearance of which was surely the cause of many thousands of impossible gaps. Armiger had separated children from parents, generations from generations, as surely as had the grenade thrown by some local malcontent into Maurice and Erna Balazar's apartment in 1958.

Nick had reached a case holding documents of the *kahalim*, or ruling community elders, of seventeenth-century Poland-Lithuania.

"You get off on having this stuff being here, under your control, don't you?" he said. "These represent the wanderings of your ancestors over several hundred years. And it's all yours, all neatly labeled. Those lives, those pasts . . ."

"Please, join me." She gestured toward the room from which she had emerged. "We have much to discuss."

"Did you 'discuss' things with Max Corban before you had him killed?"

"In a way, I envy him." She turned and walked through the double doors.

Wondering how to read her non-admission of guilt, Nick followed her into an octagonal room. The only light here, too, came from small round windows. At the far end was a rococo writing desk, with one simple chair behind it, one in front. The desktop was bare, except for a picture in a splendid old silver frame, and a tiny gold pillbox, exquisitely embellished with a scene too small for Nick to make out from a distance. They sat down.

"This is where I do my thinking," she said, scanning the room, seeming to see through the walls to the beautiful grounds beyond. "Nothing to distract. No conference calls, no faxes, no computers, no servants.

When my husband was alive, after he became too ill to leave the house for his adolescent games—golf and horse racing, primarily—this is where I sought refuge. Where I reclaimed my health after my heart attack, three years ago."

"That photo almost does justice to your daughter."

Zola, in the radiant bloom of young womanhood, sheathed in layers of taffeta and lace, curtsied with support from the white-gloved hand of a tuxedoed man who was out of the frame.

"My favorite," said Natalie Armiger. "It was her debut."

"I understand why you like it out here: it's a perfect microcosm of your life. Secrecy, absolute power, beauty masking . . . let's just say, something not so beautiful."

"Always searching for significance, aren't you, Nick? I admire that—to a certain degree. The building and the artwork were lucky finds, a package deal. Many years ago, I learned of a Hungarian family in financial difficulty; they were agreeable to my purchase of their collection, and they threw in this lovely children's playhouse from their Lugano lake estate. I had it reassembled, piece by piece.

"I have donated many of the Renaissance pieces and the Impressionists to institutions around the world—too much simplistic piety and naive optimism." Her wide mouth puckered in distaste. "But I am particularly fond of those works that you saw downstairs. They speak to me in a special way. As for this lovely property, it once belonged to an African order of Catholic sisters. My Natchitoches ancestors would be shocked, I'm sure, if they knew their most successful descendant spends much of her time in the precincts of a convent for black nuns?"

"There's a lot about you that would shock your family—below ground and above. Where did all the genealogical material come from? You can't just buy that stuff at your local bookstore."

"One of the secrets of my success, Nick, is that I make use of experts on the scene. When searching for values in small-capitalization companies in foreign markets, for instance, I find someone local whose talents and word I trust, and turn the affair over to her. It has been the same with my genealogical acquisitions. There are many like you who correctly value quality of life over philosophical niceties."

She gave him a gloating smile that telegraphed the message: *I've got you pegged, little man.*

"That was Corban's problem, right?"

"He had the choice," she replied. "As long as it was just a question of money, I could deal with him. He chose to dwell on . . . certain other themes."

"Such as your daughter's real parentage?"

She hesitated a moment, obviously caught off guard, weighing her next words carefully.

"Knowing your adversary's weakness can sometimes be your own undoing," she said. "Attack calls for counterattack. You have just brought our little game to a new level. Very well, then. Yes, Max knew about the tragedy of Zola's parents, a tragedy I relive daily. I was very young and immature when it happened. Something of an anti-Semite myself, I suppose. My own parents had just died, leaving me sole guardian of the family's wealth and social position. You see, I was a Fulke-Bruine."

Nick heard the pride as she uttered her maiden name, which, he now recalled, was chiseled over the portals of several buildings on the campus of Freret University. She was a Balazar, too, he wanted to remind her. But she had selected her own myth of ancestry. He'd seen it many times. Genealogy, for all its hard facts and systematic rules, is finally a subjective study, a handy tool to create a past that fills some present need. The difference in her case was that she was taking away the choice of others who would follow her.

She went on to say that her Balazar cousins

continued to write to her over the next decade or so. She never responded. But when she learned of their murders, and of Zola's survival, something new and wonderful was born in her soul that could not form in her womb.

Listening to her, Nick could feel some of the transforming power of the sudden love for the orphaned child. He wondered: Was this the only time she'd ever allowed love to disrupt her life?

"In some way," she said, "Max obtained a great deal of information that I had been assured would be kept confidential forever. Can you blame me for trusting those international organizations, which seemed better than the rest of humanity at the time? In those days, adopted children rarely went looking for their birth parents. Personally, I think it is a regrettable practice today. But that is beside the point.

"The amnesia of a few key officials at state and federal agencies was easy to purchase. Some records merely vanished; others, like a birth certificate, came into being. My husband and I faked a short pregnancy and a premature birth for my daughter. Our friends were completely taken in. Therefore, I had never concerned myself with the question until Max began his threats. Soon, I found that there was nothing I could propose to satisfy him. Only bringing back the dead would have done that."

Nick said, "You need me to ensure no one can make the jump to the line that leads to Zola's real parents. This had nothing to do with any fear of anti-Semitism, did it? You knew it was a hot-button issue for me. You reeled me in with that bait."

"The revelation of—how shall I put it—my interesting family background, could have been put to rest eventually. The Jewish question, shall we say? The public has a very short memory. And, of course, I don't need to tell you that if one goes back far enough, everyone is related. Back to our ancient mother, Lucy, or beyond, to a bubbling primitive pool of amino acids."

"A subversive thought, Mrs. Armiger."

"Perhaps. Surely you understand. Zola would never forgive me—what I did, or didn't do, about her real parents when I had the chance to make a difference. I know her so well, Nick. Oh, she would pretend nothing had changed, but she would freeze me out of her life. Forever." Armiger swallowed a few times before continuing. "She believes such moral issues are black and white; she can be ruthless, in her doctrinaire way."

"With Corban dead, you think the story of the adoption will submerge once again."

"I will see that it does, whatever the cost, your relationship with my daughter notwithstanding."

Nick got the creepy feeling that Armiger had a camera in Zola's bedroom, that she knew every whispered intimacy her daughter and he shared.

"What are your intentions toward my daughter?" she asked. He knew this was a little more serious than a first-date interview with the parents.

"I have no intentions. My love life is not a strategic exercise, a leveraged buyout. I don't plan these things for profit and loss. And I don't have to answer to you."

"I think you intend your relationship with Zola to protect you. That would be a mistake. I will do anything to protect my daughter, Nick. Anything to keep from her knowledge that might damage her."

"Damage *you*, you mean, Mrs. Armiger? You can't tell the difference between love for her and love of yourself."

"You're being a fool, Nick. Like Max."

"'Motley's the only wear,' when people like you feel justified in committing any crime."

"*Who are you to judge me?!*" She stood up. The scraping of her chair on the floor was like a scream. "Another's failure is so comforting, isn't it?! But what would you have done, in my position? How easy to judge from a distance, to be an armchair moralist! You have never decided the future of anyone but yourself, and that not very often, or very well!"

She struggled to bring her voice back to a normal level; she sat down again.

Then she took a small pill from the gold box and placed it under her tongue. Gradually, her pinched demeanor relaxed a little more.

Ah, so there is a weak spot in her armor.

"Emotionalism is not the answer," she said, after a minute or two. "The head must rule the heart in these situations. That reference you just made was to a Shakespeare play, wasn't it? *As You Like It*, I believe. Are you surprised that I should know that? You specialists think you have a monopoly on learning.

"A useful metaphor for our discussion, that play. Bad things happen to good people, liars and cheats win sometimes, pain and sorrow often reign supreme before order is restored. Some must die so that others may live.

"I have an empire, Nick. Thousands of human beings whose livelihoods, whose lives, depend on me. Decisions of such magnitude are foreign to your experience. I don't think you understand. This is more than merely evaluating student papers, deciding on increments of grades, lifting rocks to find some titillating genealogical centipede. I must occasionally play God."

"Even a deity can have a bad-hair day, right? Like when you betrayed her parents?"

"I made a judgment that they would be better off in Europe, and that my family and my company would be better off, as well. Yes, I knew that I was in all probability their only relative left alive. No, I could not foresee what would happen to them. But I have altered my plan to compensate. Is there no room in your world-view for divine improvisation? Zola is living a life she could never have imagined, full of accomplishment, excitement. I made that possible, and only I can continue to make that possible."

Her forehead uncreased; her hair moved back imperceptibly. When she spoke again, her voice was a razor of decisiveness: "You are the only variable remaining, Nick. Where is the information I hired you to find? There is a glass case out there waiting for it."

"I haven't finished my research yet. You wouldn't want me to do a sloppy job?"

"Your time is running out, as is my patience. It would be a pity if you were to suffer a freak accident. Goodbye, Nick."

❑

He drove to his office, more convinced than ever that it was up to him to make Armiger pay, one way or another, for her hubris. Max Corban and Ivanhoe Balzar would have accepted no less.

❑

"Find out where a guy named Shelvin Balzar is," Nick said to Hawty, who was busy on her computer in the outer room she had transformed into an office for herself. "We need to talk." He explained to Hawty where she was likely to find Shelvin.

All of the furniture in this outer room Hawty had directed Nick to push against the walls, allowing her an unencumbered central area in which to navigate.

"Where have you been?" she asked. "We're just going to have to get you a beeper, that's all there is to it. You can't keep running from the twentieth century like this, especially since it's almost over. No, even better than that, let me order you one of these new personal digital assistants—"

"No microchip the size of my fingernail is going to order me around. Anyway, what's so urgent?"

"Well, I need to ask you where I'm supposed to look for Indian records."

"Try the Federal Records Center in Fort Worth," Nick said, "or the Oklahoma Historical Society, if you're interested in the Five Civilized Tribes. Are you working on the family groups for that guy from Ohio?"

She nodded. He instructed her to check the

National Archives for Eastern Cherokee records, and just for the hell of it, the Carlisle Indian School files and the *Eastern Cherokees vs. United States* court records; and the card indexes for estate files at the Bureau of Indian Affairs. Then, she ought to look at the transitional rolls between 1880-1890, and, of course, the Dawes Rolls.

"Oh, remember that non-Indian spouses were usually not listed in Indian census rolls," he reminded her.

"Is that *all*? That shouldn't take more than a year. What if this stuff isn't available online?"

"I doubt much of it is, even though you're constantly telling me how indispensable those damn computers are. Get the Plutarch to rush-order the microfilms. In this business, Hawty, dear, there are still times when you have to use your brain instead of your computer."

She gave Nick a good-humored harrumph of mock indignation, and then said, "Oh, yeah—your lady friend. She's called something like five times. That's when I stopped counting."

Nick rocked back in his wobbly chair and began to peruse a large glossily illustrated coffee-table book on Natchez that had just arrived from a publisher.
Hawty rolled her chariot up to his desk. "Well? You going to call her?"

"Nah. Got a date in a few hours. Besides, I want to surprise her. We're going to Natchez. I want to introduce her to somebody." He chuckled, but didn't tell Hawty why. *Some body.* "Mind the store for a couple of days, will you? And make reservations at Hotel Portager for tomorrow night."

"How many rooms? . . . Oh, never mind; sorry I even asked. Awwwwwww! . . ." Speechless in disgust, she held a hand in front of her face, as if warding off some malignant spirit. All she could manage as she yanked her chair around and wheeled toward her room was, "Men!"

Chapter 23

Bright and early the following day, Zola's red turbo Volvo effortlessly cruised along I-10 and then ran like a deer through the twisting roads north of Baton Rouge. They searched for the famous plantations around St. Francisville, Audubon's stomping grounds; they sought out a self-effacing but legendary filling station/diner in an isolated hamlet.

As they followed back roads hemmed in by fields of ten-foot-tall sugar cane, without warning they would come face to face with the monumental Mississippi River levee, looming over them like an ancient tumulus of a giant race.

"The river!" Nick exclaimed, sipping an after-lunch beer and pointing to the levee's grassy hip. "It should remind us what a farce our mean dreams are. In our city, surrounded by human artifacts, we miss the elemental significance of the river. We're lured into a false sense of mastery over the world, over ourselves. The river may be plain for all to see in New Orleans, but it's become merely a prop for the tourism industry. There, *there* is the essence of history in tangible form! The river and history flow oblivious to our desires and efforts. Mortality, change, time, dimensions we only vaguely understand . . . the river can teach us. Ah, and the levee . . . signifying a huge green bank on the cosmic pool table that limits our elaborately planned but ultimately doomed trick shots . . . what are you laughing at?"

"The metaphysical ramblings of a drunk

genealogist who thinks he's Mark Twain and Thomas Wolfe combined."

Laughing until tears came, Zola opened the sunroof and turned up the CD.

She drove aggressively, pumping the pedals and jamming the stick with a European fondness for quick bursts of blazing acceleration. She didn't dwell on the rear-view mirror any more than necessary for safety. The rest of her life was like that, too; Nick hated to change that about her. He banished unpleasant thoughts about the reason for their visit and watched Zola work, realizing for the first time how erotic a woman shifting gears could look.

Three heedless young girls, heartbreakingly innocent and lovely in Catholic school uniforms, stepped from a hidden road in the cane; Zola slowed from 50 mph to zero before the girls had to release each other's hands. Nick murmured a thank-you to the Almighty Gizmo whose spirit lived in the braking system.

They made good time to Natchez.

After checking in to Hotel Portager, a gaudy relic of the Gilded Age, they made love joyfully in their big overpriced suite.

Later, languorous and thirsty, they spent the rest of the afternoon at the Nextdoor Bar, a small grungy place with good drinks and a great jukebox, which doesn't pretend to be anything else. Around dusk, they strolled over to the nearby Mississippi to watch the sun setting over flat, fertile Louisiana. Then, among the antique shops, tearooms, and vacant storefronts downtown, they found a hardware store just about to close.

"All right, now really, Nick," Zola said. "What in the world are these for?"

They'd arrived at her car, which was parked on a steep street beside the hotel. He was maneuvering two shovels and a pickax into her trunk.

"Okay, I'll tell you the truth. No more kidding around. I'm about to give you a crash course in genealogy. Not just any genealogy, but your own. We're literally going to dig down to your ancestral roots. Real hands-on genealogical research. Tonight, my lovely, you're going to meet Mulatta Belle."

❑

The mounds and slopes of the graveyard were barely discernible as blacker-than-night features of a strange dreamscape. The ground beneath Nick felt vaguely unsettled, as if the bodies themselves below the verdant carpet of grass were rolling toward the precipitous, ever-crumbling bluffs of the Mississippi, to fall in finally and be free of their remembrance of earthly life. Not the handholding type most of the time, tonight Nick was glad to share his clammy fear with Zola.

She thought this was all a joke. "I bet you used this trick in high school, so the girls would snuggle up. Well, if that's your ploy . . ." and she snuggled up, her head on his shoulder. "It's working."

Then he told her about Hyam Balazar, Jacob and Euphrozine, (her great-great-grandmother, he claimed), and the Mulatta Belle-Ivanhoe line; about the surviving Natchitoches Balzars, Shelvin, and others spread out across the country; about her mother's original contention that knowledge of this hidden family history would be used by bigoted clients as a reason to drop Artemis Holdings; that the issue of their Jewish ancestry might negatively affect the Armigers' social life in New Orleans' stratified caste system; and finally, he told her about the injustice Jacob and Euphrozine began by dispossessing Ivanhoe and his half-brothers of color, an injustice she and her mother were perpetuating.

"You've asked me before to help you explore your family history," Nick said. "This should jump-start your research."

He wasn't sure how she would take it all. He couldn't see her face; she'd turned away.

Nick wanted to strike back at Armiger, stop her looting of the past, prove to her that he, too, could use

knowledge as a weapon. If she didn't already know of
the drama of Ivanhoe and Jacob—and he suspected she
didn't—she would soon, through her own daughter.
Zola would be his sling, and what he believed he was
about to dig up would be his rock, against a modern-day
Goliath in Chanel. It was a dangerous move, he knew.
Armiger had murdered Corban for attempting the same
thing.

Zola asked some skeptical questions, which Nick
answered almost accurately; then she lapsed into a
troubled silence again. Crickets chanted their fugal
songs; frogs played staccato castanets; in the distance,
a dog barked at his own echo; tugboats discreetly piped
below on the river.

She stared at him. "Are you telling me that I have
Jewish and black ancestors?"

"You're half right. Your direct ancestor Hyam Balazar
was Jewish at one time, but Mulatta Belle and Ivanhoe
Balzar were not lineal relations."

"Nick this is all . . . well, it's incredible. I'm not
sure I understand."

"In genealogy, we call your temporary confusion
the E.G.O. factor—for 'eyes glazed over.' It's a complex
measure of how long it takes for a person to lose track
during the discussion of a complicated lineage. There's
a second part to it, the ego of the narrator: to what
degree he notices that the victim's interest is flagging.
On a scale of one to ten, I'd say this case is an eight.
But when you see it all written down, it will come
clear."

She didn't laugh; she hadn't been listening to his
last words. Her face hardened into anger. "Incredible
and insensitive. I mean, you just drop this bomb on me,
with absolutely no consideration for my feelings. I
resent it that you've played games with my emotions.
You've kept this from me. Why? You've been using me,
haven't you? I get it: you've been promised a cut from
these people in Natchitoches. Let's all sue Artemis
Holdings for something that may or may not have

happened over a century ago!" She sprang up and stood over him, giving him an unnecessary reminder that she was deadly on the tennis court—and in bed.

Her voice shook with emotion now. "I don't know what my mother has to do with this, but I bet you've been using her, too!"

"Zola, calm down. This is your chance to do some good, to correct a wrong. Isn't that the goal of Artemis Holdings? Isn't that what *you* are all about?" His words had no effect on her.

"You lied to me, Nick. I should have seen what was happening. You've been so peculiar about helping me do genealogical research, you led me on with that story of a grant . . . I wonder if you lied about your feelings for me."

"No, Zola, I didn't."

"I'm leaving. And I'm going to find out from Mother what's really happening here, what both of you were up to. How can I ever trust you again? Find your own damn way back to the hotel!"

She stomped off toward her car. "Oh, in case you didn't know, desecration of a grave is a crime!" she shouted before slamming the door.

He heard the tires clawing gravel and the engine screaming at the rpm redline. When the noise faded, the peace of the night filled the vacuum.

"You be sleeping on the couch tonight, for sure," said a deep male voice.

"Ahhhhhhhhh!" Nick screamed in the breeze, losing several heartbeats.

He turned his flashlight on a hulking figure that seemed to be a bas-relief on the surface of the darkness, not two feet away: Shelvin.

"Oh, man . . . Shelvin," Nick said, recovering some breath, the adrenaline still churning through his veins. "You, you almost *killed* me."

"No. You'd a knowed it if I wanted to kill you. Learned how to night stalk like that in the Army."

"Great. I'm beginning to wonder about my tax

dollars," said Nick.

"Look here," said Shelvin, "how come every time you open your mouth, you sing a different tune about somebody else fucking-over my family? Only way to catch you tellin' the truth is to sneak up on you. Tell you what I ought to do. I ought to beat the shit out of you, cracker, and then get me a good NAACP lawyer to sue your white ass."

"You were going to hear basically the same story I told her. It's the truth." *Mostly.* "Look, didn't I get you to meet us here?" Nick asked him.

"Yeah, I suppose so."

"Okay, then, cut the macho crap and listen—one of the new skills you're going to need in this future we're going to discover tonight. Down there lies your great-great-great-great grandmother."

"You mean, what's left of her."

"Yeah. I believe she's been keeping something safe for you, something that will give back what is rightfully yours."

They shone their lights on the tombstone.

ঙ Belle Reyaud ও

b. 1812 Georgia

d. April 14, 1869 Natchez

His sweetest dreams were still of
that dear voice that soothed his infancy.–Southey

"I bet those lines were Ivanhoe's touch," Nick said. He was sure Ivanhoe would have become familiar in Hyam's study with England's popular poets. Seeing Shelvin's confusion, he added, "Ivanhoe Balzar, your great-great . . . oh, anyway, your ancestor, okay, and this woman's son. He bore the name of one of Sir Walter Scott's most popular characters, and probably suggested those lines of poetry." He picked up a shovel and lobbed it into Shelvin's waiting hand. "Let's get started. This is going to take a while and I don't plan to get caught by the sun."

"Hold on a minute," Shelvin said. "You telling me you expect me to dig up a grave? No way, man. Not me. I don't care if she *is* my great-great whatever."

"Scared?" Nick asked, smiling, enjoying the irony of the big man's sudden qualm. "You're not worried about getting arrested, I know. I remember your performance with that deputy up in Natchitoches."

Shelvin scratched his bare scalp as he made his decision. Then he attacked the ground as if he were digging a foxhole under fire.

Their tools bit through the thick mat of grass, making an awful ripping sound that made Nick think of limbs being pulled out of sockets in a schlocky horror movie. The rich, moldy black earth piled up around them, and soon there was room for only one person to work efficiently in the rectangular hole. The two of them alternated. Shelvin made much greater progress with his well-conditioned body.

It was during his shift that they reached the right level. At first, as Nick shone a flashlight on the papery rotted wood, he had a second of panic. Had Ivanhoe buried his mother in a simple wooden box that was now decayed to such a degree that nothing was left inside?

No, there was something else there.

Shelvin used his hands to clear away debris, and to Nick's relief, he saw below the crumbling wood a zinc lining, which was a common burial practice in those days for prosperous families. Nick surmised that Hyam had left Mulatta Belle quite well off and that their son, Ivanhoe, did not stint on his mother's burial—for a reason besides love, he hoped.

He jumped down with the tire tool he'd brought, and when Shelvin worked free the several bolts with an evil-looking assault knife, Nick prized the lid off.

The corpse did not cackle and fly into the air. It was

just the leathery, bony husk of life they saw. Nick's momentary revulsion gave way to fascination. Insects had found ways into the coffin, and heat and moisture had done the rest. There were fragments of lace, the dust of an outline around the bones.

"That was probably her favorite dress," Nick remarked. Mulatta Belle's mortal remains lay before them. Did her delicate skull smile in gratitude at Nick, or was it just a trick of the light and shadow? He wasn't sure, but he was too excited to care.

Below her gruesome arms and hands crossed on her chest was a lovely small velvet Bible, considerably damaged . . . and a sealed cylindrical glass jar, the kind barbers often use even today.

Nick held the jar up to his light. He'd guessed right: the family Bible and important documents were never far apart in the Balzar family. Inside the jar was a rolled-up piece of paper. He gingerly took it out and read to Shelvin the letter, in Hyam Balazar's own hand, bequeathing to Ivanhoe Balzar, his son by Mulatta Belle, 1000 acres of Mitzvah Plantation; to Jeremiah Putnam, a slave, his freedom and 500 acres; and to Chapman Winn, 250 acres. The letter was dated May 16, 1859—two days before the making of the nuncupative will and Hyam's assumed death date.

❑

They had reburied Belle as best they could.

Shelvin drove Nick back to the hotel in his truck. Nick said that he would have a rare-documents specialist make certified copies of the letter. He would keep the original and send copies to the Balzars.

Shelvin hesitated but agreed.

Crusty with dirt and sweat, the two of them staggered into the lobby at three-thirty.

"Get that lawyer," Nick said to him, in farewell.

❑

The door to the bedroom in the hotel suite was closed. Nick crashed on the couch.

At dawn, without a word to him, Zola emerged from the bedroom and left, slamming the door.

Nick took a bus back to New Orleans.

Chapter 24

A prearranged workshop gig—a paying one, of course—took Nick to a regional conference at a hotel in Memphis, where in a small, over-air-conditioned room, he expounded for a week on the genealogical treasures of New Orleans to shivering empty nesters, retirees, widows, and widowers. He also schmoozed with a few star speakers of the genealogy conference circuit, hoping to become one, and literally bumped into Gwen at a booth selling books of interest to Louisiana researchers.

Gwen tearfully confided that since her precious work had mysteriously gone up in flames in Natchitoches, she hadn't been the same. As she swallowed a handful of antidepressants with a gulp of diet soda, Nick, in a sudden attack of remorse, begged her to let him to do what he could to help reconstruct the material that—still unknown to her, thank God!—he'd incinerated.

On his way back to New Orleans, Nick hit as many county courthouses in Mississippi as he could for a new client's project, until his car broke down in Hattiesburg. He tried to handle the exorbitant repair bill with Natalie Armiger's credit card. *What's she going to do, fire me? I should be so lucky!* But the card had been canceled. He wrote a check that possibly wouldn't bounce.

At last, he headed home, having done a lot of thinking.

❑

The Armigers' premier downtown property was

the city's tenth tallest building. It stood sentinel over the river at the foot of Canal.

"So, this is the famous Artemis Holdings?" Nick said to Zola's beautiful visage on a color monitor behind the security desk in the lobby.

She'd called him that morning, three weeks after their trip to Natchez, summoning him to her office. It was a sparkling fall day, the first truly temperate one of the season. He'd walked here from his apartment, his steps unconsciously quickened by his repeated, mumbled rehearsal of what he wanted to say.

"Nick, thanks for coming," Zola said, from the monitor. "I'll meet you on thirty."

The guard hung a visitor's tag on Nick and directed him to the proper elevator. Thirtieth through thirty-fifth floors. After a rapid ear-popping ride, he emerged into what sounded like a college football game. Actually, he found himself on a sort of catwalk; there were offices with glass sliding doors behind him, each with two or three people clutching several phones at once. Below him, in an auditorium-sized room, were a hundred or so men and women at banks of keyboards and monitors. Digital displays and clusters of large screens with rapidly shifting numbers and graphs dangled from the high ceiling.

The scene reminded Nick of the gothic Boschian representations of the damned, occupying themselves with their imbecilic activities or suffering the torments of divine judgment.

Zola stepped from another set of elevators down the catwalk. Her dark hair was coiled at the back of her head; she wore a rather staid suit. But her grace and beauty shone through even this business disguise. She walked up to Nick, grasped his right hand in both of hers and gave him a friendly kiss on the cheek.

Friendly, and no more than that.

They had to step aside to let several hurrying workers pass. Nick caught snatches of their conversation, which seemed to be mainly about an Asian currency crisis, a shortage of ship capacity, and the very good coffee crop somewhere.

"Just part of the company, the stock, bond, and commodities trading pit," Zola said of the scene below them, indicating that they should walk toward the elevators to the higher floors. He could see she was amused by his inexperience in this world arena, and proud at the same time of this termite hill of capitalism. But there was something else behind her eyes, something Nick sensed he would hear before this morning was through.

He fondled the small box in his coat pocket for reassurance, for courage.

"On the floors above us," she said, "are our departments for private investment banking, property management, and insurance. I think we have time for a short tour, don't we, Gloria?"

Zola checked her watch and glanced for confirmation at the young woman who was shadowing them. Gloria shrugged with good humor and went to work rearranging her boss's schedule on an electronic office-in-a-pad.

❑

Thirty minutes later, he sat with Zola in her office on the top floor. It was a big circular room that resembled the windowed observation decks atop airport control towers. Was he crazy or hung-over, or was the whole place . . . rotating slowly? He struggled to remember how much wine he'd drunk the night before. Too much, obviously.

He'd gone through most of the Armiger cash with

disconcerting, guilty speed, buying books and documents that interested him, paying off several years' worth of debts to merchants, credit-card companies, the IRS, his ex-wife—and buying cases of rare Burgundy, single bottles of which in previous days he would not have even picked up in any shop for fear of dropping them.

"The rotation? It's very gradual. Most visitors notice it, if at all, only much later," Zola said. "After an hour or so you get used it. But the view of the city *is* breathtaking. Sometimes I forget to even look, and it takes someone else's surprise and delight to bring me to a new appreciation of it."

"This building used to be, uh"—he snapped his fingers trying to remember—"what was the name of that company?"

"International Maritime Consortium," she said, "New Orleans' attempt to emulate Lloyd's of London. Went bust a few years ago, and we snapped up the building at an RTC auction. Yes, there used to be quite a renowned bar up here, the Sextant Club, which I'm sure you frequented at some time in your reckless youth."

"Ah yes, back when I was a shipping magnate. I recall many a fine Havana and glass of cognac enjoyed here, discussing the price of bauxite."

Their forced, hollow laughter soon died. Zola looked down, seemingly unable to say what was on her mind. He leaned back in the chair, his arms behind his head. That was a mistake, because he got a dizzying sensation of perilous movement, accompanied immediately by an irrational feeling that he was about to plummet thirty-five stories.

He straightened up quickly and focused on the things moving around with him. The outer ring of circular floor was divided into two segments by the arrangement of furniture, art, and plants: one segment was the domain of Zola, the other of Mrs. Armiger. At certain points in the rotation, he could see that Armiger wasn't at her desk. In an unmoving island in the middle of the large room were the elevators and several desks used by the personal staff of the two women.

Nick marveled at the quietness that encapsulated them. He reached in his coat pocket and removed the jewelry box. He concealed it in his hand, below the edge of Zola's desk.

If you don't do it now, you never will.

"Noise-cancellation technology," Zola said. "We're underwriting a start-up company that specializes in it. We wanted to try it out for ourselves. It's really amazing. Research being done with Freret. You see how we're able to do away with isolating walls and partitions. We think this is going to be a tremendously successful product. More coffee?"

She signaled a secretary; the young man quickly brought the cup and returned to his desk.

"Nick, I have a problem."

"I know. Should you get me the Breitling or the Rolex for Christmas?" She'd taken him to task often for having no watch.

"No, no," she said, laughing sadly. She put on a serious face. "Sometimes your flippancy can be so annoying. I'm trying to talk about something important, here. It's this situation with the Balzar family . . ."

"Your family, remember?"

"Well, yes, I suppose so," she said. Her hesitant tone told Nick that she'd been looking in the rearview mirror a lot lately; her audio technology couldn't cancel that. "But really, I don't feel at all close to these people. It's a terribly distant connection. Merely a line on a pedigree chart. I just don't think it merits all this controversy, and cost."

She showed him a small back-page clipping from the *Wall Street Journal*, describing a class-action suit against Artemis Holdings, and Natalie and Zola Armiger personally. Nearly forty provable heirs of Ivanhoe wanted the equivalent of 1000 acres—with a hundred-and-thirty-odd years of interest and damages. The article speculated that a big chunk of cash could be on the line. The opposing lawyers were preparing for battle, which could go on for years and years. Nick thought of Dickens' *Bleak House*.

"Mother says that your original project was simply to investigate some vague family rumors she'd heard as a child, about this alleged Natchitoches ancestor of ours. She felt it was time to know the truth."

"'Alleged'? You don't believe me? Is having a Jewish ancestor such a problem for you, too?"

"Of course not. But in Mother's day, and even now, for people like us . . ." She set her coffee cup down and held it with both hands, as if seeking answers from it. "The point is, why are you doing this to us, Nick?"

"It's a long story I don't want to go into now. But this much I will say: your saintly mother paid me $50,000 to obscure your family history, not to bring it to light. The truth was never part of our deal."

"'Obscure'? What does that mean? My knowledge of genealogy is deficient—thanks to you—but that doesn't seem possible. You've been completely unsupervised on the project she gave you, and you've failed to make timely reports to her. Mother was your client, yet she had no idea what you'd found. We now think that in the course of your research, you uncovered this somewhat controversial past of ours, and then decided to make some money from it.

"This is all your fault," she said. "Far from obscuring our presumed family history, I understand you told the Balzars where to look for a fast buck: at the last of our line of the family, the only line, apparently, with any wealth. That seems highly unethical to me. We're considering a complaint to the genealogical certifying body—whatever it is."

Zola stopped talking and took a deep breath. Waiting for a denial, Nick thought. But he kept quiet and rubbed his hand over his mouth. He would blurt out too much if he started at all. He would tell her what her beloved mother was really like, what she had done, what she was capable of doing, why he was striking back in the only way available to him. He would try to persuade her to break free of Armiger's poisoned protection, to find the truth on her own, to let him share the joys and sorrows of that search. He had worked it out in the past few days—their escape, sailing away in a magical galleon on a river of red wine . . .

He slipped the box back into his pocket.

Zola was saying, "Mother wanted to make an offer, handle this affair as quietly as possible. I insisted that we go through the legal system. I was wrong. This thing has turned nasty. We're hearing very insulting whispers here and there, at our clubs, at restaurants, at parties. I never thought people could be so horrid. We've already lost a good deal of business." She lifted a few pages from a stack of reports on her well-ordered desk. "Investors aren't sure what our liability is. Confidence is a big issue. This should have been stopped before it became public."

"You're beginning to remind me more and more of your mother every day."

"Meaning?" she countered testily.

"I can see your idealism gradually transforming into her style of moral sophism."

"Please, Nick, don't try to turn me against Mother. She is a great woman, a pioneer in this industry. You don't know her. She's been terribly upset by this. In fact, she's quite ill and hardly comes to the office anymore. Her doctors have advised heart surgery. What gives you the right to speak of her in such disparaging terms? Who are you to preach to us? You've lied to me and others; you've accepted money under false pretenses. In spite of our . . . friendship, you're not part of our family, even at the remove of these Balzars."

"Sometimes family ties aren't all they're cracked up to be."

She shot a raised eyebrow at him. "Nick, our relationship has become a problem for me. I think maybe we should let things cool off."

Nick had felt this was coming, but knowing did not make the impact hurt any less.

"Zola, these months we've been together have been . . . what I mean is, um . . . look, this isn't easy for me to say: I don't want to lose you."

She turned her chair to look out over the river. Huge ocean-going freighters slid by as if they were models only inches from the windows.

"I think this is best, Nick. Maybe when this has all blown over . . ."

"Yeah," he said, standing up. "Sure. Thanks for the tour and the coffee. And the past few months."

As he stepped onto the stationary center of the room, he looked back at her. She was already on the phone, shuffling reports, slowly moving in her own orbit, and then out of view.

❑

At the river's edge in Woldenberg Park in the Quarter, Nick threw the engagement ring into the brown water churned up by a departing paddle-wheeler. Then he dropped the light-blue plastic jewelry box into a trashcan. *Mustn't litter.*

Zola would have commended his public spiritedness.

Chapter 25

Two opposite streetcars had screeched to a halt. The drivers angrily clanged the bells. Impatient passengers stood up for a better look and shouted insults in the direction of the gray Ford blocking both tracks.

"Get in the back, asshole, or you're dead meat." Nick's massage therapist, the blond goon who'd held him against the wall, pointed a black pistol at his abdomen from the open front-passenger door of the car. Nick had been enjoying an afternoon jog on St. Charles Avenue, the day after his unhappy audience with Zola. The goon behind the wheel, cool as a cucumber, gave the finger to the irate drivers and passengers.

Though the two men ignored his questions as the car hurtled across town, Nick was certain of the destination.

❑

The iron gates at Armiger's lakeside estate swung open. The gray Ford sped toward the munchkin chateau.

"That meter must be off?" Nick said, stepping from the car when it stopped. "I think you're padding it. Last time I use this taxi company."

"You're a regular David-fuckin'-Letterman," the

blond goon said. "Wonder how funny you'd be with your dick in your mouth. The lady's waiting for you."

❑

Armiger sat where Nick had last seen her, similarly attired, a different pattern to her caftan. But she seemed years older, not a woman you'd see in the pages of *Town and Country*, mingling elegantly with other society bigwigs. Now she reminded Nick of a very sick patient in the waiting room of a doctor's office, prepared for the worst possible news.

The framed picture of Zola and the gold pillbox were close at hand.

Her real religion and hope for salvation. The weak spots in her armor.

She was deep in thought and didn't seem to notice the incongruity of a nearly naked slob walking into the severe formality of the room. Nick sat down.

When she finally looked up, in the instant before she composed herself, he saw that weariness, worry, and physical anguish distorted her face. She seemed to have crawled out of one of the canvases of abstract horror downstairs.

She began in a scratchy near-whisper: "This has become more serious than I had imagined, Nick. This claim of heirship. I had never *heard* of these people before you turned them up. These Balzars."

"Ironic, isn't it?" Nick said. "Our crimes give birth to their own justice. You tried to put one genie in the bottle, and let another one out."

Very Miltonic, Nick thought; Dion would love it.

"You don't realize what you've done. Not only have you caused an estrangement between my daughter and me, but you have also nearly destroyed what I have struggled so hard to create. Merely with the discovery of one illegitimate union! It would have been much better if my ancestors had cleaned up their own mistakes, as I have," she said, a deep bitterness slicing up her words. "Never have I seen such an outflow of funds from Artemis, not even in the great bear market of 73-74. The company is in serious jeopardy, which, fortunately, the financial press hasn't discovered yet."

Why is she telling me this? Am I going to walk out of here alive? In the intervening silence Nick formulated and rejected ten scenarios of escape.

"I liked you," Armiger said, as if he had spoken his thoughts. "Again, my emotions led me astray. I admire talent, intelligence, stubbornness against daunting odds. Repeatedly, I warned you. But I should have seen: people like you make their own rules, take no advice from those who wish them well. Or ill. We are, after all, Nick, much alike."

"You must not be looking in the same mirror, lady."

"My penchant for the underdog has been costly," she said, pressing on in what seemed to Nick more and more like a prepared speech. "Now I must attempt to repair the damage that I am responsible for, just as much as you are. I have had you brought here today to give you a last warning. I am not a monster. And I understand your moral dilemma perhaps better than you yourself do.

"Turn over the Balazar documents to me, documents which I now know you possess—I have my sources in Natchitoches and Natchez. You've been wise not to part with them. There is a letter, I understand, about which I can do nothing—for the moment. You were foolish enough to share that with the opposing camp. But without documentary evidence of my descent from Hyam Balazar, the case will be nearly impossible to prove. When I have what you discovered in

Natchitoches, I will no longer *be* a Balazar, as far as anyone can tell. My unfortunate pedigree will cease to be a liability."

"I've been thinking," Nick said, "maybe I'll go to the police? Tell them about Corban and the woman from Poland. The whole sorry spectacle of what your family did to the Balzars pales in comparison with murder. That'll cost more than any lawsuit. A lot more."

"You're smarter than that, Nick." She gave him a condescending smile. "Who would believe you, a third-rate hack hungry for publicity, a plagiarist? A man who has stolen public documents? The police are more likely to charge *you* than me. And where do you think those young men work?" she said, feebly pointing outside.

The two goons are cops!?   A sudden onset of vertigo made him grab the arms of his chair. Somehow, the idea that they were cops made him more frightened than if they'd been ordinary civilian assassins. He was alone in this mess, with no authority to back him up. The climactic scene from *North by Northwest* flickered into his consciousness: Cary Grant hangs by one hand over Mount Rushmore, Eva Marie Saint dangling from his other hand, as Martin Landau steps harder and harder on his knuckles . . .

"I would know the instant you contacted a detective," Armiger was saying, her voice having regained its customary confidence. "You wouldn't live long enough to drive to police headquarters."

As usual, she had all the answers before he even asked the questions. A tricky situation: keeping the documents hurt the Balzars' case; releasing them, leading to the inevitable discovery that he'd stolen them, would land him in very hot water—certainly he'd be drummed out of the genealogy corps; and giving them to Armiger doomed the documents to perpetual imprisonment, perhaps destruction.

But of all the reasons he could think of at the moment, the most important was that the documents he'd stolen were his ticket to continued health, since Zola had broken off with him. He wished fervently that he'd never accepted Armiger's money in the first place. Nick struggled to sound unrattled as he began to present the strategy that had come to him in a previous jogging session. "Look, Mrs. Armiger, Zola is no closer to the real story because of what I've done. Agreed?"

"You're treading on dangerous ground," Armiger warned.

He swallowed hard and continued. "She has no reason to doubt that she's your daughter. I've even bolstered the idea that she's Hyam Balazar's direct descendant. I don't want to hurt her. I happen to be in love with her, but let's forget that for now. All those glass cases"—he nodded toward the gallery—"make it unlikely she could follow the European line to her parents, either by chance or deliberately. You may not have everything there is out there, but what you've gathered would certainly stymie even an experienced genealogist. I've worked with a few adoptees; the desire to know birth parents should come from within, not outside. For Zola it's a matter of identity, and I would be wrong to tamper with one that satisfies her—regardless of your role in the matter. Give me some credit on that score, okay?

"With the Balzars, it's a financial question—much easier to resolve for a businessperson of your talents. Settle with them. You'll never have to go to court, and the Natchitoches crap will become moot. As a bonus, you'll never hear from me again."

Unless I find a way to nail you for two murders.

He was pleased with his performance; his nervous

sweating had stopped, and his damp T-shirt was cold. Had he won her over?

She seemed ready to agree but finally shook her head. "They are unreasonable. Their demands escalate every day. Absurd allegations—"

A telephone chirped somewhere. Armiger pulled a cellular from a drawer of the desk. She listened for half a minute, then replaced the phone in the drawer. A new surge of pain hit her.

"Genealogists spend too much of their time in the company of dead people," she said. "It affects their judgment. I suggest you give more thought to the living. For Zola's sake, if not your own."

"So you refuse to consider the Balzars' claim?"

"I will take care of their claim!" she shouted, her anger flaring through the icy grip of pain. "Give me the documents, or you will be killed. And never mention Zola's past to me or anyone else again. You have a week. Get out!"

❑

Not the most successful meeting he'd ever sat through.

The two goons were gone when Nick got downstairs. He was supposed to get back on his own, it seemed. But he was relieved that he wouldn't have to spend more quality time with them today.

At the iron gate, the security guard was conspicuously absent.

He replayed Armiger's final statement over and over again in his mind as he searched through the guardhouse for a way to open the gate.

"I will take care of their claim!" Ominous, very ominous.

In his gym shorts and ragged Fortescue College T-shirt, Nick walked, jogged, and thumbed along

Lakeshore Drive before he caught a ride with a man driving a new, but phone-less, Cadillac. The man made a shy, lewd proposition as the car stopped twenty minutes later on St. Charles, in front of Audubon Park. Nick exited the car quickly, not bothering to shut the door. He jumped into his own car and floored it into the thick traffic without looking.

❑

At the next K&B drugstore, he called his office. No answer.

Then he drove like a madman, weaving from the street to the neutral ground, dodging joggers, dog-walkers, and streetcars, honking his horn as he sped through intersections.

❑

But he was too late.

A fleet of police cars blocked the street in front of his office building. Three ambulances waited with open doors and flashing lights.

Nick charged inside and bounded up the stairs before any of the officers could stop him.

Pieces that had once been Hawty's high-tech chariot littered the stairwell. On a landing, two paramedics were carefully placing Hawty herself on a gurney.

She was in a neck-brace, a leg was cocooned in an inflatable cast, and her bloody face was already swelling.

Tears of rage jumped into Nick's eyes.

"Hawty, baby, how bad is it?" he asked, nearly choking on the words.

"How should I know? My body didn't work so well before this," she said, not much of her usual spirit subdued.

The female paramedic reassured Nick with a nod

and a kind touch to his shoulder. She finished taping an
IV tube to Hawty's arm.

"Shelvin's upstairs," Hawty said, but broke off,
overcome by sobbing. "And Ronald. It happened so
fast. Ronald got it bad from two guys. White guys—a
blond one and a dark-haired one—I think. Never seen
them before. I've already told the detectives. We were
coming back from lunch, and they just appeared from
nowhere and pounced on Shelvin and Ronald from
behind. Somebody kicked me down the stairs. They
must have been just leaving our office, and we surprised
them. *Please*, go find out how they are, Nick. They
won't tell me a damn thing."

The paramedics started slowly down the stairs
with her.

She and the Balzar brothers, Shelvin and Ronald,
had struck up a friendship, as now and then the two
young men dropped in at the office, and planned aloud
what great things they were going to do with the money
the family was expecting from Artemis Holdings.
Trouble was, the young men reported, the lawyers were
having trouble finding out anything about this Hyam
Balazar. *Imagine that.*

For all his bluster, Shelvin was really a nice guy;
Ronald—lighter in color, slightly shorter, and less
athletically honed than his older brother—was the
charmer of the pair, the dreamer, and the one who
seemed on the way to conquering Hawty's impetuous
young heart.

Nick had known they were going to lunch
together. When he began to suspect that Armiger had
summoned him primarily to get him away from his office,
he immediately began to fear for their safety; he'd had
a bad feeling about that upsetting phone call she took.
Indeed, during the meeting in which Armiger delivered

her ultimatum, the two goons were busy: they turned over his temporarily empty office—and his apartment before that, he later learned but didn't report—and attacked Shelvin, Ronald, and Hawty when caught in the act. The phone call must have been the goons' report of the unintended battle and of their failure to find the Natchitoches material.

"I'll come see you later, Hawty . . . and I'll do what I can for Shelvin and Ronald." He watched until the group made a corner and sank out of sight.

Then he sprinted upstairs, taking two, three steps at a time. *This is your goddamn fault! Still playing both sides of the game, like Armiger. Playing God.*

In his hallway he saw uniformed cops and plainclothes investigators milling around; to the right, toward his office, paramedics worked frenziedly on a large, squirming human heap on the floor. Shelvin. He seemed to be still fighting off his attackers.

"My brother! Where's my brother?! Let go of me!" Shelvin shouted over and over again. He knocked over a paramedic with a sweep of a bloody arm. Someone got a needle into him. His shouts faded to incoherent bellows and then to moans. Finally, he was quiet.
Blood pooled the hallway floor, particularly to the left of the stairwell, where one paramedic pumped a precise rhythm on Ronald's chest, as another one tried to stanch the bleeding.

A young uniformed officer approached Nick. "Sir, this is a crime scene. I'll have to ask you to—"

"That's my office," Nick said to him. "They're my friends. The injured girl downstairs works for me."

"You'd better come with me into the office. One of the detectives will need to ask you a few questions."

Nick was as uncommunicative as he dared be with the detective who interviewed him. How could he trust *these* cops? What of his own crimes? Any accusation he fired off was likely to ricochet and land him in jail. Or worse.

Surreptitiously, he checked the rug over his hiding place; Ivanhoe's diary and the original letter were undisturbed.

Chapter 26

Ronald died in surgery about two the next morning.

❑

In an echoing tiled hallway of the hospital, an emergency room doctor almost young enough to be Nick's son explained that Shelvin would probably live. He'd lost a lot of blood and his heart had stopped twice, but he seemed out of the woods now.

"Were they shot?" Nick asked. "Can I see him?"

"Knives," the doctor said over his shoulder as he hurried to another scene of emergency-room carnage. "Or maybe chain saws. Five minutes."

Ghoulish humor, but Nick understood. For someone who glimpses every day the horrible secret—that we're just fragile bags of blood—it must keep the madness at bay.

❑

Shelvin lay on a tall wheeled bed in Intensive Care, amid a forest of bags, tubes, and wires. Softly humming machines on carts generated green lines and red numerals of vital signs. Nurses ministered to maybe twenty other patients in the dimly lit room, talking to the semiconscious ones as though they were children, ignoring their pitiful pleas and odd requests. Odors of blood and antiseptic competed to nauseate Nick.

Shelvin stared at the low ceiling of acoustic panels, as if counting the holes. He breathed slowly, deeply, through his wide nostrils. His finely chiseled full lips quivered occasionally against each other. Thick gauze bandages covered his neck and arms and hands. His face and smooth scalp showed bruises and abrasions, but they had escaped the ravages of the knives. Except for his powerful, naked shoulders, an elevated sheet hid the rest of him.

His eyes, now unnaturally black, suddenly darted sideways, fixing Nick with a piercing gaze. "You don't have to tell me. I know. He's dead."

Nick looked down. The floor shimmered behind a veil of sorrow and shame. He could say nothing.

"Give me your hand."

Nick walked the remaining step to Shelvin's bed and took the injured man's bandaged right hand with his left. Shelvin was weak; his listless forearm was heavy in Nick's grasp.

"I want you to go up to Natchitoches," Shelvin said, in a low monotone. "See to it my brother gets buried proper. Do what you can for my mama and daddy." He ordered Nick to spare no expense and told him where in New Orleans he could charge what he needed.

Sick people have a lot of time to obsess over details, Nick realized for the first time in his life.

Exhausted, Shelvin paused for a few breaths, before his muscular brows knitted together in concentration. He turned his coal-black eyes again to Nick. "If we'd never heard about Ivanhoe Balzar and how his own family turned on him, my brother would be alive, and I wouldn't be here, all cut up . . . Hawty okay?" he asked, anesthesia-belated concern for her pushing aside the point he was struggling to make.

Nick nodded. Contrition welled up within him, threatening to break the dam.

"But I don't have no blame for you," Shelvin said.

"We weren't who we thought we were, and that ain't healthy for the soul. You had a duty to tell us, and you did it. Things needed setting right. Still do."

Shelvin closed his eyes. His brows relaxed a bit. Must have been a load off his mind, Nick thought, knowing that his parents would be comforted by—dare he say—a friend.

Nick gently laid Shelvin's hand on the sheet, and then started to go quietly. A nurse headed their way, tapping her wristwatch.

"You know who did this?" Shelvin asked, his eyes still closed.

Nick stopped and turned around. "I think so."

"When I get better, you're going to tell me. And then I'm going to kill them."

❏

"The material you gave me, Nick, remember? The night of the play?"

He'd picked up the phone on the fifteenth ring. Una had been talking for a few minutes, but he couldn't get the gist of her words. Sleep's gravity still tugged at his awareness.

"Wake up; it's eleven o'clock in the morning," she said. "The material you asked me to put in my safe-deposit box."

"What, the night of the play? Uh, yeah. Just a second."

Nick went into his bathroom and splashed water on his face.

He'd stayed with Hawty until eight a.m., trying to assuage her grief for her dead friend and her worry over Shelvin.

"You're going to be angry," she said. "It's gone."

"Gone? What do you mean? How could it be gone? Did the bank blow up?"

"I screwed up. I temporarily stored the material in the departmental safe. But I forgot about it, until this morning. I've had so much on my mind, Nick. The new semester, our departmental fall symposium . . . I'm so sorry. When I went to retrieve it this morning, it had vanished. The secretaries swear they don't know what I'm talking about. Something's strange, here. But I take full responsibility for—"

"Tawpie," Nick muttered, now thoroughly awake, sitting in his boxers on the side of his bed. Armiger's goons probably knew Una was one of the few friends he saw the night of the play, after he'd returned from Natchitoches. It must have just occurred to her to track Una's movements during the following days. Frederick Tawpie no doubt told Armiger that Una had deposited something in the safe. Armiger certainly did have her "sources," everywhere, it seemed.

Now Nick was that much closer to being expendable. Armiger had everything she feared. Or so she thought.

"What?" Una asked. "I didn't catch that."

"It's okay," Nick said. "I know where the stuff is. It would be better if you didn't mention this to anyone, because I don't want you . . . because there's been more violence. Hawty's in the hospital—but she's going to be all right. Shelvin, one of the Balzar heirs from Natchitoches suing Artemis, is in pretty bad shape. And there's another man dead."

Una was flabbergasted. She fired off a dozen frantic questions Nick wouldn't answer. He did tell her which hospital Hawty was in, and asked her to go keep her company, when she got the chance.

"This is awful, Nick . . ." The shock of all the bad news had temporarily stunned her, and Nick could tell she was on the verge of tears. "Oh, I really hope Hawty

isn't hurt too badly. Do you think she'll recover? Where
are you going? Will you be all right? You'd better come
stay with Dion or me. You could be next."

"Una, just do what I ask," he said. "I'll be busy
for the next few days."

Chapter 27

Ronald's funeral in Natchitoches was a big affair. And sad.

Relatives and friends lingered over the open casket, discussing how handsome he looked. The knife wounds and the autopsy damage were for the most part well disguised. On Shelvin's instructions, Nick had purchased a new Brooks Brothers double-breasted pinstriped suit in New Orleans. The morticians had been impressed. Nick's own touch for Ronald's final costume was a tasteful boutonniere for the lapel.

Just visible below Ronald's clasped hands were a brand-new small Bible and a sealed aluminum tube with a black ribbon. The tube contained Hyam Balazar's original letter, which Ivanhoe had buried for safekeeping with his mother in 1869. Dora had bravely seen to this detail, with the help of a plumber friend. It was a form of insurance, Nick had told her.

Erasmus was completely broken up by his son's death. Dora had her hands full taking care of him and the old man, Twice, who of course didn't know what was going on. He would erupt now and then in the little rural Baptist church during the minister's sermon with a demand for ice cream. The choir sang many rousing hymns throughout the long standing-room-only service; powerfully moved, Nick hummed along to "I Love the Lord, He Heard My Cry," "Amazing Grace," "We'll Understand It Better By and By," and other gospel favorites he wished he'd grown up hearing. Ronald's sister, five childhood friends, a couple of coworkers (he had been advancing in a Dallas telecom company), and three high-school teachers delivered tearful eulogies.

Later, in the cemetery behind the church, Nick stood at the edge of the crowd, indulging his passion, guiltily, even in the midst of this tragedy. He was reading headstones, traveling back in time, wandering farther and farther from the group; but no one paid any attention. All eyes focused on the burial.

In a neglected, overgrown section of older graves he found Ivanhoe and his wife. The headstones were just marginally legible. He was fairly sure Erasmus and Dora were unaware that these ancestors were buried here.

Well, Nick thought, Ivanhoe will once again know where his precious letter is.

❑

The next day, the minister allowed Nick to graze in the old church records and scrapbooks, where he discovered, among other interesting things, that Ivanhoe Balzar had been gunned down in an argument with Chapman Winn, his own half-brother, the son of Mulatta Belle and the white gambler. Nick supposed that Chapman had second thoughts about having sold his own letter and Portion to Jacob at a discount. Maybe he thought Ivanhoe had some chance of getting the thousand acres Hyam had promised his love child, and wanted a piece of that pie. At least Nick now understood why the diary came to such a sudden halt.

❑

At a convenience store outside New Orleans, Nick walked by a newspaper box. The headline caught his eye:

"Artemis Holdings Near Failure?":

A bitter dispute over ownership of the company and wave after wave of capital flight have left one of New Orleans' financial empires shaken and on the verge of collapse. Federal and state authorities, responding to a chain reaction of complaints, descended on the landmark office tower of Artemis Holdings yesterday afternoon, carting away hundreds of boxes of documents and computer records. Many in the investment community believe this is the beginning of the end for Artemis, long hailed as one of the region's top money-management and venture-capital firms. Calls to the company headquarters for comment have gone unreturned. Regulators fear thousands of investors may face tremendous losses. . . .

Nick called the company, but he did no better than the reporter. A recording said all client service representatives were busy and politely suggested he try again later, or "select one of the following options." He slammed down the pay-phone handset. Voice menus drove him nuts. He would just have to make his own appointment time, unilaterally.

Must be lots of worried people trying to get through, he thought; then again, it might just be electronic stonewalling.

Good thing he'd put his money in Burgundy.

❑

When he got to the lakefront driveway of Armiger's property, he noticed the guard in the gatehouse was still missing. What the hell, he thought, a few more dents couldn't hurt. He stomped the gas pedal and crashed through the gate, leaving clumps of his car clanging on the ground behind him.

He sped down the winding road and parked in front of the elegant little building. The blond goon limped toward him, his gun drawn. One arm was in a sling, three fingers of the other hand were wrapped securely. Tape and plastic hid his nose, and what Nick could see of the rest of his face looked like a well-bruised melon.

"Easy, pal," Nick said, stepping from his car, his hands raised, as if approaching a skittish alligator. "I'm not armed. She asked to see me. The gate was open, so I just—didn't she notify you?"

"No. No she didn't." He seemed confused, probably still seeing stars from his recent run-in with Shelvin and Ronald. Maybe it was the painkillers. "Come 'ere."

He stuffed his gun in his pants waist and frisked Nick perfunctorily, wincing from what Nick suspected were broken ribs.

"It shoulda been you, motherfucker," he said to Nick. "Okay. Go on in."

He limped back to his car.

Inside, Nick felt surrounded by a disturbing new species of silence that brought to his mind images of a suspended heartbeat, a blade raised, or a gun cocked. There was a new glass case upstairs. He walked up to it, and wasn't surprised to see the documents he had stolen from Natchitoches, the documents Una had stored in the departmental safe a bit too long.

All these silent witnesses thus imprisoned strengthened Nick's determination to get Armiger out of the genealogy business—forever.

Natalie Armiger sat in her accustomed place behind the ornate desk. The silver frame and the gold pillbox were there, too. The chair seemed too big for her now, though, slumped and indrawn as she was. Her elbows supported her on the arms of the chair, and her hands gripped each other before her face.

"Praying, Mrs. Armiger? Not your style, exactly. You usually just place an order with God, a market transaction."

Nick thought that mouth of hers seemed less malignant than pitiable now, a jagged, fatal wound. He had no pity for her. She was a murderer, of human beings, of genealogy.

"You should not have come back," she said. "I had envisioned a happier fate for you."

"Mrs. Armiger, you don't direct fate. You never did. The past and the future are beyond your control. Your delusion is a convenient excuse to do what you want—save this one, kill that one, as if the world were your personal ant farm. You don't really believe that? Maybe it's worked so long that you do. I'm here to tell you that you're wrong. You have to pay for what you've done."

She seemed momentarily amused. A brief smile played across the surface of her lips and was gone, like fugitive sunlight on a cloudy, windy day.

From her lap she lifted an elaborately inlaid, silver-and-gold double derringer. Nick thought it might have belonged to Euphrozine, her great-grandmother, or to Jacob Balazar; it might even be the one Ivanhoe mentioned in his diary. But he didn't doubt it was capable of a modern killing.

"Justice, payment for our sins, 'a divinity that shapes our ends,' I believe Hamlet says. What a quaint archaic concept of life, Nick."

He wanted to point out that she was the one who'd named her company after a Greek goddess, but his mouth was too dry.

The weak spots in her armor, he kept telling himself, hoping his poker face was better than his cards.

"Zola and I will survive our difficulties, lawsuit or no lawsuit, here in New Orleans or elsewhere. You could have lived to know how lucky you were to have occupied a brief space in our hearts—and our checkbooks. Now you are the one who has overreached; in *your* delusion, you are an agent of Nemesis. When the media report your death, it will be something like this: crazed Artemis investor with a petty grievance breaks into Armiger estate, where he is shot dead by security guards. Don't worry, we'll open an account for you."

Nick could see her finger beginning to move the trigger.

He found his tongue. "If you kill me, Zola will find out about her adoption, what you allowed to happen to her parents."

"I told you never to mention that again!" Her outburst drained her; she panted as her wild eyes searched the room for the strength to continue. Her caftan seemed to be devouring her, inch by inch. "You're bluffing. You have no proof. You merely put together some odds and ends, some coincidences. No, that story died with Max. The immediate danger is . . . one day, I will gather those records, as well. But now, your threat will die with you."

"Odds and ends, coincidences, vague patterns—genealogy defined," Nick said, talking rapidly, all the while looking down at her finger on the trigger of the derringer, three feet away. "So spread out, so powerfully free, that not even you can gather them in to your glass cases of revisionism. I put Zola's story on a dozen computers, timed to be released online—if I don't live to stop it. No matter where she is, it will follow her. At first not many will notice, just the cybergeeks. But eventually thousands of people will start to ask thousands of questions. One day, maybe years from now, she'll turn on her computer or pick up a magazine, and there will be her real past, pointing the accusing finger at *you*."

In all Hawty's rhapsodies about the information superhighway, something had stuck in his memory. He hoped it sounded convincing.

A sudden pain made Armiger inhale sharply; she fought it. Each sign of her increasing anguish made Nick bolder.

"I don't believe you," she said. But he could see she did.

The gun drifted slightly. She was calculating profit and loss.

After a moment's reflection, she asked, "For the sake of discussion, if you are telling the truth, what do you propose?"

"My quaint archaic concept. All is chance and necessity, Democritus said. Ancient Greece again; you should feel right at home. What do I propose? Has your chance reached the limit of necessity? Have the things you can alter met the things you can't? Let Fate—with a capital *f*—decide our contest here."

Something twisting her insides made the veins in her neck stand out.

"The legal system you mean? I am to turn myself in, confess? Do you really believe that I would be indicted of anything more serious than jaywalking? My means are not inconsiderable, even now."

She picked up the pillbox and tried to open it as

she continued to cover Nick with the pistol. Her trembling hands fumbled with the box, revealing to Nick the depth of her crisis. But her finger never left the trigger.

That pill, she needs that pill!

"The legal system's not what I had in mind," Nick said. "Allow me." He stepped forward and took the pillbox from her unresisting hands.

"If you live long enough to do what I propose, you'll have earned my silence." He slipped the box in a pocket of his corduroys. "I'll accept that judgment."

"How do you know I don't have more medicine here?"

"You would be reaching for it now. Here's my deal. Make a settlement with the heirs of Ivanhoe Balzar—immediately. Fifty million dollars. Next, establish a foundation at Freret University for the study of the Holocaust. Another fifty million. Donate the documents in the display cases out there to the foundation—call it the Maximilian Corban Foundation. Finally, leave the past alone—never again damage the historical record. That's it. I drive a hard bargain, remember?"

"You have thought of everything, Nick. I cannot kill you . . ." Her words trailed off into rapid breaths.

"And you're having a heart attack," he said, finishing the analysis of the royal flush he'd laid down. He wondered if she'd heard him.

At last, she met his gaze. Nick saw in her eyes the helpless power of a dying lioness. Her voice was faint, barely audible.

"You would stop this . . . broadcasting, this revelation? I have your word?"

"The word of a third-rate hack and a plagiarist? Yes. Zola will never know the truth from me, and I'll do nothing to make it more likely that she'll ever find out."

She put the gun on the desk and dragged her hand from it.

He had beaten her—for Corban, for Ivanhoe, for Ronald, for Shelvin, for everyone whose past she had sought to erase.

She listed to one side like a sinking ship. "I have always thought that fear of financial ruin was exaggerated. One is never truly bankrupt while dignity remains. Death is a bankruptcy, too. You will allow me to retain my dignity, Nick?"

It's more than you did for anybody else.

He watched a moment more. Then he turned and unhurriedly walked toward the doorway, half-expecting to feel a bullet. But if this worked, it would have to work his way.

After all, he was entitled to some dignity, too—dignified revenge.

❏

The blond goon now sat in the driver's seat of the car, reading the sports section. The door was open. He wasn't all that interested in Nick's exit from the chateau.

A human being with the silicon soul of a computer-game demon, Nick thought: he kills only on command. Armiger had not yet instructed him to get rid of the pesky genealogist—and never would, now.

Nick walked past the front of the car. As if a thought had suddenly occurred to him, he took a few steps back.

"Hey, you know CPR?" Nick asked, casually.

"Huh? Yeah. Why?" His head snapped toward the chateau; then he hoisted himself to his feet and ran growling with pain into the building.

Nick removed the pillbox from his pocket and

drew his arm back to throw it into the meandering pond of a restful Japanese garden extending back from the parking area. The engraving on the pillbox caught his eye. "Genesis 27," he could barely make out on the cover. The tiny scene depicted Jacob kneeling at his father Isaac's bed, receiving the blessing meant for his brother, Esau.

He let it fly. There was no way to be sure, but he wanted to believe that the box, too, had belonged to Jacob Balazar.

Chapter 28

"The rumor is he can't buy a new Mercedes-Benz this year," Una said.

"Tragic, tragic," lamented Dion, from deep in his glass of Young's Old Nick Ale.

The bizarre label on the bottle of English brick-red brew pictured the devil in Edwardian evening clothes. They had all ordered one to toast the flesh-and-blood Nick on his recent triumphs. The Folio featured hundreds of such odd beers from around the world; for years, Nick and Dion had been trying to drink their way through the list.

"Here's to Nick," Hawty said. "*Our lucky devil.*"

"Lucky to have such pals," Nick added, choked up as they drank.

Natalie Armiger had not outlasted the wail of the ambulance siren that ushered her to the emergency room. Soon, official inquiries uncovered startling facts about Artemis Holdings. Armiger had been a loose cannon not only in her private life, but also in business affairs. The catalog of her securities transgressions and other crimes over the course of several decades ran to more than a hundred pages.

Her death and, in the following weeks, the implosion of Artemis Holdings would not have been earthshaking news in the insular world of Freret University—another high-roller benefactor would be found—except that a professor of high rank in the

English department was among those who had lost life savings in the debacle: Frederick the Usurper Tawpie. The student-run newspaper did a hard-hitting issue on the scandal, and the word was that Tawpie lurked about campus confiscating any stacks of the free publication he found.

It was two months after the crash.

"But there *is* something good that's emerged from these ashes," Nick said to his friends. "The lawyers have salvaged a generous deal for the Balzars. Twice, the old man, has cable television and all the ice cream he can eat; Erasmus has better health care; and Dora has a new kitchen."

"And Shelvin's much better," Hawty added. "I visited my family over Thanksgiving break, and I stopped by Natchitoches. I think the boy's gone crazy, but now he wants to be a cop! He's already applied to the police academy here in New Orleans . . . can you believe it? After what those"—she clamped her mouth shut until her anger allowed her to continue in civil language. "After what *they* did to him and Ronald." She looked intently at the beer bottles on the table, perhaps to hide the mistiness in her eyes; but after a moment, she sniffed away the outward signs of her sorrow. "Dora puts fresh flowers on Ronald's grave every Sunday, rain or shine."

Ivanhoe's heirs had indeed won a substantial settlement; though considerably less than the fifty million Nick had demanded from Armiger, it was an impressive figure, nevertheless. There was to be no Max Corban Foundation; but Nick hoped that, through his efforts, the old man's soul was now at peace.

In a separate matter, the state highway department had re-examined a certain land deal in Natchitoches and had discovered old and more recent fraud. Several Chirkes were headed to the Louisiana State Penitentiary at Angola. An anonymous call—from a K&B payphone—to the attorney general's office had done the trick.

"Let's not forget the diary," Una said, bragging about Nick's latest literary feather in his cap.

He'd persuaded Coldbread to finance publication. The day before, he'd received a letter from the quixotic, crotchety scholar, who was in Paris, hot on the trail of his idée fixe. Coldbread had found that the man he was searching for had actually been called Balayeur, not Balazar; a series of transcription errors was responsible for centuries of misidentification.

"Thus, you must not expect half, or indeed ANY, of MY TREASURE!" Coldbread had written Nick. "However, if OUR book about Ivanhoe Balazar does well, I would be amenable to employing you on other such NON-SENSITIVE projects."

Dion leveled a searching gaze at Nick. "You're going to have to tell us one day. We can't be put off forever. Were you working for the Bad Witch or the Good Witch or the family in Natchitoches or the old Holocaust survivor? Come now, we're your friends."

"Yes, and how did you know so much about the old man's demise?" Una said.

The two goons were arrested not long after Armiger's death. Nick had given a tip to the detectives working Ronald's murder; Hawty later provided positive ID on the suspects. They were, in fact, rogue cops, with reputations much worse than the tarnished norm of NOPD. Now they were ratting on each other, competing for plea bargains on murder raps and a few dozen other charges. There would be cells at Angola or a federal prison waiting for them, as well.

Nick had scrupulously kept Zola's name out of

everything.

"Hey, I plead client-genealogist privilege," he said.

His three questioners groaned in disappointment. A series of beeps emanated from Hawty's new chariot. "E-mail," she said. "For you, Nick. The computer system we ordered is ready. The shop wants to know when we'll be at the office for delivery."

Una and Dion looked at Nick in silent raillery.

"Your apostasy shocks and grieves me," Dion said. "How many times have I been witness to your philippics against the growing hegemony of the Almighty Gizmo? Yea, even here in our beloved Folio, in this hallowed retreat"—he spread his arms wide in practiced Shakespearean hyperbole—"the very name of which suggests our guiding humanistic ideal of the unique glory of the individual in history. Nick, you were one of us, once! Have you now abandoned us, your erstwhile fellow humble servants of knowledge?"

"Forgive him," Una said. "He hasn't been able to flex his rhetorical muscles today. His first class isn't until this afternoon. But tell us, seriously—you haven't mentioned your Miranda. What happens to her now that she's cast out of her island paradise?"

"I'm not sure," he answered. "I got a letter about two weeks ago, from one of her secretaries. She wanted to know the appropriate places to send all that genealogical source material I told you about, all the stuff in those cases. Since then, nothing."

"Oh, so it was a professional matter?" Una said. "You aren't . . . seeing each other?"

"Seems that way," Nick replied, making sure to give a lovelorn sigh.

"Look," Hawty said. "Is that who I think it is?" The Usurper, in a dark far corner, gesticulated impressively in intimate conversation with an enthralled female student probably less than half his age.

Nick caught the attention of a waitress. She wore the current youthful uniform of drab castoff clothing hanging from her like skin in the process of being molted.

"See that red-haired man way over there?"

"Uh-huh."

"Please take him and his companion another round, and leave whatever money's left." He gave her a bit too much money for the drinks, along with a generous tip. "And tell him—now this is important—'Keep the change. You need it.' You got that?"

"Uh-huh." She wandered off.

"Hey, you three," Nick complained, "what's happened to the communicative skills of the students since I left? They're sliding back into a pre-verbal stage. You're teachers of English, remember? Aren't you supposed to be the life preservers keeping our civilization afloat in the rising tide of imprecision, claptrap, and technobabble?"

"Carlyle lives!" Una said. "Would you, sir, consider lecturing my classes on your theories of social decline? That is, if we can disguise you sufficiently to get past dear Frederick, who hates you almost as much as you hate him."

The waitress, for all her seeming earlier inattention to Nick's request, was now delivering the drinks and the message across the crowded barroom. Tawpie at first seemed to think there was some mistake; but he soon realized someone was making fun of him. He scrutinized the dark, cavernous barroom for the culprit.

Nick waved, flashing a big phony smile. He could

just detect Tawpie's jowls jiggling as he launched a fusillade of invective his way.

Tawpie's curses were drowned out by the laughter of the four friends and by a new song whining at high volume about the difficulties of being twenty.

"All right! The Rotting Fish-heads from Pluto!" Hawty shouted, waving her arms to the frenetic beat. And then to Nick, who was the only one close enough to understand: "I played that. A local band. They've really hit it big. I think they're hot!"

Una and Dion put their fingers to their ears.

Nick almost explained that he'd seen the band live—with Keith Richards—in the company of Zola, and that he now owned the entire Rotting Fish-heads output on cassette . . . but he decided to keep quiet. He just smiled and nodded, tapping his foot under the table. After all his elaborate lies, they probably wouldn't believe the simple truth from him.

Chapter 29

Nick walked down Zola's street in the cold drizzle. The latest catalog bauble of the rich dripped limply from porches—large boldly colored flags with cutesy elves, Santas, and evergreen motifs.

Human beings are the flag-waving species, Nick was thinking. Even in our fads, even when there's nothing worth dying for, we declare allegiances, choose sides, form tribes. It's innate.

Other than the flags, the houses were about evenly divided in displays of Christmas and Hanukkah decorations, blinking at him in syncopated costliness. The for-sale sign in front of Zola's house seemed to Nick at odds with the clubby cheerfulness of the neighborhood. Here was someone who wanted out of the game, or perhaps was no longer welcome. The house itself seemed to have lost its purpose, its unity and personality, now merely a collection of boards, bricks, and nails.

Inside, he dodged moving men as they made their way past, hefting boxes or last pieces of furniture. The place looked even bigger than he remembered it, now that it was empty. He looked into the study, to see only depressing barren shelves.

"You'll be getting a box of those books next week," Zola said, behind him. "I know there were some you especially liked."

He turned to face her. She wore blue jeans, a man's baggy button-up shirt over a black turtleneck, and work gloves. She might have been any woman moving out of her apartment, except for the fact that few women have the luck to look so good, so artlessly. Nick detected a new dimension to her hazel eyes, reflecting the clarity of mind and serenity of spirit that often follow the purifying fires of illness. She was certainly grieving for her mother, but had the innate grace to keep her grief as private as she could.

"Thanks," Nick said. "Weren't you going to say goodbye?"

"No. I thought this would be better. After the way I treated you. After I refused to believe that Mother was—not what she seemed to be. I'm ashamed of her, ashamed of myself for not realizing how out-of-control she was. She did terrible things, Nick. The police have finally run out of questions. But I haven't. I know there's more that needs to be exposed."

Nick shrugged. No point in making her suffer for her mother's wrongs, those she suspected, those she didn't. As far as she and anyone else knew, her mother's crimes were the desperate attempts of an unbalanced mind, first to hide the family's Jewish ancestry, and then to defuse the Balzars' suit.

Maybe, Nick thought, the ancient harvest of sour grapes has ended for this family; there would be no more teeth on edge.

"You were good to me, Nick," she said. "You tried to protect me from the pain of the truth as long as you could, but not from the truth itself. When you offered to show me, I ran away. I was a coward."

There's more pain out there for you yet, Zola. You're on your own now—no revolving office in the sky, no more lackeys cringing in your footsteps, no more tea-parties with disingenuous corporate do-gooders with their hands in your bank account, no more Mother-in-

shining-armor.

They had walked over to the large living room, where two shrouded wing chairs faced a cold fireplace. They sat down.

"I'm leaving New Orleans," she said, looking around the barren room as if she missed it already. "I don't know when—if I'll ever come back. Nick, I just keep seeing the image of Mother, all alone out there in that beautiful setting, physically sick, obsessed with protecting the family name, in her disturbed way. If she'd only confided in me."

"Yes. A terrible thing," Nick said. Armiger deserved everything she got; but of course he couldn't tell Zola that.

"If only I'd known how devastated she was by the difficulties—and that's what they were, really. Just difficulties. None of this needed to happen. Our more sophisticated clients didn't give a damn about that suit, or the story behind it; they also happened to be our most important ones. And the $10 million figure I finally agreed on with the Balzars was better than I'd hoped for. The media had exaggerated the scope of the whole affair. In fact, I've sold the company for just a bit less than it was valued before all of this. We've always had buyers waiting in the wings. Maybe you read about it."

Nick had. He'd been pleased to learn that the division over which she'd exercised direct control was untainted by fraud. He could tell she was proud of her deal-making abilities; but sadness returned to displace her momentary swagger.

"I just don't have the heart right now to run that kind of organization."

Zola was quiet for a few moments.

"She kept so much inside, so many secrets," she said. "How can a mother and her daughter be so close and know so little about each other?"

"Some people are like that," Nick replied, trying to be sympathetic and opaque at the same time.

"I loved her; you know I did," Zola said. "But now I realize what a frightened woman she was. Frightened of the past. I don't want to be like that . . . oh, damn it!" Her eyes squinched shut and tears seeped out; she found some tissues in a shirt pocket. "I didn't want you to see me doing this."

Nick unclenched her hand from the chair arm. "Here's my final lecture for this semester," he said. "You have the power not to be frightened of your past; it can't hurt you unless you think it can."

"Like those monsters under my bed when I was a child," Zola said.

Nick wiped away a rolling tear she'd missed. "Lots of people stop me in family history research when I uncover the first scoundrel. They think a bad apple in the ancestor barrel is a curse, condemning them to misfortune. I don't believe in curses—not that kind, anyway. It's all chance and necessity: some things we can change, some we can't. And we don't know which are which; that's frightening sometimes, yes, but it's also *liberating*. I say learn and live. Begone, all monsters under the bed! Scram, all you skeletons in the closet!"

He'd produced the intended reaction in Zola. She smiled tentatively.

"So what's going to happen to the little chateau?" he asked.

"Do you know, she didn't allow me out there? Her 'special place,' she called it." She sighed, shaking her head. "Oh, I've given it to Freret University, along with those atrocious pictures and sculptures. Part of the deal with the government. But I'm really not supposed to talk about that."

"Hey, I know how it is. Got a few secrets, myself. What about the genealogical treasure trove in those cases? I suppose you'll be sending that to the places I suggested."

He wanted it all himself, but he knew it had to be repatriated. Zola had solved his anxiety over returning the Natchitoches material by offering to pay for the relocation of the courthouse's neglected subbasement archive to the Plutarch Foundation in New Orleans, where future genealogists would have the opportunity to scurry around in it like happy dung beetles. Nick's pilfered Balazar documents were unobtrusively added, and no one was the wiser.

"Well, not exactly," Zola said. "My lawyers have told me not to reveal where I'm going, or what I'm going to do, but between us," she drew closer, continuing in a whisper, just a glimmer of her old fun-loving self in her eyes, "I'm bound for Europe to deliver those items myself. I've decided to take some time off, figure out a new direction. In the meantime, I intend to devote my energies to the study of—drum roll please!—genealogy. Learn and live, isn't that what you said?"

"You know," said Nick, "maybe I should have been a teacher."

She gave him her address in the small alpine country where she would be setting up house—or castle, rather—and made him promise to visit.

"Oh, wait." She ran into another room and returned with a gift-wrapped package. "Merry Christmas *and* Happy Birthday! I was going to send it to you. Go on, open it."

It was a Breitling wrist chronograph so complex he was afraid he'd never be able to make out the time, much less the altitude—a negative number in New

Orleans, anyway.

"No microchip. Excellent!" he said.

"Slightly antiquated, but very charming. Like you."

"Hey, no fair. I didn't get you anything."

"This is all I want," she said, and kissed him.

Eventually the moving men gave them unsubtle hints that they were about to be loaded onto the truck.

❑

Nick crossed the street, heading for St. Charles and the streetcar downtown. His car had received terminal injuries in its joust with the iron gate. He stopped on the opposite sidewalk and faced the house. He recalled a particularly important passage from Ivanhoe's diary, possibly written on a typical dreary Louisiana winter day like this one.

"Zola, my love," Nick said softly, "may you safely cross all the impossible gaps on your journey."

Chapter 30

❖

From *The Diary of Ivanhoe Balzar: Mulatto Barber of Natchitoches*

December 21st 1873. Jacob, my half-brother, passed today. I was with him at his deathbed. He held my hand. Maybe he did not recognise me. Maybe he did. The Lord Almitey forgive his sinning soul! Euphrozine, my half-sister, would not let my Mary come in the big house, making her keep to the kitchen with the servants. The plantation house look very bad indeed, and the fields gone to seed mostly. I don't even beleve Jacob saw to plantin anything this year at all, cept for some vegetables that critters got. Euphrozine married a man from up East a few years back, and spend most of the time over in New York. But lately I hear tell she and her husband doing some cofee trading down in New Orleans. His family can't deal in slaves no more, like they did before the War. But I think Euphrozine is not as bad as Jacob; nobody has to be bad, unless they want to be. She says to me, after we bury'd poor Jacob—I hate this cankrous, rotting, barren place, Ivanhoe! I don't care what happens to it. It makes me so melonkolie.—Well, I wager we won't be seeing much of her round here nomore. I'll miss her. She never hated me, tho, least not as much as that devil of a man Jacob. These past few years been almost enuf to make me deny my dedly pedigre. I'm ready for some Peace. The influenca broke out again, and is spreding. I hear

some folks died over near Isle Brevelle. Froze hard
last nite and killed three old cows to tuf to eat even.
Loaned Logan Younce $6, for two plows, at small
intrist because he is my friend. Tom Oliviette has
proposed to me a part of a barge that he want to run.
I don't know if I am willing or not. Cut ten heads
today, which is about rite for the time. Folks got to
go to Church. My prentice cut just four, tho.
Erasmus is coming up to three now. All the world is
afore that child. I won't let the Past stand in his way.
He can chuse his own Futur the Good Lord tended
him to have. *

*All excerpts from J. N. Herald, ed., *The Diary of Ivanhoe Balzar: Mulatto Barber of Natchitoches* (New Orleans: Coldbread Press, 1997). The Plutarch Foundation in New Orleans possesses this extraordinary diary (Manuscript 895). Herald's book has received awards from the National Genealogical Society, the American Society of Genealogists, and the Association of Professional Genealogists, among others.

Chapter 31

January 1, 1995--3:16 a.m.

From a shadowy canyon of deserted warehouses, stacked rail-sea containers, and barbed-wire fencing, police cars shot blinding spotlights down a rocky embankment to the crime scene below. Two bodies lay in thick, clammy fog at the edge of the Mississippi River, halfway between the French Quarter and the Industrial Canal.

Emergency lights flashed alternating blue and red spasms of diffuse illumination on the crime scene, enveloping the living and the dead alike in a disorienting plasma, as if the fog were a contagion spreading the violence that had occurred here across the city, to cling to the beloved architecture and ancient trees, to suck life from the hallowed traditions, to infect the souls of unsuspecting, innocent residents and tourists.

Muted revelry of diehard New Year's Eve celebrants in the Quarter reached the cold ears of NOPD uniformed officers and plainclothes detectives, paramedics, and crime-lab technicians as they worked the murders. Two men had been shot at close range. No witnesses, no suspects, just a nameless phone tip.

Dark river water visible near the bank eddied into man-sized whirlpools and unexpectedly flowed backward in isolated pockets; toxic foam the color of dead eyes scudded across the turbulence; unidentifiable shapes lumbered by just under the surface.

A tall black cop stood apart from the methodical dance

of evidence gathering. The star-and-crescent badge over his heart reflected the pulsing glow of the emergency lights. In short-sleeves despite the damp chill, his shaved head bare, he clenched and unclenched his big fists like a fighter just before a bout, or just after a knockout victory. Vicious scars scored his thick, ropy forearms. He seemed transfixed by the Orleans Parish assistant coroner's examination of the blood-caked bodies of the two dead men sprawled like broken kites on gray boulders lapped by the river. His jaw muscles rippling, he brought his right hand to his neck and rubbed under the collar of his light-blue uniform shirt.

A beefy white detective by the name of Gus Roulé found footing on the rocks next to the black cop. Everyone called Gus "Bons Temps," after Louisiana's Cajun-inspired unofficial motto: *Laissez les bons temps rouler!*, or "Let the good times roll!"

"You don't look so hot, Balzar," said Bons Temps. "What's wrong, you never seen a stiff with half its head missin'?"

"Maybe more of them than you, man," Shelvin replied, without looking at the detective. "More than I can count, in the Gulf War."

"No shit?" the detective said, easing off his gibing tone of superiority. "I was in Nam, myself. Long time ago. You wouldn't recognize me." He laughed, slapping his bulging stomach. "Sometimes I think this damn city's worse . . . so, Balzar, what the hell you doing here? My information is you're Sixth District."

The 'Bloody Sixth,' it was called, encompassing the Magnolia and St. Thomas housing projects, war zones festering with such mayhem that cops drove their cruisers to calls rather than present themselves as easy targets in the open courtyards.

"Got detailed to the Eighth up until Mardi Gras," Shelvin said. "Like I told your partner, I heard the call on my radio, figured I could get here as quick as anybody else. Over in the Quarter, most of our professional criminals already gone to bed; all them other folks just too messed up at this time of night to do anything real bad."

The detective grinned and nodded in agreement. "Yeah, you right. I been wantin' to meet you, Balzar. Word goin' round is you don't take no shit from nobody. They say you haven't missed a collar yet."

"Well, tonight could be a first for me, then."

"Could be. Whoever did this got away clean. Execution style. No way we'll ever find the gun, but it was a mighty big one. Forty-five or 10mm. If only that ole river could talk, huh? The poor bastards were kneeling down, lookin' right at their killer. Looks like somebody evened up a score here, big time."

"Looks like a drug deal gone bad to me, man," Shelvin replied, searching Bons Temps' fog-obscured face for unasked questions. "But you're the detective."

Another detective summoned Bons Temps aside; they spoke together and examined notebooks by flashlight as a train thundered by on tracks beyond the warehouses.

Shelvin removed his flashlight from his belt and joined other officers in the search for evidence.

Soon the assistant coroner rose from his uncomfortable crouch and directed his team to bag the bodies and put them in the "meat wagon."

Then he began a stumbling climb up the rocky bank, cursing the lateness of the hour and the discourtesy of the victims in getting murdered here.

Bons Temps found Shelvin a few minutes later. "We just got positive ID on the victims," he said. "Kirk Dagget and Harvey Baspo. I thought maybe that's who they were, but from what was left of 'em, I couldn't be sure. Names ring a bell with you?"

Shelvin didn't answer.

"Let me jog your memory. These guys were on the force. Uniforms, like you. In their spare time for extra dough they did strong-arm work for Artemis Holdings. Like we all do a little security work to make ends meet, you know? But these guys were real bad news. Made us all look dirty. They got busted about a year ago, after the Armiger woman died and that genealogist gave the powers-that-be the leads they needed. I wouldn't think you'd have any trouble remembering 'em, seeing as how they sliced and diced you and your brother."

"Yeah," Shelvin said, watching the two coroner's men heft a body bag up the rocks, "I didn't recognize them either . . . you got a point, here, Bons Temps?"

Shelvin had pronounced Gus's nickname right—a rare thing for a rookie cop—losing most of the ending consonants. Bons Temps seemed flattered.

"Matter of fact, I do. Lotta guys on the force probably think the shooter did us a favor, getting rid of these creeps. They had plenty of enemies; hell, they even screwed me on a transaction or two. The Feds cut 'em a sweetheart deal to spill their guts about their former co-workers—us. They been under house arrest all these months. Nobody's seen 'em for a couple of days."

"I read the paper and watch TV," Shelvin said.

"I realize I'm probably going over old ground with you here. What I'm sayin' is, Balzar"—and here Bons Temps swiveled his tree-stump of a head to make sure no one was within earshot—"we all got certain little secrets best left unknown. Sometimes, the lines aren't so clear, and we all crossed over 'em in our careers. You got to, to feed your family. Howya like that, them two pointin' fingers, after what they done?" Bons Temps leaned forward to deliver these words, driving a fat index finger into Shelvin's chest: "Least I never *killed* nobody for money, like them."

Shelvin glanced down at the rubber-gloved finger and

then up at the detective's face. Something in Shelvin's eyes made Bons Temps remove his finger and back off a few inches.

A new police superintendent had taken over in October 1994, with a mandate to clean up the notoriously corrupt department and end the city's unwanted claim to the title of Murder Capital of America. At his Gallier Hall swearing-in celebration, the new chief received a briefing from an FBI agent on investigations and stings in progress to root out the vice rampaging within NOPD.

"Lotta things gonna change in the department, Balzar," Bons Temps said, from a safer distance. "But one thing'll always be the same: you need friends when the shit starts flyin'. I watch your back, you watch mine. That's the way it works."

"Yeah, I hear you," Shelvin said.

Bons Temps slapped Shelvin's ox-like shoulders. "Good man. You a fast learner. They sure don't grow 'em dumb up there in Natchitoches, do they?"

The detective removed a plastic bag of white powder from a pocket of his dark-blue, yellow-lettered rain parka and dropped it amid the rocks.

"Hey!" Bons Temps shouted to the others, "come look see what our Balzar done found!" He turned to Shelvin, a big grin on his face. "You right, Balzar. Sure *does* look like a drug deal gone sour. Guess it's another cold case for the bottom drawer."

Reyaud

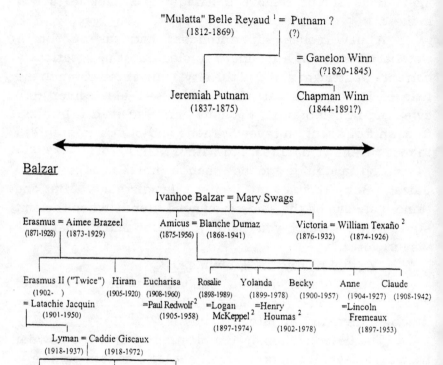

"Mulatta" Belle Reyaud [1] = Putnam ?
(1812-1869)   (?)

= Ganelon Winn
(?1820-1845)

Jeremiah Putnam
(1837-1875)

Chapman Winn
(1844-1891?)

Balzar

Ivanhoe Balzar = Mary Swags

Erasmus = Aimee Brazeel
(1871-1928)   (1873-1929)

Amicus = Blanche Dumaz
(1875-1956)   (1868-1941)

Victoria = William Texaño [2]
(1876-1932)   (1874-1926)

Erasmus II ("Twice")
(1902-)
= Latachie Jacquin
(1901-1950)

Hiram
(1905-1920)

Eucharisa
(1908-1960)
=Paul Redwolf [2]
(1905-1958)

Rosalie
(1898-1989)
=Logan
McKeppel [2]
(1897-1974)

Yolanda
(1899-1978)
=Henry
Houmas [2]
(1902-1978)

Becky
(1900-1957)

Anne
(1904-1927)
=Lincoln
Fremeaux
(1897-1953)

Claude
(1908-1942)

Lyman = Caddie Giscaux
(1918-1937)   (1918-1972)

Erasmus III
(1935-)
= Dora Brown
(1936-)

Verlinda
(1936-)
= Sam
Takato [2]
(1930-)

Amelie
(1937-)
= Reuben
Bienvenir [2]
(1936-1967)

Shelvin
(1961-)

Ronald
(1964-1993)

Winfred = Stephen Whythall
(1965-)   (1963-)

---

1. Several graves of unnamed infants in Natchitoches and Natchez indicate births from other Mulatta Belle unions. She must have been a slave at the time Jeremiah was born, since Ivanhoe in his diary states that his half-brother Jeremiah was once a slave. The slave system mandated that the child inherit its mother's status. No record of Mulatta Belle's pre-war manumission has yet been located; however, because Ivanhoe seems never to have been a slave, Mulatta Belle must have gained her freedom before his birth in 1839.

2. Children will be found under the husband's surname. See charts in Herald, *The Diary of Ivanhoe Balzar.*

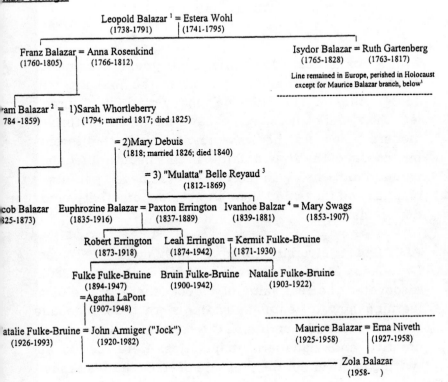

Leopold Balazar [1] = Estera Wohl
(1738-1791)   (1741-1795)

Franz Balazar = Anna Rosenkind
(1760-1805)   (1766-1812)

Isydor Balazar = Ruth Gartenberg
(1765-1828)   (1763-1817)

Line remained in Europe, perished in Holocaust
except for Maurice Balazar branch, below[1]
----

am Balazar [2] = 1)Sarah Whortleberry
784 -1859)   (1794; married 1817; died 1825)

= 2)Mary Debuis
(1818; married 1826; died 1840)

= 3) "Mulatta" Belle Reyaud [3]
(1812-1869)

cob Balazar   Euphrozine Balazar = Paxton Errington   Ivanhoe Balzar [4] = Mary Swags
825-1873)   (1835-1916)   (1837-1889)   (1839-1881)   (1853-1907)

Robert Errington   Leah Errington = Kermit Fulke-Bruine
(1873-1918)   (1874-1942)   (1871-1930)

Fulke Fulke-Bruine   Bruin Fulke-Bruine   Natalie Fulke-Bruine
(1894-1947)   (1900-1942)   (1903-1922)
=Agatha LaPont
(1907-1948)

atalie Fulke-Bruine = John Armiger ("Jock")
(1926-1993)   (1920-1982)

Maurice Balazar = Erna Niveth
(1925-1958)   (1927-1958)

Zola Balazar
(1958-   )

1. For exhaustive treatment of this line, traced back to pre-Roman Jerusalem, see *The Balazars of France, Germany, and Poland,* by Zola Balazar-Armiger (Geneva: the author, 1999). Charts begin on p. 1,480, v. II.

2. Invaluable source material relating to this family's early Louisiana years is housed at the Plutarch Foundation, New Orleans; see The Balazar Collection.

3. Children from other Reyaud unions on following chart.

4. Balzar chart follows. Descendants of this union listed there.

About the Author

Jimmy Fox is from Alexandria, Louisiana, a dynamic city of about 50,000 population situated on the Red River in the center of the state. Louisiana's many distinct cultures have left their marks here; some have managed to thrive into modern times. As he was growing up in this interesting microcosm of the state at large, in this beautiful recreational wonderland, he was fortunate to have parents who emphasized ideas and their expression, creativity, and self-determination.

At Tulane University (B.A., English major, 1977) and at Louisiana State University (M.A., English, 1980), he discovered the real value of a good liberal-arts education: learning how to learn. Later, for more than a decade, he worked at the Alexandria NBC television affiliate, in various creative and managerial capacities. Here, he honed his writing skills under the pressure of constant deadlines.

He has been writing, in one way or another, all of his adult life. When he became fascinated by genealogy, he knew he was onto something that could be the stuff of great mystery fiction. He continues to study extensively in the field of family history, both in a personal quest to trace his roots and in an effort to enhance the authenticity of his mysteries. Genealogy by its very nature is detective work, and his sleuth, Nick Herald, will have no shortage of cases to keep him busy for many years to come.